INCRIMINATED

Also by M. G. Reyes

EMANCIPATED

INCRIM

INATED

M. G. REYES

KATHERINE TEGEN BOOKS

Katherine Tegen Books is an imprint of HarperCollins Publishers.

Incriminated

Copyright © 2016 by Reynolds Applegate, Inc.

www.epicreads.com

ISBN 978-0-06-228898-1

Typography by Carla Weise
16 17 18 19 20   PC/RRDH   10 9 8 7 6 5 4 3 2 1

First Edition

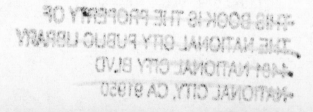

For my daughter, Lilia,
the first teenager to read *Emancipated*. May your own
writing always bring you challenge, excitement, and joy.

CALIFORNIA FAMILY CODE SECTION 7120-7123 EMANCIPATION:

7120.

(A) A MINOR MAY PETITION THE SUPERIOR COURT OF THE COUNTY IN WHICH THE MINOR RESIDES OR IS TEMPORARILY DOMICILED FOR A DECLARATION OF EMANCIPATION.

(B) THE PETITION SHALL SET FORTH WITH SPECIFICITY ALL OF THE FOLLOWING FACTS:

(1) THE MINOR IS AT LEAST 14 YEARS OF AGE.

(2) THE MINOR WILLINGLY LIVES SEPARATE AND APART FROM THE MINOR'S PARENTS OR GUARDIAN WITH THE CONSENT OR ACQUIESCENCE OF THE MINOR'S PARENTS OR GUARDIAN.

(3) THE MINOR IS MANAGING HIS OR HER OWN FINANCIAL AFFAIRS.

GRACE
EL MATADOR STATE BEACH, SUNDAY, MAY 31

It was all going wrong between the housemates. Grace was the one who decided to put things right. But not everyone was in the mood to play along.

"Really?" Candace peered down from the cliff path at El Matador State Beach. With maximum snark she said, "You couldn't find a busier beach?"

Dismayed, Grace eyed the crowded sand. "It'll thin out, you'll see. It's almost four thirty. It has to." The other five housemates paused behind her on the path, beach bags and coolers dangling from their fingers, surfboards under Maya's and Candace's arms.

"We should have come later," John-Michael muttered. "Who sets out for an evening beach barbecue at four in the afternoon?"

Grace had persuaded her housemates it was time for a day trip away from their Venice Beach house, where lately all they did was eat too many grilled cheese sandwiches and stare at the TV. They had to get out, get together in a place where nature and tranquillity could work on their senses. Where the distractions of everyday life wouldn't snap the housemates apart and send them flying for the corner pockets like a rack of pool balls on the break.

She'd even cajoled John-Michael and Candace into helping her put together a picnic. One or two of them grumbled about going to "just another beach," but so what? What they needed was different air and a different horizon. A place where they could breathe without the taint of uncertainty and suspicion that had settled around them. This was about being together. With its coves wrapped by the cliffs of the Pacific Coast Highway, its crystalline waters and soft golden sands, El Matador seemed like the ideal getaway.

Grace bit her lower lip. Her housemates' complaining was pretty annoying. But she wasn't going to be so easily ground down.

To her relief, Paolo caught her eye. He noticed Grace's frustration and replied with a comforting half grin. "I'm glad we're here while there's still some light. I like to watch the kitesurfers."

Grace gave Paolo an appreciative smile and her stomach knotted in response. It happened way too often. One of these days her feelings were going to show in her eyes, in the twitch of her lips, and then what? Then she'd be the stupid girl who fell for the ridiculously gorgeous, unattainable guy.

"Kitesurfing, on this beach?" Maya said, skeptical.

"You'd have to be pretty crazy to risk that."

Paolo shrugged. He could see at least one bright pink sail dragging a surfer across the water, about a hundred yards out. "It's not so windy."

"Because, *cliffs*," Maya said, pointing at the wall of rock that bordered the cove. "If a strong gust picks you up you could get slammed against a cliff and killed."

"No one's getting killed," Paolo said, his voice tinged with admiration. "Just look at that guy, he's a mile out!"

This time, Grace couldn't hold back a warm smile. Paolo, at least, was trying. He had been a little down, too, since Lucy rejected him; hadn't exactly jumped at the idea of the picnic. But once they'd gotten moving, his mood had improved.

She paused for a moment, watching Paolo take the steps two at a time. He looked as good as ever. It was pointless, she told herself. You had to make the effort to avoid boys like Paolo. Too cute, and he knows it. Better to keep him as a friend.

When Grace looked up it was to see Lucy's eyes on her; curious, considered. "Hmm," Lucy murmured with a knowing nod.

"What?" countered Grace. She could feel a blush rising and couldn't do a thing to stop it.

Lucy smiled gently. "Don't sweat it. Guys are dumb but they figure it out eventually."

Grace, for a brief moment, was too stunned to move. At least one housemate wasn't fooled by her charade. Moving somewhat mechanically now, she followed her friends down to the beach.

Candace and Maya rode out into the waves on their short surfboards while Paolo swam nearby. The ocean was still too cold for any but the most hardy, but Paolo didn't seem to care. The water was as clear as a freshwater spring in the middle of the woods. Out on the wide blue expanse, two kitesurfers crisscrossed as their boards bounced and skated over the water.

Grace stayed on the sand, between boulders and the cliffs. Most of the time, she stared out over the water, John-Michael beside her, the two of them silent.

It could be that way with two people looking into the sea, Grace had found. All her life Grace had lived in San Antonio, Texas, more than one hundred miles from the coastline. She'd never known the calming effect the ocean could have on her mind. The past five months, living a hundred yards from the water's edge, had brought the revelation of shared silence.

Grace doubted that she could ever go back.

She thought about the first days of living in the Venice Beach house she shared with Maya, Lucy, John-Michael, Paolo, and her stepsister, Candace. It had taken a few months, but they'd grown close; a synthetic family on Venice Beach. It wasn't something they'd taken for granted. Yet, recently, there were tensions.

It was no surprise, given what some of them had brought into the house. Secrets, deceptions, crimes. Grace watched

Candace rub lotion onto her arms, and felt a familiar flash of guilt. She had confided in John-Michael a secret she was still keeping from her own stepsister.

Grace had kept silent about the true identity of her father, Alex Vesper, for years. How would Candace react if she knew that her stepmother was once married to a convicted murderer, a man on death row? Would Grace's relationship with Candace survive, if that truth ever came to light? Without Candace, Grace was pretty sure she wouldn't be able to keep pretending that being emancipated was as easy as everyone liked to believe. It didn't help that the housemates had more or less all agreed to keep their parents at arm's length.

If Candace were to find out the truth about Grace's father from anyone but Grace, she'd feel betrayed. She might even begin to pick through her memories and wonder what other things Grace had lied about. Grace could already imagine her own response, begging to be believed that there were no other secrets and that even this hadn't been her choice but her mother's.

She lowered her eyes before Candace noticed. No. She couldn't risk it, as tempting as it sometimes was to confess. Like her mother always said: "It's not just *your* secret, Grace."

Grace had confided in John-Michael, a week ago, on Memorial Day. She still wasn't exactly sure why she had. When one person shared something private, it felt right to share something back. At least, that's what she told herself.

It was the reason why she'd brought John-Michael in on her own buried treasure—the truth that her father was "Dead Man Walking"—the death row prisoner she'd been writing to for years.

But John-Michael had shared a secret with her, too. One about his own father's death, which hung like a dagger above his head. The police had arrested John-Michael on suspicion of murder, but he'd been released without being charged. A week ago things had come to a head. Rather than benefit one more day from his father's pride and joy, John-Michael had driven his father's Mercedes-Benz convertible off the Pacific Coast Highway. Only Grace knew the real reason he'd done it.

She didn't agree with the morality of assisting a father's suicide—especially when it involved holding a pillow over your father's face until he stopped breathing. She could never have done it herself—however terminal the medical diagnosis. But John-Michael was her friend, and he'd trusted her with the truth. She would *never* tell, and she knew he would do the same for her.

After sunset, the moms and dads, grandparents and toddlers began to pack up and leave. The disposable barbecues began to glow in the fading light. From the tiny plastic bag within her first aid pouch, Grace pulled fibers from cotton balls to use as tinder while John-Michael lit a match. His practicality often surprised and impressed her.

"When I was living on the street," he said, "there were

days when I'd have shivered all night long if I hadn't been able to make a fire."

When the tinder had caught a flame, he tossed a burning cotton ball onto the teepee of sticks he'd carefully arranged. He dropped onto his belly, mouth no more than six inches from the nascent flame, and began to blow. Within a minute, the sticks had caught fire, too. They began to crackle and blaze. In another minute, they had a real campfire.

Candace approached, drying her shoulders and head with a towel. She knelt in the space between Lucy and Grace. After a moment she leaned her head on Grace's shoulder. "This is so great. Why've we never done this before?"

Paolo sat down on a rolled straw beach mat and peered up at her. "You're the one who's always working on your TV show over the weekends."

"Candace is right," Maya chipped in. "This is really fun. It's been a while since we just hung out together." She reached for the cooler and took out cold cans of soda and foil-wrapped cheese-and-meatball hoagies. Paolo caught the Diet Coke she lobbed at him and turned to John-Michael. "Dude, did you bring the rum and the limes? I wanna make a Cuba libre."

Grace felt the beginnings of a warm glow within her. The easy vibe that had once existed between the housemates wasn't quite there, not yet. But maybe it was a good thing that their secrets had begun to come out into the open. In the flame-heated air that connected the six friends around the fire, she could sense them coming closer together.

Maybe Lucy would finally reveal her own secrets. *If only.*

Lucy didn't know it, but she had the power to change Grace's entire life with a single action. She just had to tell the truth about the murder she'd witnessed as a child.

There had to be some way to get Lucy to talk. Grace knew that John-Michael had already told Lucy about Grace's father—she'd suggested it herself, to see if it might get Lucy to confess. So far Lucy had said nothing. The question was—had she made any connection between Grace's father's situation and what she'd witnessed as a child?

Grace couldn't be sure. No, it would have to begin with Grace sharing her side of the truth with Lucy first. She had to tell her that Alex Vesper, the man on death row for the murder of Tyson Drew, was her father.

Grace sighed. Then Candace would find out that she'd been lying to her all these years.

If only there was another way.

PAOLO

Paolo King was sitting at the country club bar, as he often did after a training session with one of the club's tennis students. It was late afternoon. Some kind of mellow jazz played in the background. Paolo had no clue what the tune was. He rarely heard that kind of music outside the club.

This particular student was somewhat older than the usual women who favored Paolo. She was in her forties, with perfectly styled blond hair that settled high on her neck. Her tennis skirt showed off tan, athletic legs that were crossed at the ankles.

He knew her only as "Jimmy's mom."

Paolo had once played a game of tennis for money with Jimmy, her idiot teenage son. He'd been tricked into swindling the kid out of a forty-thousand dollar Corvette. Even though Paolo had been basically blackmailed into the con by a guy who'd long since hit the road, Jimmy's mom held him responsible. She'd agreed to keep the matter away from the cops, but only if she and Paolo got on *real* good terms.

He'd been doing a pretty good job at keeping up the pretense—minus one small detail. Somehow, her name had eluded him. She'd told him once but he'd forgotten. Now that they'd been intimate it seemed just plain rude to ask her again. Paolo had hoped that they'd never meet again. But no. Today, she'd lain in wait for him at the club.

"Your hair looks great," Paolo said as Jimmy's mom switched his Diet Sprite with the Tom Collins cocktail she'd ordered for herself. He picked up his new drink. "Are you sure you don't want this?"

"Better not." She smirked. "I'm driving."

So was Paolo, but in this woman's company he was wary of saying anything that might annoy her. The subject of Paolo's age—sixteen—was a sketchy one between them, on account of how they'd slept together. Technically, it was illegal, but this wasn't Paolo's first time with an older woman. He was pretty sure she'd drag out the names of all those other women he'd slept with at the tennis club, if he tried to use their relationship against her. He didn't want that.

He took a sip and tried once again to remember her name. She would be annoyed that he couldn't remember.

"I enjoyed watching you play against your coach." She smiled. "But my dear, it's exhausting. I thought he had you beat for sure."

Paolo humored her. "Victory tastes sweeter when you snatch it from the jaws of defeat."

Jimmy's mom would have known that if she'd stuck around to watch the whole match he'd played against her son. Darius, Paolo's doubles partner that afternoon and the architect of the entire scam, had made sure they'd let themselves be held down, almost until the end. A classic hustle. Jimmy had fallen for it, and hard.

She gave him a long, thoughtful look. Paolo avoided looking back, feeling the full weight of the years between them. He thought back to their last encounter. He already felt uncomfortable, the way you did when a girl came on to you and you knew you were going to deny her in the end. He did it all the time with girls from school who seemed to think he was some kind of trophy—to be snatched up and displayed.

"Are you quite sure that you can't move your class to another evening?" she asked suggestively.

Paolo's fingers closed around his glass. "I really can't. My student's already here—I saw her car in the parking lot."

She pouted. "Too bad." There was a hesitation, as though even she had some qualms about broaching the subject of their one-time affair. Then her voice dropped. "I've been thinking about you, you know." She tried to look him in the eye and couldn't. Suddenly, she seemed almost vulnerable.

Paolo struggled to maintain an even expression. She wanted him to say something similarly flirtatious, he could tell. When she noticed his reluctance, a smile spread across her lips.

"Come along, Paolo, don't be so bashful. We're hardly Mrs. Robinson and Benjamin, now are we?"

His eyes narrowed in puzzlement. "And they are?"

"You never saw *The Graduate*?"

"*The Graduate*?" He shook his head and took a sip. "No."

Jimmy's mom sighed patiently, as though dealing with a slow but fondly regarded student. "It's a marvelous movie, a classic. Mrs. Robinson is the bored, wealthy housewife and Benjamin is a recent college graduate, the son of her family friend. They get together. Ben's very shy about it all, at first. And then he starts to like it. Just the way you did, Paolo, that afternoon we spent together."

"How does it turn out?" Paolo asked, dreading the answer.

She shrugged. "Not altogether well. Benjamin runs off with Mrs. Robinson's daughter."

Paolo fumbled for words. This conversation was getting pretty bizarre. He wasn't sure what he was supposed to say. "Are . . . you not happy with Mr. . . . with Jimmy's dad?"

She leaned back in her seat, regarding him. "Happy? Paolo, you really believe that a happily married woman takes a sixteen-year-old tennis coach to bed?"

"I guess I don't know a lot about married people."

She touched his hand affectionately. He found his eyes drawn inexorably to the place where her fingers had lightly landed on his.

"Why would you? You're just a kid. Out of your head with testosterone, maybe, but that'll calm down, in time. I'm guessing you don't have a girlfriend?"

"Why'd you say that?" The words, too defensive, were out before he could stop himself.

She gave a curious smile.

"I don't have a girlfriend because the girl I want isn't interested."

A flicker of genuine interest. "Ah. Unrequited love, is it?"

"I don't know about love." Paolo could hardly believe he was talking about these feelings to a predatory stranger. It was as though she'd mistaken him for one of her girlfriends, someone with whom to share a confidence. Just the same, he tried to give a helpful answer. Jimmy's mom could still cause a lot of trouble for him. It was better to keep her on his side.

"I like this girl a lot. We kind of hooked up once and she wasn't into it. I thought I'd be angry. But I dunno. Somehow, it just made me want her more."

Jimmy's mom gave a satisfied smile. "My, my. Sounds to me like your little girlfriend has you exactly where she wants you."

"It's not like that." That didn't describe Lucy Long at all. He'd had enough experience with women to be able to tell when a girl really wanted him. Lucy hadn't shown those signs, not really. Not until she kissed him and it seemed like she finally wanted to get close to him . . . until she didn't.

"What I think," he said carefully, "is that she didn't like me, not that way, at least. She only wanted to hook up with me to forget about everything else happening in our lives. The timing was all wrong."

"Well, now," murmured Jimmy's mom, evidently surprised. "How unusually perceptive of you."

She pulled out her credit card as the waiter dropped the check. Paolo craned his neck until he could make out the name on the card.

Meredith Eriksson.

Her name was Meredith. Wouldn't even have been in his top ten guesses. Paolo sank into his seat, barely holding back a sigh of relief.

"Perhaps you need to get that girl out of your system," she continued. "You know the saying; the best cure for an old love is a new one."

But you and me, we can't ever be in love, Paolo wanted to say. It had been a one-time thing only to stay out of trouble, nothing more. He nodded a little and sipped nervously at his Tom Collins, quickly thinking of a way to let her down. "Meredith," he started, tentative with the use of her name. "You got any daughters? Maybe we can totally Mrs. Robinson this whole situation."

"Come near my house or my family, and it's good-bye to your tennis career," she said, with a sharpness that felt like a slap. "And as for law school, a few calls to some lawyer friends of mine would put an end to that, *Mr.* King."

Paolo played along, pretending it was a joke, but he knew it wasn't. "I'll be sure to remember that," he managed to say after a while.

"All right," she said, her tone crisper now, formal.

"Paolo, where would you say this leaves us?"

He glanced up, bewildered. "Us? I thought you said . . . ?"

"I know what I said, but I expect some flexibility, naturally. Given the extent of your misdemeanor, I mean. The total cost of your little scam."

"It wasn't just me," he added resentfully.

"Yours and Darius's, then," Meredith said, widening her eyes. "Darius was rather more effective than you at making a hasty getaway." She leaned closer and smiled. "He's also far less attractive."

There it was again, the calculatingly ravenous look that made Paolo feel as though he were a strawberry cream pie.

"You cost me upward of forty thousand dollars, Paolo King. And as memorable as our afternoon was, on reflection, one time doesn't quite cut it."

Paolo felt himself swallowing his revulsion. He wasn't at all sure that he could make himself go through a repeat performance.

Reluctantly, he said, "What did you have in mind?"

"I have your number. When the mood strikes me, Paolo, I'll give you a call." Meredith stood. "Don't worry. I could be good for you. I suspect that when it comes to young women, you've a lot to learn. What we have is fun, but I wouldn't be averse to helping you win the girl of your dreams."

She touched his cheek thoughtfully. After a second or two, it turned into a caress. "Don't look so worried.

I guarantee that you'll have a great time." She leaned in like she wanted to kiss him but remembered where they were. She brought her mouth close to his ear instead and whispered, "Grow your hair longer, and use a little bit of product. You're looking so good these days, Paolo, I could scream."

CANDACE
CULVER STUDIOS, WEDNESDAY, JUNE 3

"Candace Deering? This way, please."

It was too easy, nothing like the other times. No line, no crowd of girls that made her wonder if she was a clone. She'd been escorted to the audition room by someone who actually knew her name, and when she entered, there were only two guys inside.

One of the guys stood behind a desk manning a short tripod and a video camera. The second leaned against the door frame, silent. He was in his midthirties, about six feet tall, dark-haired with greenish-blue eyes. The stubble on his chin lent him an unkempt look. Candace recognized him right away.

He turned, deliberately casual, to look at her. His eyes flicked up, then down. A two-blink checkout. "Thanks for coming to audition for us. I'm Ricardo Adams."

Candace smiled. "I know who you are," she said, figuring flattery was the way to go. "I watch *Deadbeat*."

"Always nice to meet a fan," he responded with an

artificial grin. He eased aside to let Candace pass. She went to close the door behind her, but Ricardo caught the edge and held it open. "We're not all here yet." Cool professionalism oozed from his every pore.

Candace practically held her breath until a moment later she heard a cheerful yell from down the corridor, *"¡Oye, asere!"*

Into view came a guy, a little under six feet tall, about twenty years old and of African descent. He was lithe and slender with a stylish, layered pattern shaved into short dark brown hair. His features were delicate; high cheekbones, almond-shaped dark brown eyes with curly lashes and a perfectly sculpted jaw. He was ludicrously handsome. Beaming a 100 percent gorgeous smile from a face as sweet as his body was perfect, he sauntered into the room, did some kind of bro-hug with Ricardo, then leaned in and surprised Candace with a friendly kiss on the cheek.

"Yoandy," he said, his voice low and sultry. He squeezed her right hand. *"Encantado."*

His accent. Light, yet definitely Latino. Was he Dominican? Cuban? Colombian?

"Candace Deering," Ricardo said formally, "this is Yoandy Santiago."

She nodded, trying not to look at the muscles playing under the flawless, smooth brown skin of Yoandy's shoulders. Most of his upper torso was exposed by the tight, sleeveless white top that he wore over faded, ripped blue jeans with cream-colored Chuck Taylors, unlaced and with the tongues pulled loose. There was no sign of any tattoo or other marking on him, but his throat was adorned with a doubled necklace of tiny red and white beads. He had the physique of an athlete or maybe a dancer.

Candace was pretty sure she'd have recognized him if he had been on TV before.

"I like your show," Yoandy said, amused. "You're Gina! She's so badass."

"How have you seen *Downtowners*? It hasn't even aired yet." Candace glanced at Ricardo for confirmation.

"I showed Yoandy some of your work," Ricardo said. Something about the way he bit off the sentence made Candace wonder. Had Yoandy's approval been important? Required, even? She struggled to remember the name: Yoandy Santiago. Was he already a bigger star than her?

When she focused again, Candace realized that Yoandy was staring at her, looking positively charmed. "I *loved* when you killed that guy with your bare hands."

Candace pulled herself straight, recovered her poise, and smiled at Yoandy calmly. "He got what he deserved."

Yoandy burst into laughter. "I like this girl. Ricardo, give her the part."

"Give her the part?" Ricardo echoed, disgruntled. "*You* haven't got the part yet, so why don't you zip it?"

"Dana will whup you if I don't get to play Sebastian," Yoandy said with a smirk. "And *I* say you hire Candace for Annika."

She would have been appalled if anyone else had said

that. But then again, she'd never met anyone quite like this guy. Charm radiated off him like some kind of magical power.

"Uh, hey—who's Dana?" Candace asked, pretending that she hadn't already scoured the internet for details of Ricardo Adams's private life.

"Dana Alexander," Yoandy explained. "Ricardo's wife. The British movie star?"

"Of course," Candace replied. "I love her work, especially when she played Lady Macbeth. I'm crazy for Shakespeare movies."

"Yoandy is a very good friend of Dana's sister, Kay," Ricardo said. "And Kay has persuaded Dana that Yoandy is the next Jaden Smith. The *Latino* Jaden Smith. So she got Dana to *insist* I get him a part on my show. Which is why you're gonna have to tolerate the lousy bum at least if you want to work on *Prepped*."

Yoandy beamed another radiant smile at Candace. "You see how he talks to me? And we're almost family."

Almost family. A very good friend.

Candace made a conscious effort to suppress a frown. Here she was, about to land a huge TV deal and she was getting anxious. Was it because Ricardo mentioned that Yoandy was "good friends" with Kay Alexander? Could good friends mean something more? And did the fact that she cared mean she was jealous? But this *never* happened to Candace. Guys crushed on her—not the other way around.

It was too bad. With every passing moment she was

coming to the conclusion that Yoandy was the sexiest guy she'd ever seen in her life.

"Hi, I'm Lowell, one of the directors." The other man's voice broke across her thoughts. He'd been standing politely to one side with a clipboard in one hand, observing the interaction between Ricardo, Candace, and Yoandy. But now he spoke up, rather firmly. "A couple of questions. It says here on your résumé that you're emancipated. But you're still in high school, is that correct?"

Candace forced her attention away from Yoandy, who had turned to exchange a few quiet words with Ricardo. "Oh, uh, yeah. I'm at Hearst Academy. We break for summer vacation at the end of the week."

"That's excellent. We plan to record over the next month, break for about three weeks around July Fourth and be back at work by August. You'd have more lines, so the schedule's gonna be heavier than for *Downtowners*."

Candace nodded. This was all good news. More work, more money, more face time on TV . . . more Yoandy.

The director put down his clipboard. "If you're ready, Miss Deering, I'd like you to improvise a combat sequence with Mr. Santiago. Then we'll try the second scene."

Yoandy gave her a reassuring wink. He was taller than her by about four inches, and heavier by at least forty pounds. Taut biceps, the outline of a six-pack clearly visible beneath the thin, ribbed fabric of his shirt.

"You're my combat partner?" she asked.

"Don't worry, *nena linda*, it's just like dancing," Yoandy

said with affection. "And all Cubans know how to dance."

"You're Cuban?" she said, secretly wondering what *nena linda* meant.

Ricardo snickered. "I guess she's never heard of you, lover-boy."

Ignoring him, Yoandy took her by the hand, as if to lead her to the exercise mat on the other side of the room. The skin of his palm was bone-dry, smooth and soft, and his grip was the ideal balance between control and gentleness. A little dazed, Candace found herself following. She wasn't quite sure what was happening. She could feel her breath coming a little faster. She focused on looking anywhere other than Yoandy's face or body, but her eyes were drawn to him with an irresistible pull.

When she finally willed herself to break the trance, she saw the director make a note in his smartphone. Then he glanced up at Candace. "Could you go from the top, do the scene, and go straight into the fight?"

"Improvise the fight?" she asked, eyes widening.

"I never did this before, either."

"But at least you're a dancer."

"It's just confidence," Yoandy said, and placed a palm on her shoulder as he looked directly into her eyes. "Candace, I've seen what you can do on *Downtowners*. You're a fantastic actor, in the physical scenes, too. You can do it. I promise."

Candace shook the tension out of her hands. Despite her mixed-up feelings for Yoandy, she was a professional.

She kept her features sharp, determined. "Let's get started."

"I'll give you some basic choreography to rehearse," Lowell said. "Now, as Yoandy pointed out, we saw some really great physical stuff in your role as . . ." He fumbled for the name of her character on *Downtowners*.

"Gina," offered Yoandy. He and Candace shared a knowing smile.

"Right. Let's see some of Gina, but with some inner geek. Annika is not just a pretty girl-fighter, she's a scientist, too. Remember, the show takes place after the apocalypse and a de-aging virus has just been released into the water supply. You're a thirty-six-year-old woman who's suddenly back in the body of a teenager. You need to give us a hint of that experience and expertise."

"Hidden depths." Candace nodded. "I got it."

"Don't worry about playing a middle-aged woman who looks seventeen," Yoandy said in a conspiratorial whisper. "The guy I play is, like, fifty."

"All right," said the director, "let's talk choreography. Yoandy, he hits first; a left hook. You duck, then get up, swing in a kick, parry a punch, and then let him roll you over his back."

"Duck, swing-kick, parry, back-roll." Candace nodded again. "All right." She bounced lightly on the balls of her feet. *What the heck is this?* No one had said the combat would be rolled into the same audition. No one had warned her to expect Ricardo Adams, the star of the new show, at the actual audition. Nor that he was already lining up other roles on the advice of his movie-star wife. Either her agent was totally incompetent, or the studio was playing mind games.

Yoandy continued to smile at Candace. It was a very natural, sexy smile. She made herself look at him from the corner of her eye, like when you tried to catch a glimpse of the sun during an eclipse. She probably should have been creeped out by this guy, who was most likely in a relationship, coming on to her so strong. And yet, she could somehow tell that he wasn't exactly doing that. It was just his natural charm, his unguarded reaction to Candace. Or maybe he had so much charisma that it couldn't be contained, even by the shackles of whatever it was he might have going on with this *Kay*.

Kay Alexander. Candace didn't know who the girl was, but already she couldn't stand her.

PAOLO
CHEVY MALIBU, FRIDAY, JUNE 5

As things turned out, Meredith didn't wait very long to make her move.

The call arrived while Paolo was driving his house-mate Candace to a TV studio in Culver City. She'd loaned her own car to Grace, whose team had a beach volleyball match. Paolo allowed no more than a quick glance at his cell phone before he slipped it back into his shirt pocket. Just enough to see who was calling.

Meredith.

He turned to Candace. "Would you hate me if I just drop you off? Could you maybe get another ride home . . . ? One of the tennis pros had to cancel on a student. He's wondering if I'd take his lesson. But I'd have to bail on you."

Candace groaned. "Fine, be that way, but if you won't support me on the way up, don't expect any invitations to red carpet events."

"You without a date for a red carpet event?" he said. "Never gonna happen."

"Hmm," she mused. "You have a point." The car pulled up to the parking lot of the TV studio. Unfastening her seat belt, Candace groaned, "Go teach your lesson," but then her lips revealed a smile. "I bet you're real popular with the Friday-night crowd. Then after, maybe you'll take one of them out for a drink, am I right? Maybe they'll suggest a hotel?"

Normally, Paolo would have laughed it up. Now though, Candace's accusation held a little too much truth. If the request had really been for a tennis lesson—from just about anyone—he'd have turned it down. But with Meredith, Paolo sensed that "no" wasn't on the table. So he said nothing. Candace opened the passenger door. Her joking expression had vanished. She looked a little concerned.

"Hey, King, everything okay? You seem a little antsy."

He forced himself to smile. "I want to hang out with you. But the truth is, I need the money."

"Got it, good deal." Candace moved away from the car and waved good-bye. "Don't stay out too late, y'hear?"

Paolo was already reversing the car. He grabbed his cell phone and plugged in a set of earbuds. Then he touched the phone screen, returning the last call.

"Hello, gorgeous," said Meredith's silky voice. "Where are you? I'm in the mood for a drive."

"A drive? Where to?"

"We've got an adorable little cabin in the pines, up in Malibu Creek. My husband's away for the night. I'd love to take you down there." He heard the anticipation in her voice. "Or rather, to have you take me down there. I've had a little too much Pinot. It's better if *you* drive."

"You want me to spend the night?"

"It's perfectly safe, Paolo. The place is in the middle of nowhere. My husband is in Sacramento until Sunday. Now stop being a baby and come pick me up at the club."

Pursing his lips, Paolo ended the call. He turned back onto Venice Boulevard, heading north. Ten seconds later, the phone rang again. He answered without looking at the screen. What could she possibly want now?

"What is it?"

"Sorry," he heard Lucy say on the other end, making him jump a little. "I guess now's not a good time."

"Oh, sorry. Just, I'm driving. Sorry, what's up?"

Lucy hadn't reached out to him in weeks. She'd barely even spoken to him. Paolo had been the one making all the effort to be nice since two weeks ago, when they'd almost had sex. Not that they ever talked about that. They were getting along fine, so long as they avoided the topic. Paolo wondered why Lucy was calling him now.

"When d'you think you'll get home?"

"Late."

Lucy went quiet again for a moment. "Oh. I was hoping we could hang out. I—I want to talk to you about something. Or rather some*one*."

The words made Paolo sink in his seat but he tried to hide his surprise. "Huh, mysterious. Who? Can you tell me now?"

A pause. Then, "Nah. This is better face-to-face. Also . . ." Another hesitation. "Are we good, Paolo? I mean, since . . ."

Since we kinda sorta hooked up but didn't? he thought. "Of course. We're friends." The last thing Paolo wanted was for Lucy to have any clue how much her rejection had stung. Better that she thought it had all been lighthearted fun. "It can be with benefits if you like, obviously, I mean that's always on the table, but . . ."

"Yeah, all right, glad we're okay," she said, her voice brittle. "Not that I don't appreciate the offer," she added with a touch of sarcasm.

"I can't wait to hear what you're gonna tell me."

"You dying of anticipation over there? Talk to you tomorrow."

"I'm dying of something, that's for sure," he laughed as Lucy ended the call.

When he pulled into the parking lot, Meredith was waiting for him in the passenger seat of her silver BMW, fixing her lipstick in the mirror. Paolo parked alongside her car. Wordlessly, he watched her. After a moment, she turned to face him, blew a kiss, and smiled. "Get in," she said. "You're driving."

From a distance, she looked like a super-attractive mom being sweet to one of her son's friends. Paolo remembered when he'd first started noticing a difference in the way grown women looked at him. It had happened sometime around his fifteenth birthday. It was subtle. Not anything he could put his finger on. Just something speculative in the way other people's moms and even a few teachers watched him, *wondering.*

Paolo got out of his own car and into the driver's seat of her BMW.

She kissed him on both cheeks. "Hello, Paolo."

It was the first time he'd noticed her making an effort to look good for him. She wore a simple powder-blue silk shift dress that accentuated her slim, athletic figure, under a tight, indigo denim jacket. Her blond hair was freshly washed and blow-dried, her eyes made up with dark gray eye shadow that gave her a knowing, confident air.

When their eyes met, he could already see her desire. Despite himself, he felt the dull ache of his own interest awakened.

This was twisted, he thought grimly. *He* was twisted.

He went for distraction. "What's the deal with this cabin?"

"Hotels are never entirely safe. Good ones, I might get recognized. Crummy ones, the walls are too thin." She fixed him with a sensuous smile. "I'd rather enjoy the opportunity to feel totally uninhibited."

Paolo reversed the car. Uncomfortably, he wondered how much more uninhibited she could possibly be.

They continued a little farther north along the coastal

road, and then turned off onto Malibu Canyon Road. Meredith selected a Madonna playlist, pushed her seat way back, and leaned toward Paolo, her eyes and lips relaxed from the wine.

She reached for the glove compartment, fiddled around for a few seconds, and smiled with satisfaction as she found what she'd been searching for–a half-smoked joint. She used the car's cigarette lighter to light up. Deeply, she inhaled–a sound like a sigh. Paolo glanced across at her. He wondered if she'd even stay awake long enough to tell him how to get to her cabin.

The road started to twist, carving its way through the canyon as hills appeared around them. To their right, below the road, a creek flowed alongside. Dusk began to fall. The slopes of the hills and mountains glowed deep ocher as the sun descended, contrasting with the higher, deep blue of the sky. Every now and then they passed curves on which a scrub of parking area contained the occasional car that had stopped to allow the passengers to admire the scenery. Other times they passed improvised stalls selling firewood, strawberries, and bonsai trees.

A peaceful silence settled between them. Meredith finished the stub of joint, cracked open the window, and let the wind take what was left. Paolo checked on her again after a few minutes. She was close to sleep. He stretched a hand out to the car's touch-screen controls, trying to change the music. For a split second his eyes flicked away from the road.

The next thing he heard was a blaring horn. His fingers froze in midair. A gigantic truck was approaching, flashing its headlights. To his horror, Paolo realized that he was halfway across the road, heading straight for oncoming traffic. He yanked the steering wheel over, swerving out of the way of the truck.

The truck sped by, mere inches to his left. Shaken, Paolo slowed down, pulled over in a tight swerve, and came to a full stop at the side of the road. His heart was pumping, he could feel a fresh film of sweat under his arms. His breathing began to slow. He looked over at Meredith. She was awake, her eyes open, wild and staring.

"Omigod . . ." she slurred, fumbling for the door.

Paolo put a hand out, trying to restrain her. She shot him a look of pure disbelief, pushed his hand away. The passenger door swung open. Meredith staggered against it, almost fell into the road.

"It's fine, get back in the car," he tried to tell her. But she wasn't hearing him. Instead, she swayed for a second and began to move around to the driver's side of the car. She rapped against the window with her knuckles, shouting, "Get out, you maniac. I'm gonna drive. You almost killed us."

Paolo kept the door locked. Meredith glared at him, eyes totally unfocused.

"Don't be crazy," he said. "You're wasted. Would you please get back in the car?"

She straightened up, her features twisted with anger.

Paolo slowly pushed open the driver's door. He had to get her back in the car. They were less than twenty yards from a blind corner. As the door opened, she backed farther into the road.

A white SUV appeared from around the corner. It slammed into Meredith, sent her body arcing through the air. He heard brakes screeching, hard. The noise seemed to last for several seconds. But the vehicle didn't stop. By the time Paolo was out of the car and at the roadside, the white SUV had already disappeared into the distance. Barely able to make himself look, Paolo turned toward Meredith. She lay in a crumpled heap farther up the road, straddling the shoulder, the golden tan of her bare legs contrasting with the gray asphalt.

He slammed the driver's-side door behind him, rushed to her side. Her eyes were still open, staring blankly into the sky. Paolo slumped to his knees. His fingers felt numb. Ice seemed to have crystallized along the length of his spine. He tried to say her name but no words would leave his mouth.

Blood pooled about her head like a wine-colored oil slick. Paolo looked down. He was trembling with shock. The right side of her head had been crushed—he could see the horrific dent. He couldn't bring himself to touch her.

Meredith was dead.

Desperately, he stared into the road. Two neat tire tracks marked the surface, a black smear that led to and away from a broken body. There was a faint smell of burnt rubber. Unsteadily, he rose to his feet, backing away. Panic was beginning to grip him. Pieces of a hideous puzzle were falling into place around Paolo. Police. Jimmy. Jimmy's dad. Eventually, maybe even the con Paolo had played on them with Darius. He was convinced that if anyone made even the smallest connection between him and Meredith, her death would be blamed on him.

Paolo knew, with blinding insight, the law would not protect him today. If he didn't get out of there fast, a world of legal consequences would surely descend.

MAYA
VENICE BOARDWALK, FRIDAY, JUNE 5

Maya took a moment to check out the blond guy on her doorstep, wearing faded blue Levi's and an untucked, mint-green polo shirt under a shabby, brown leather jacket. He looked more put together than the typical Caltech student. He smiled back, a surprised little grin, like he'd also expected someone else but was kind of delighted by the sudden turn of events.

"I'm Jack," he said in a British accent, offering his right hand. With a measure of self-consciousness he added, "Jack Cato, your new tutor."

They had decided to meet up at the beach house, but after a few minutes it became obvious to her that was a bad idea. The kitchen/living room was the only communal space other than the balcony and it didn't feel right to monopolize either. It also didn't feel right to invite Jack into the bedroom Maya shared with Grace and John-Michael. Instead, she suggested they head for a nearby café.

A warm breeze greeted Maya and Jack as they left the

house. There was salt and the fine dust of sand in the air. She breathed it in contentedly. Days like this, she loved being in the house. If she could only succeed in getting her school situation straightened out, she'd be so happy.

Two days ago she'd been called to see her homeroom teacher, Mrs. Geary. Math and chemistry were the problem, it seemed. With the long summer vacation coming up, her teachers didn't feel confident that Maya could afford the break. She was weak in both subjects and chem was the only science she was taking. Physics was just more math, and since Maya had a "thing" about cutting up animals, biology wasn't an alternative.

Geary had asked, "Do you think that the difficulties you're having in math and chemistry might stem from your dyslexia?"

Well, duh. Maya had just smiled sweetly. "Maybe." Or maybe it was just that she didn't have enough time to properly study, what with all the coding, but she guessed it was best not to mention that. There was extra funding available for dyslexia-related issues. But for spending-all-your-spare-time-developing-apps, not so much.

"I'm told that you're a gifted computer programmer?"

The comment had put Maya on her guard. No one at school—apart from Lucy—knew just how much of Maya's spare time went into coding.

Geary had continued, "I'm assuming you hope to get into a good college? With some improvement, that is a possibility."

She remembered how she'd reacted then—stared hard at the pattern of yellow-and-blue plaid on her skirt and pretended to be deep in thought.

The teacher had pressed the point. "Google, Facebook, all the top Silicon Valley companies; they recruit from the best colleges. Wouldn't hurt to get yourself on the road to all that. Your math and chemistry teachers think you just need a bit more study time. Maybe over summer vacation, with a private tutor?"

That had drawn a quick-fire, disbelieving response. "I have to come to school over summer vacation?"

"If your mother signs the permission slip he can tutor you in your home, which I understand is not with her. Is that right?" Geary had handed over a business card. "I'm going to recommend a young man we've used before. His name is Jack Cato. He's majoring in chemistry at Caltech. Very clever, and he's only seventeen. His agency will invoice the school."

"But he's not, like, a psycho or anything?"

"Jack's references are excellent; his tutorial agency has run all the background checks. He's a nice guy, by all accounts."

Now, with Jack beside her as they strolled along the boardwalk, Maya took a few moments to observe him. He wasn't particularly tall, only a few inches taller than her. He had a heap of dirty-blond, unruly, collar-length hair that reached down to his eyes. Slender and narrow-hipped, his clothes practically hung off his bones. Darker, prominent eyebrows lent intensity to his pale blue eyes. He didn't look any older than fifteen.

Maya had never talked to a British guy before. His manner was quite disarming. Distractingly so. He had a way of grinning while saying rather serious things, and rubbing an ear or his chin at the same time, or otherwise giving the impression of being deeply uncomfortable, laughing.

"You went to Eton College. Isn't that where, like, both the princes studied?"

"It is," he replied with a friendly grin.

"So do you know Prince Harry?" Maya asked, a little flirtatiously. "You sound a lot like him."

Jack guffawed. "Do *I* know him? No. Harry's *army*. We—ah—we don't exactly move in the same circles."

"I thought Eton College was some super-fancy prep school. Aren't you 'posh'?"

"Me? God, no. I'm a scholarship boy. No aristocratic blood, no 'new' money. Very ordinary. Sorry about that."

"Why should you be sorry?"

Jack glanced at her for a second, as if to check if she was being sincere. They'd arrived in front of the coffee shop. He opened the door and stepped aside to let her through, with a gentlemanly flourish that Maya found impossible to take seriously. A little later, Maya realized he *had* been serious. It wasn't that she wasn't used to the occasional bit of macho charm. But boys like that were often looking for something in return. It was unusual to meet a guy of Jack's age who was so self-effacingly gallant.

Unusual and kind of intriguing.

"So, Miss Soto, you're having problems with math and chemistry? Where would you like to begin?"

She eyed him quizzically. "'Miss Soto,' really?"

Jack looked immediately taken aback. "Do you not like that? Would you prefer Maya?"

"Miss Soto is, like, a teacher's name."

"Maya, let's do whatever makes you happy. Okay, tell me what's going on. What do you find particularly challenging?"

Maya opened the blue plastic folder that she'd brought along and removed some worksheets.

"Okay, so, acids and bases. Molarity and pH and stuff. It's chemistry, but there's some math, too. Basically, I'm clueless. To be honest, I don't really like chem." She shrugged happily. "Sorry to be so down on your entire existence."

Jack peered at her for a moment, his lips twitching as though they weren't sure whether to form a grin or a frown. "You're not giving it a real chance," he said eventually. "Chemistry is *immense*. And before we're done, you're going to think so, too." He took a black-and-red notebook from his own messenger bag and began to write. "There's a very easy way to make this stuff simple. What you need to do is keep the idea of moles in your head. You know what a 'mole' is, right?"

"It's a chemistry thing to do with molecules? I get confused between moles, molecules, molarity."

Jack smiled gently. "In that case, let's start with that."

He waved the waiter down and ordered two café lattes and chocolate chip cookies.

A steady breeze swept across their table from the beach. Maya could suddenly smell Jack's mingled scent of bergamot-and-lemongrass-tinged deodorant and a hint of something muskier. Together with the watery blue intensity of Jack's scrutiny, Maya felt a definite impact. It took several moments before she was able to decode what she'd experienced.

Gradually, every word out of Jack's mouth came to seem utterly fascinating. And yet, as engrossing as those words were, Maya found it almost impossible to process what he'd been saying. Chemistry with him was going to be amazing. But she was still going to struggle.

PAOLO

MALIBU CREEK STATE PARK, FRIDAY, JUNE 5

Underneath the bend in Mulholland Highway, the firm dirt of the slope gave way to gravel. Paolo began to slide. Arms stretched out for balance, he half fell, half scrambled down the side of the hill. By the time he reached the bottom of the gully he was covered in dust, palms grazed, mouth dry from the parched earth. He looked up. The road where he'd left Meredith was about twenty yards above him. It was still light enough to see without a flashlight. Anyone who stopped by her body would only have to throw a casual glance in his direction to spot him. About fifty yards away was the edge of a pine grove. It was the nearest cover.

Paolo turned and sprinted hard toward the pines. Behind him, he heard a car speed right past the spot where Meredith had fallen. Some people were soulless dirtbags. But for once, that was working in his favor. He kept his eyes down. The ground was full of rocky obstacles. Every yard brought hazards. This was hiking country, not a running track. But he couldn't slow down.

Thirty yards to go. Twenty. The sound of a car slowing down. Noises amplified by the dry terrain. If they stopped their engine they might even hear his footsteps.

Ten yards, five. On the road behind him, a car door opened.

Paolo dashed behind the thick trunk of a pine. He pressed up against it, tight to the bark. His chest rose and fell, burning. He spat dusty saliva, picturing the scene on the road above.

He'd left the BMW's driver's-side door open. Meredith's body was on the ground about ten yards along the road. To anyone who stopped, it would look like she'd been alone. Tests would show that she was drunk. A drunk-driving accident.

My fingerprints are all over the steering wheel.

But what would even make them think Meredith wasn't driving?

Paolo raised his hands in front of his face. They were shaking. He interlaced his fingers as though in prayer, breathing in through his nose. He exhaled slowly. Apart from his fingerprints, there was no sign he was ever in that car. No reason to suspect she wasn't alone.

His heart thudded against his ribs. He could feel blood draining from his head. Panic rising from nowhere, threatening to engulf him.

Think. Be still, and think.

He closed his eyes and thought of *deuce*. Match point to the opponent on deuce, his own second serve. Blow this and you blow everything. Be calm. Becalmed, like a sail-boat. There's no wind. The sea is like a mirror. This boat is going nowhere. *Breathe.* Pull back your racket and serve.

Paolo's eyes opened. The sounds from the road carried with absolute clarity across to where he stood hidden. At least two cars had stopped now. Raised voices. Phone calls were being made.

There's no sign I was ever in that car.

He clung to this thought as he began to navigate through the trees. Every step took him farther into the wilderness. Roads and hiking trails twisted across these hillsides every which way. He'd be sure to run across one, eventually. And then what?

Clumsy, ambling movements eventually became a reg-ular strolling pace as Paolo adjusted to the minimal light. In the east of the sky, a pale, greenish tinge hinted at the approach of the full moon. He wasn't wearing a watch, as usual, and so he checked the time on his cell phone. It was a little after 9:40. He pocketed his phone again and peered into the gloom of the gulley into which he'd stumbled. It was impossible to see more than a few feet ahead. The ground was dry and cracked beneath his feet. Dry scrubby grasses lined the route. Somewhere to his left, Paolo heard the trickle of water. The vaguely clear path that he was fol-lowing veered in that direction. The grasses closed in, until Paolo had to brush them aside as he walked.

It struck him then that terrain like this might house rat-tlesnakes. Paolo stopped and made his way back to a cluster of trees that he'd passed minutes ago and began, carefully, to examine the ground for any kind of stick. He found a twig no longer than his forearm and he used that to scratch around for another, longer specimen. It took longer than he'd hoped, with the dim light challenging his eyesight. His senses became more alert in the quiet, magnifying every tiny noise, and made him jolt to attention. Eventually, he found a stick, about a thumb thick and a yard and a half in length.

Making his way back along the trail, Paolo swept the staff before him, clearing the path, just in case any snakes were dumb or sleepy enough not to scoot out of the way at the sound of his footsteps. The sound of water became stronger, but never reached more than a healthy gurgle. If this was a river, then it was mostly dry, like many rivers in the California desert.

For the first time since he'd left Meredith, Paolo allowed himself to relax, just slightly. It couldn't take more than an hour or so in any direction to happen across one of the crisscrossing roads. The whole area was a national park, so there would have to be some kind of visitor parking lot, eventually. He wasn't exactly lost, but he still needed to find a way home.

Paolo felt for his cell phone and then stopped. The cops could trace cell phones, if they're used. If they were scanning for calls, hunting for the hit-and-run driver, they might use the GPS on his phone to place him at the crime scene. They might connect Paolo to the accident. They might even find the hit-and-run driver—who would tell the cops that Meredith wasn't the driver.

The parking lot at the country club. Paolo's breath caught in his throat as he struggled to remember. Were there security cameras? He was pretty sure there were. If he'd been recorded getting into her silver BMW, then it was all over. He'd have to make some kind of excuse—say that Meredith gave him a ride somewhere, dropped him off.

But why would he need a ride if his car was right there?

Paolo could feel desperation swelling his chest. He needed to do something about his car. But how? If only he could call someone. John-Michael would help him. John-Michael kind of owed him for going halfway to San Francisco to pick his ass up after he totaled his Benz. Not to mention that like everyone else in the house, Paolo was keeping quiet about the fact that John-Michael had driven it, quite intentionally, off the coastal highway.

He urgently needed to call John-Michael. But Paolo couldn't risk using his phone.

The trees grew more densely as the slope began to rise. Paolo's progress slowed. He paused to get his bearings. Mulholland Highway was still right behind him. He was about one hundred yards away now. Still no sign of a trail. He pressed on. There was barely enough light to see by. The crickets creaked loudly in the undergrowth. It was the worst time of day for snakes. They'd be coming out now, slithering across his path. The best strategy was to make as much noise as possible to scare them away. But Paolo wasn't sure if he dared to make loud, human sounds. All it would take was for one person on the accident scene to wonder if there had been someone else in the car and the police might come looking for him.

Who's gonna tell? Not me.

The hit-and-run driver wasn't likely to come forward, either. Paolo felt a queasy sensation as he realized—he and Meredith's killer were now in this together. If one of them were to come forward, it would immediately trigger a hunt for the other.

It was a pretty solid bet that the driver wouldn't be the one to come forward. But what if the guy got a sudden attack of conscience? Or realized that he might get caught and decided not to risk getting charged with a more serious crime, like trying to get away with it?

There could be no relaxing about this. Paolo had to do everything in his power to avoid being linked to Meredith's death.

To his left, Paolo could hear the nearby creek trickling, an anemic sound compared to the heartier gurgle higher up the gulley. From over the rolling peaks in the east, a dazzle of moonlight now lit up a whole sector of sky. He looked up hopefully. Maybe soon he'd have enough light to be able to see a road. He was pretty sure he'd spotted the occasional red taillights streaking past, a long way ahead. Paolo stepped out with confidence, determined and optimistic.

His footstep landed on the sandy ground but didn't rebound. Instead, it sank farther, broke the apparently dry surface, and gave way beneath him. The momentum of his walk carried his second foot inexorably into the same position. Both his feet were immobilized, one just below the surface, the foot completely submerged. Paolo felt panic clutch at his chest. He cried out. Terror swept through him as he struggled to understand what was happening. It only took him a few seconds to figure it out, yet those seconds passed slowly, vague thoughts infiltrating his mind.

I'm stuck. I'm stuck in quicksand.

Moments after he'd felt that first foot slump underneath him, Paolo began to realize that he was sinking deeper. He pulled hard at each foot, twisting this way and that. With every movement he sank a little more. Now he was submerged to the knees. The deeper he went, the more he panicked. The dual sensations of being trapped and of sinking were simply overwhelming. Any minute now he'd be in up to his waist. Then he'd have no hope, none whatsoever. The slowness of it all only added to the horror. It was like witnessing his own demise in slow motion.

With a flash of good sense, Paolo reached into his pants pocket for his phone and transferred it to the slim, tight pocket of his polo shirt. His right hand then dropped to the surface of the quicksand, which was dry and crumbly. He stared hard at the area around him. The surface of the gloopy mud gave absolutely no indication of what lay beneath. Experimentally, he stuck three fingers into the quicksand and quickly pulled them out. They were coated in thick mud the consistency of whipped heavy cream.

The mud now reached the top of his thighs. Paolo looked around. There was nothing for him to do but yell for help. Even that wasn't likely to bring anyone. And if he were found, how would they even get him out? He might be stuck for days.

I might be on the point of death by then.

Paramedics would be involved, the cops, too, most likely. Questions would follow. Where had he come from, what was he doing here?

It dawned on Paolo with a burst of clarity—the only way out was to get someone to come for him. He'd have to contact John-Michael. Even if it meant risking the phone.

For the next few minutes, in the darkness and silence, Paolo weighed the risks. Dying of dehydration under the California sun. Immediate exposure to the cops, with questions sure to follow about Meredith. The phone was a far lesser risk, he could see that. Yet, who really knew what they could tell from cell phone data? Paranoid libertarian types were always bleating about how the NSA could figure out what you had for breakfast from your data trail, but how much of that was grade-A wingnut nonsense, and how much was true?

Paolo faced up then to the fact that he really didn't know. But if he wanted to stay out of prison, he probably shouldn't use his phone.

Which left only one option. He had to accept that no one would come to help him. Paolo had to get out of the quicksand, alone.

PAOLO
MALIBU CREEK STATE PARK, FRIDAY, JUNE 5

Paolo swung both arms around, trying to find anything he could grab on to. There was nothing. His stick was partly submerged, poking out from the dry surface. Paolo pulled it out and wiped off the mud that coated the top ten inches. He tried swinging it around, hoping to catch on to something in the nearby undergrowth that might be rooted deep enough to hold him. But whatever he did manage to hook with the stick came out of the ground at the slightest tug.

He stopped swinging. The movement had taken him down even farther. Now the mud reached his belly. Paolo's breath became ragged. He could hear the blood rushing to his head.

I'm not gonna die. Worst-case scenario is prison. Absolute worst.

The idea of prison was terrifying. Paolo had some idea what prison would do to a good-looking guy like him, someone with zero connections in the criminal world.

He simply could not allow that to happen.

"I'm getting out of here," he said aloud. A little louder,

he added, "I'm not going to prison. No one is ever going to find out about Meredith. Everything is going to be fine."

For a few minutes, determination pulsed through him. He lay the stick down ahead of him, across the surface of the sand. It didn't break the crumbly layer at the top.

The surface. I have to spread my weight.

Bending himself over at the waist, Paolo positioned the stick just below his chest, perpendicular to his body. With both hands, he grabbed the ends of the stick, which was about a yard and a half across. His torso fell across the surface of the quicksand, broke it in places. Now his chest was covered in the thick mud. But to his immense relief, he didn't sink far, no more than an inch or so. It was frightening when he was forced to touch his face to the top layer of quicksand, but even then, only his chin disappeared into the mud. Meanwhile, behind him, Paolo was kicking hard with his legs, resisting the thick suction of the mud as he drew them up closer to the surface behind him. The sheer effort had him panting and sweating within two minutes. His entire body was covered in mud now, his arms buried fist-deep at the surface, his face smeared from chin to forehead, his torso completely coated.

But when Paolo tilted his exhausted face to the sky, he realized that he was mostly lying on the surface, with much of his body submerged by less than a foot. Like some slithering creature, he could crawl across the patch of quicksand using the stick for leverage, until he reached dry land. He took a few deep breaths and gathered his strength. He could do this. He was going to be free.

He let his weight fall forward, spreading himself as wide as possible with his arms. He squirmed, but still he resisted the final submission of burying his face in the slime. The tendons in his neck strained from the effort of holding his chin a fraction of an inch away from the mud. But when he relaxed, he was crushed to see that he'd made almost zero progress.

Desperation shot through Paolo like an arrow. He gulped down a huge breath. This time he flung himself into the mud, no resistance whatsoever. His face sank beneath the surface. He wriggled and put every ounce of his energy into twisting his hips, bucking upward to free his legs. Thirty seconds later he dragged his head free and gasped loudly, dragging down another breath. He was tiring fast. A little more of this and he'd be wrecked. They'd find his mutilated body days from now, perhaps. His eye sockets would be empty—he knew that much. Buzzards went for the eyes of weakened prey.

This final thought was what pushed him to the edge. With a final burst of concentrated effort, he tossed and turned in the mire, until finally he felt his legs freeing enough to allow him to roll onto his back. His neck rested against the edge of the riverbed and—finally—solid land.

After resting for another five minutes, Paolo hauled himself to his feet. He checked his cell phone. It was dirty but mostly dry. The tight fit of his polo shirt's pocket had protected it.

He began to walk, shuffling now, like a swamp zombie, until the sandy mud trapped beneath his clothes began to grate his skin. He stopped and stripped off his clothes, until he was wearing only boxer briefs, socks, and sneakers. He shook the jeans and shirt until he'd gotten off as much mud as possible. He had to do something about the rest of the mud, now, or else it was going to make movement impossible.

To his left he could still hear the creek, but the knowledge that there was quicksand in the area made him anxious. In the end, Paolo decided that he had to reach the water. Now even more cautious than before, he approached, tapping the ground in front of him until he'd reached the trickle of water. He knelt down and dunked his whole head in the cool water, almost sobbing with relief. Soon enough his clothes were all rinsed through and wrung out. He dressed in the damp garments and pocketed the cell phone and the wallet he'd removed during the washing. Once again, Paolo began to walk. And as he walked, he made a plan.

Finally, he came to a narrow country road. It was overhung by trees with low branches that cast a trellis of shadows in the dusky light. The temptation to check the GPS on his cell phone was extreme. Fear restrained him. He followed the road to his left, walking just to one side so that any passing cars might not spot him. In the twenty minutes he spent on the road, only four cars drove by. The road bent and twisted on itself several times. Eventually he arrived at a crossroads. On the opposite side was a sight that made him feel light-headed with hope.

A Department of Parks and Recreation parking lot. From here he could follow a road out of the park. It would take hours to walk to the coast, but he was easily fit enough. Once he was out, he could find a bus to take him closer to Venice.

There was still the problem of his car, parked in the lot of the country club. That was the priority now. He had to get ahold of John-Michael.

Paolo approached the parking lot cautiously, staying in the shadows. A few vehicles were parked in a largely empty lot. There was a public restroom, a vending machine that sold water, sodas, and candy. And a pay phone. Hands trembling, Paolo checked his wallet. He only had two twenties and a five. He examined the parked cars. One was open, the male driver leaning against the passenger door, smoking.

Paolo doubted he could risk a simple approach, like asking the guy for change. In soaking wet, mud-stained clothes he'd be way too memorable, when what he needed was to be invisible. Desperately, Paolo forced himself to review his options.

He could ask for change and make the call to John-Michael. Both actions could be traced to him. He could ask for a ride back to the coast. Another witness, right there.

There was nothing he could do that wouldn't in some way incriminate him.

Nothing *legal*.

The key was to avoid using any *traceable* method of contacting John-Michael.

He needed access to someone else's cell phone. He'd delete any record of the call and no one would be the wiser.

Paolo went to the hut that housed the restrooms. He waited by the vending machine, careful to keep his face turned away. After ten minutes a woman approached with a little boy around three years old. As they entered the ladies' room, Paolo turned to see which car they'd come from. It was a navy-blue Buick LaCrosse. There didn't appear to be another passenger in the car. He approached, trying to remember if he'd heard the woman activate the lock. He didn't think he had. Nor had the headlights flashed. Paolo increased his pace. He felt a surge of hope.

He reached the side of the car. He checked back at the restrooms. No sign of the woman and child. Inside, he could see the blinking light on a cell phone. It was lying right there on the passenger seat. He put a hand on the passenger door. It opened.

He reached for the phone. Then he froze. A girl around ten years old lay asleep in the back of the car. The shock jolted him. He straightened up fast, slammed his head against the roof of the car. The girl didn't budge. Paolo pulled back clumsily. The cell phone was in his right hand. He just about had the presence of mind to close the car door as he made a hasty retreat, as quietly as possible to avoid waking the girl. Ten seconds later he was behind a tree at the edge of the parking lot. He looked across to the car. The woman was on her way back, the little boy's hand in hers.

He didn't have much time to make his call and drop the phone back into the car without being seen. Paolo dialed quickly—the only number he knew by heart, the house landline. Candace's mom had insisted they get one for emergencies.

Please pick up, John-Michael. Please pick up.

Only John-Michael could help him now. He was practical, calm—the only housemate who wouldn't ask too many questions.

His friend's pleasant, tenor voice answered, "Hello?"

The air left Paolo like a gust of wind. "John-Michael, thank God. I need your help. This is serious, man. It's *extreme.*"

"Go ahead, dude. I got your back."

"Get the spare keys to my Chevy. Take a taxi to a gas station in Malibu, but don't stop right at it—walk the last part. Pick up a five-gallon container of gas and a baseball cap, pay for it in cash. Take a second taxi. This time, you're wearing the baseball cap. Keep it low over your face. You got that? Baseball cap. Don't make the taxi wait, get another one. Take that taxi to the Malibu Lawn Tennis Club. You'll see my car in the parking lot. I want you to put the gas in my car."

"Paolo . . . you sound awful. D'you need medical help?"

He felt himself nodding hard. "I'll be fine, JM. Just listen. Keys. Taxi to a gas station in Malibu, but get dropped off before you're actually at the station. Gas container.

Baseball cap. A second taxi. The country club. Put gas in my car. Drive it home. Stay there. Now, repeat that back."

Paolo waited, motionless, as John-Michael stumbled his way through the instructions, twice. "Okay. Good. Also—don't call my cell. Don't call this number."

"I won't."

"One last thing, John-Michael. You're me. You got that? I'm the one going to the gas station. I'm the one taking a taxi to the country club. I'm the one putting gas in my car. My car is out of gas, that's why I had to go to pick up gas. Then I drive home. That's all. *You're me.* So borrow my clothes. I'm wearing blue jeans, gray shoes, and a pale yellow polo shirt. Do the best you can."

There was a momentary pause. "That's a pretty messed-up set of instructions."

"I don't have time to explain. You get what I need you to do?"

"I got it," John-Michael said. "What about you?"

"Don't worry about me. *You're* me. Tonight, I got gas for my car, which I had to leave at the tennis club. Then I went home."

"Dude, I don't look anything like you."

"That's why you wear my clothes and the hat."

A sigh. "All right."

"And don't tell the girls what you're doing."

There was a hollow laugh. "Hell no, we don't tell *anyone.* I don't know what you've got going on, Paolo, but I already don't want to find out."

LUCY

Lucy had just settled down to catch up on some episodes of her favorite TV show, *Grey's Anatomy*, and was secretly glad when her housemates had all gone to their rooms for the night so she had the entire couch to herself. Just as she was getting comfortable the doorbell rang.

Lucy visibly slumped with shock when she opened the door. A wave of cinnamon-scented air wafted past her nose. Nicotine chewing gum. The scent took Lucy right back to those first weeks at rehab, going cold turkey, getting rid of all the stimulants on which her body had come to rely. Lucy froze. Her old rehab buddy from Claremont, Ariana, was leaning in to hug her.

"Dear Lord, thank goodness I found you home! I've been fretting that you'd be out with your friends."

Before Lucy could move away, the skinny redhead had wrapped her arms around her shoulders and was squeezing tight, rocking slightly. "Sure—I should have called. But some creeper stole my cell when I was asleep on the bus. I need a bed for the night. You gonna help me out, Lucy?"

Lucy counted to ten and then gently disentangled herself from Ariana. She stood back to get a good look, or maybe to check that the sinking feeling in her chest wasn't the result of some stupid dream. In front of her stood a petite white girl, slim and with dyed-red hair that reached her shoulders, dressed in tight white jeggings, a yellow sleeveless T-shirt, and a faded denim jacket. On her feet she wore a pair of scuffed red Keds. Gold bangles, hoop earrings, and a silver belt jazzed up the outfit, but made her look several years older than her almost nineteen years, like a woman in her late twenties trying too hard.

"Hope you don't mind me showin' up out of the blue? You don't look too happy! Lucy Long, I sure have missed your moody self."

In a daze, Lucy showed Ariana into the house and took the shoulder bag from her as Ariana wheeled in a carry-on suitcase. She breathed a quiet sigh of relief that no other housemate was downstairs to witness Ariana's arrival. Lucy's mind was already rifling through possible ways to get rid of Ariana.

Ariana looked slightly sweaty, hair mussed, disheveled from the bus journey. Lucy watched her old friend drop onto the gray three-seater sofa. Ariana scowled, then pulled a discarded copy of *Variety* out from beneath her. Lucy went and got a glass of ice water for Ariana, who sipped at it gratefully.

Stumbling for an easy conversation opener, Lucy said,

"You came on the Pomona bus?"

"Two changes after Union Station," confirmed Ariana, fanning herself with the magazine. She already looked irritated, as though Lucy's questions were some silly barrier against which she had to battle constantly. "It wasn't easy to show up here unannounced. But I figured, you know, I had to do it. I couldn't stay in Claremont another day. I needed my best girl, Lucy. If you'd said no, that you were busy or something, I wouldn't have gotten onto the bus. That's it. I'd still be in Claremont now, already thinking about getting some blow."

Lucy froze. She fixed Ariana with a stony glare, and then exhaled slowly, unable to speak for several seconds. "Cocaine? That's what you're into now? Ari, jeez!"

Ariana's reply was wheedling, pitiful. "At least it isn't crystal, right? Or H?"

Dismissively, Lucy said, "I'm no angel. I admit it—I've started smoking weed again, too." Her voice rose, suddenly imploring. "But Ari. You gotta stay off the hard drugs! Is that what you're spending all your money on? Is that why you can't afford a taxi or a place to stay?"

Ariana's face became serious. "You always could see through me. I'll be straight with you, Lucy. I've racked up a little debt again. Not too much," she said quickly, raising both hands as Lucy's expression of forced compassion turned into a frown. "But I needed to get out of there quick, break the habit, go somewhere totally different, be around someone I know can help me."

"So you came to me," Lucy said, struggling to keep the sourness out of her tone.

A beam spread across Ariana's face. "You never once let me down, hon."

Then she was hugging Lucy again. Over the girl's shoulder, Lucy gritted her teeth. There had to be some non-mean way out of this. As annoying as Ariana could be, she'd been a solid friend through the worst months of Lucy's life, and shown her nothing but steadfast devotion since.

Lucy cleared her throat as she pulled away as gently as possible. "How long you, ah, thinking of staying here?"

Ariana's seraphic smile reappeared. "Could I? It'd just be a couple of nights."

"Really?"

"A week at most."

Lucy plucked at her lower lip. "We don't have any spare beds."

Ariana glanced around the living room and tipped a finger in the direction of the green futon. "Isn't that one of those sofa beds?"

Lucy tried to smile. "It's just that, you know, the house is already kind of crowded. Six of us sharing two bathrooms. It gets kind of crazy on school mornings."

"Then I guess it's good that school is almost out. Look, let me help. I'll cook y'all some breakfast, and I won't shower until y'all are gone. I can take care of you a little, hon. Let me do that? C'mon, all this living on your own, you gotta be missing your family just a teeny bit, right?"

Shaking her head firmly, Lucy said, "Not even. I'm exactly where I want to be."

"But you're using again?" Ariana said with a little pout that Lucy could tell was entirely fake.

"Alcohol, tobacco, a little weed on special occasions. It's no biggie, Ari. I'm like a regular person now; I don't go crazy."

"But you're not a regular person, are you, honey?" Ariana said very gently. "You're an addict. Just like me. There's no middle ground for people like us."

Lucy didn't reply, but felt anger burn through her eyes. Ariana was right. *An addict is an addict.* But the illusion of being a normal teenager with a chemical hobby was way better.

"Listen, I'm three days clean, Lucy. But it's not easy. I knew if I stayed in Claremont, I'd fall right back off over the weekend. God knows I've tried enough times. So okay, I admit it, I didn't think about it too much, I just packed a bag and headed for the bus. Please don't let me down. If I can just get through the next week with a good friend by my side . . ."

Slowly, Lucy blinked. She could feel her resolve cracking. The other housemates were going to kill her.

"Okay. I guess. Just a few days, and you be sure to keep your stuff all neat. This is a pretty chill place, but things get nasty when people don't clean up."

Ariana shook her head fervently. "Oh, that's me all the

way, Lucy. You remember our room in rehab, right? Didn't I keep it nice?"

"Yeah, true. Between the two of us, I was the slob," Lucy said as a reluctant grin spread to her lips.

Memories of their time in rehab returned. It hadn't all been bad. The environment had been pretty relaxing: ashram vibes, dreamy music, and the odor of lemongrass everywhere. They'd donned white, waffled-cotton robes and slippers every morning before heading to the sun-drizzled breakfast room in which a dozen bleary-eyed, rich junkies would enjoy mint verbena tea with wheat toast and apricot jam made from fruit grown in the center's own orchard.

Even more impressive for someone of such modest means as Ariana, although from what Lucy understood, her people were recently impoverished. They still rattled around in some dilapidated old house in the Louisiana swamp, at the center of what had long ago been a small sugar plantation.

Lucy had often wondered where the money had come from to pay for Ariana's stay at the rather exclusive rehab center. She'd guessed that the girl had a rich aunt or something; someone who might occasionally be leaned on for a favor, but who wouldn't go as far as regular support.

"You were a slob, messing up a nice place like that," Ariana chided. "But I didn't let you get away with it, did I?"

"Guess you didn't," said Lucy, trying to smile despite

the vague sense of unease she felt at letting Ariana stay. She should really ask the others first. Still, Ariana was a rehab buddy. That was a tight relationship. You didn't even really need to like your rehab buddy, but if it came to a matter of support over the addiction, you had to have each other's back.

Ariana patted the space beside her on the sofa. "C'mon, girl, sit awhile. We need to get caught up. What's it been since we really talked–five, six weeks? What's going on with you and that tennis player, Mr. Disney Channel? Anything ever happen there?"

"Paolo? You could say that."

Ariana smiled wickedly. "Ah, it's like that, is it? You lose your cherry yet?"

Lucy sat beside Ariana, and slapped her sharply on the arm, hard enough to make her yelp with surprise. "Ugh, please. Like I would ever go for him."

Ariana laughed, rubbing her arm. "Ooh–I touched a nerve."

Lucy shrugged. "Maybe. Truth is, we almost hooked up. But I changed my mind."

"Did he get mad?"

"No, actually he was kind of a gentleman about it."

"That surprise you?"

Lucy shook her head. "Not really. But maybe he's angrier than I thought. We were gonna talk yesterday and he avoided me the whole day. Today, too."

Ariana wrapped both arms around Lucy, slow and

deliberate. Lucy kept still, but the gesture wasn't welcome. "Ari's here now, honey," she murmured, her breath warm on Lucy's neck. "We can be there for each other. Just like old times."

Lucy began to count down in her head. She'd forgotten how clingy Ariana could be. Having her around was going to be sheer claustrophobia.

MAYA

OUR LADY OF MERCY CATHOLIC HIGH SCHOOL FOR GIRLS, TUESDAY, JUNE 9

The air-conditioning in the school library wasn't working. Miss Topalian, the librarian, had opened the French doors to the patio outside. Somewhere in the yard, an argument was rumbling along. Maya could hear the raised voices of moody teenage girls and, despite the fresh air, she was sweating lightly under the tight polyester blend of her school uniform. Under the desk, she kicked off her shoes. For once, she was glad she was wearing a skirt.

She peered hard at the computer screen. Another bug. Her new program code was full of them. Each report she ordered found at least one. She sighed quietly. Was there no end to this?

Maya's idea for the Cheetr app had seemed so blindingly simple that she couldn't believe it hadn't been done before. The first version had been a thing of elegant simplicity, and had worked after only a week of debugging. That was the first time she'd seriously looked at what *else* was out there that was anything like Cheetr. Turned out to be quite a lot—people obviously loved to download free game cheats to their smartphones.

Cheetr was okay, but it was going to have to get a lot more amazing if it was going to stand out from the crowd. It was being downloaded plenty, but not enough to make more than a hundred bucks a month in advertising revenue. It wasn't even just about the money: the truth was, since Maya had found out how many similar apps were out there, her interest had waned.

Who really wanted to be nothing more than a *wannabe*? Original ideas were elusive, that was for sure. But originality was well worth the extra effort.

Maya's cell phone buzzed.

WHERE IS THE LATEST REPORT?

Yet another message from her mom about her employer, Dana Alexander.

Of all the people her mother had to work for, why did it have to be Alexander? Maya felt like putting a curse on that British movie star for soaking up so much of her time and attention.

Maya had to get her mind off her family troubles and onto her work.

It wasn't easy, though. Maya's mother was terrified that Alexander would reveal their family's secret and she would be deported. If that happened, Maya knew her mom would insist on taking her along, too. Not all parents were so ready to let their kids be emancipated—Maya's least of all.

That fear had driven Maya for long enough. Spying on her friends was no longer an option. Lying, concealing. What was the point of doing something that made your everyday existence a misery?

Being sent to live in Mexico City didn't frighten Maya as much as it once did. Now that she'd figured out why Dana Alexander wanted her to spy on the house, she was more scared of what Dana might do to keep her own secret safe.

From what Maya had pieced together, it seemed Alexander had attended the infamous Hollywood party where movie star Tyson Drew was murdered eight years ago. A drunken brawl between Grace's father, Alex Vesper, and the murder victim had taken place earlier in the evening. Combined with Vesper being the only party guest with no alibi, it had been enough to convict Grace's dad. Now Grace's father was on death row for the crime, but maybe the wrong person had taken the blame?

Lucy was at the party, too, back when she was a child star. The fact that Alexander was going to so much trouble to keep tabs on Lucy and everyone associated with her made Maya wonder if Lucy had seen someone else with Tyson Drew at the party that night. Someone Dana hoped she'd keep quiet about.

Did Lucy know something that proved Dana Alexander was the real killer?

Dana Alexander; Grace's father, Alex Vesper; and Lucy. A triangle of deceit connected them. Maya was acutely aware that amongst the housemates, she alone had access to all three points of the triangle. She alone could fit the facts together. And now Maya was scared enough to make a crucial decision.

She was done with helping *la inglesa*. Sure, she'd file the reports. But from now on they'd mislead and distract.

I'm not your slave anymore, Dana—I won't betray my friends.

Arriving at that decision had felt like a release. No more sneaking around or spying on those closest to her. It had unlocked Maya's creativity. Since then Maya had dreamed up a truly *immense* (as her tutor from England, Jack, might put it) new app—Promisr. A social app for matching favors— a promise for a promise, the barter economy.

Maya hadn't dared to show the whole app to anyone yet. They might hate it. But worse still—a lot worse—another coder might steal the idea. For now, it was Maya's secret. Sometimes, in the early hours of the morning when lines of code danced before her eyes, even when she was trying to sleep, it felt a little like her own personal hell.

It didn't take long to locate the bug in the code. When she did, Maya cursed, quietly and vehemently, in Spanish. Another unbelievably dumb mistake. A five-year-old child wouldn't make that mistake.

Maya corrected the code, recompiled the program, and started the tedious process of reloading it on the iPhone emulator.

Dyslexia. It slowed everything down. At least Jack was managing to tackle some of the academic weaknesses that arose from the sheer lack of time she had to devote to math and chemistry.

The first lesson with Jack had gone amazingly well. She hadn't been able to stop thinking about him since that day on the boardwalk when he'd laid bare the mysteries of *molarity.* She was also surprised that some of what he was teaching her was beginning to sink in.

"It's incredible," she'd marveled, minutes after solving a particularly fiendish problem. "Why don't they teach us this way at school?"

"No idea. It's how I was taught."

She'd released a huge sigh. "Thank you. Jeez, now I'm worried that I won't be able to do this when you're not here."

"In that case, you'd better try problems seven and nine," he'd told her with a wry grin. "They're even tougher. If you solve those, you'll be unstoppable."

"Should I email the answers to you?"

"Sure." He'd written his email address on a piece of paper, torn it off, and handed it to her. To her surprise, Maya had experienced the tiniest frisson as she took the address. There was something strangely intimate in knowing they had a way to communicate now, any time of the day or night. She'd never felt this way about getting anyone else's email.

In the school library, waiting for her code to compile, Maya took out her phone, looked up Jack's contact details, and began composing an email.

Hey Jack, I may not get around to sending you the latest chem problems for a few more days. Kinda distracted with my app. I'm getting all kinds of suggestions from the Cheetr users.

The return email arrived with the speed of an instant message.

You wrote an app? Seriously, wow.

Maya giggled loud enough to catch Miss Topalian's eye. "Hey over there," she called out. "I hope there's nothing inappropriate going on."

"I know," Maya agreed. "Like I need the distraction, right?"

"I hear it's all hands on deck with you," Miss Topalian said, waving a hand vaguely as she returned her attention to her own computer screen. "No talking in the library," she said to no one in particular.

Maya's phone lit up again as another email arrived from Jack.

How many downloads?

She typed back, Cheetr? A few thousand.

Amazing. So what's next?

Maya hesitated. Her latest idea was too new to talk about it, but Jack hadn't said he was a coder. She was dying to tell someone about it, at least the basic concept.

I'm working on something new. More of a social app.

Sounds like a plan. Social is definitely where it's at. What does the app do?

I'm still working on the alpha version . . . prefer not to discuss details yet.

This time there was a longer delay before his emailed reply arrived.

Not a problem. Totally get where you're coming from. It's just that I was wondering what you're doing about investment.

. . . Investment . . . ?

Have you thought about getting together with a business

angel? Some guy in the know, connected and suchlike, who'll bung in a bit of cash to get you to the next level.

Maya was in the middle of composing a reply when the phone began to buzz. It was Jack.

"Take it outside," Miss Topalian said the moment that Maya opened her mouth to reply. The librarian pointed toward the open French doors. "Bring me a diet soda from the machine and we're even," she said with a wink as Maya passed the desk.

"This is all rather exciting," were Jack's first, slightly breathless words. "How come you didn't mention the other day that you wrote apps?"

"I was trying to stay focused," Maya said. It wasn't entirely true. She wasn't sure how much of what she shared with Jack would bounce right back to the school administration. It had felt safer to keep quiet about the extent of her coding in case they tried to slow her down. Yet she sensed that Jack would understand. Guys her age understood tech in a way most teachers didn't.

"So—what's the answer to my question? Do you want to take things to the next level?"

Maya paused, felt the skin on her cheeks tighten as she blushed at the faint hint of a double entendre. Turning away in case Miss Topalian saw her, she tried to suppress her own instinct to flirt.

He's your tutor, for crying out loud, she told herself. *Get a grip!*

"I . . . I don't even know what the next level is," she said, and heard the huskiness in her own voice. "I'm just trying to write a cool app."

"Oh—well, okay. It all sounds tremendous. I didn't mean to interfere."

Maya smiled, once again taken aback by his politeness. "No—I appreciate the advice. Business angel? I'll look into that."

"What I wanted to tell you is that if you ever need a contact, let me know. I only know about them because I went to a networking thing at the Caltech Investment Opportunity Network." He gave a heavy sigh.

For a moment, Maya regretted her reaction. He seemed a little put out, deflated. "You know investors then. How come?"

"'Know' might be putting it a bit strongly. I've *met* some."

"You're still way ahead of me," she said, this time encouragingly.

"It's a long story, but basically, my rather troublesome ex, Clarissa, is over from London. Things can get a bit, y'know, awkward, so I thought I'd take her somewhere where we'd have a lot of distraction. Mainly, it's a bunch of 'angel' investor types hanging around campus. If you want, maybe you could come along to the next pitch meetings?"

"Come along with you and your ex?" Maya said, barely containing a gasp.

"Not at all," he replied hurriedly. "I mean, after Clarissa's gone back home. It would just be you and me. Truth be told, I don't have any free time until she leaves, anyway."

"Ha," Maya said, relieved. "Me? Pitch to investors? Yeah, like that's gonna happen."

"And why not?" he demanded. "What do you say? Are you in?"

Maya nodded slowly, clutching her phone to her ear. The sudden drop in his voice, the insistent timbre sent a shiver right through her. She felt a long-forgotten thrill course through her veins. When had she even last had a crush? And why did it have to be on a tutor—especially one whose "rather troublesome ex" was in town?

"Sure." Maya took a deep breath. "I guess it couldn't hurt."

LUCY
KITCHEN, VENICE BEACH HOUSE,
TUESDAY, JUNE 9

It always took a few seconds before the images made sense. First she'd notice the pale blue glow of the pool water, how the ripples radiated across the surface. Then she'd puzzle over the sight of two figures struggling at the near edge of the pool. They were almost directly beneath her. Instinctively she grasped that the tiniest noise would betray her. Frozen rigid, she could only grip the edge of the balcony with her small fingers and watch, breathless, as one of the figures fell into the water.

It looked like a game, but the silence made her understand that it wasn't. It was something private, something between two adults, the kind of thing from which kids were shooed away. Turning to leave, she noticed a hand emerge from the shadows and push down on the submerged figure's head. Long nails painted the prettiest peach shade she'd ever seen.

Later, wandering in despair, wet and unable to find the

bathroom, she bumped into the lady. A cold terror gripped her and she could only stare at the beautiful peach-colored nails.

"Charlie didn't see anything. Nothin'. Go 'way."

"Lucy?"

"Pretty lady said if I go to bed now I can get my nails painted like hers. GO 'WAY!"

"Lucy!"

Lucy shuddered awake. She felt a firm hand on the curve of her shoulder, rousing her. She blinked, bleary-eyed. "Ari?"

"You were dreamin', honey. You were Charlie again."

Lucy gave a low groan. "Oh for pity's sake." How long would she be haunted by the memory of that night at the Hollywood party? It was almost as though her subconscious was prodding her to take action.

"You're still getting the dream, huh?" Ariana said sadly. She leaned against Lucy, easing herself onto the bed alongside her friend, stroking her hair. "The one where you see the woman with the fancy manicure drowning someone?"

"Just shadows," Lucy said, lying. Ariana's interest in her "Charlie" memories was already kind of morbid. The last thing she wanted was to encourage it.

She sat up, still feeling groggy. What was Ariana doing up in Lucy's bedroom? Candace's bed was empty. She glanced at the clock on her nightstand. It was 9:20—way too late to go to school without a killer excuse.

Puzzled, she stared for a moment at Ariana. She'd put

on a little weight since Lucy had last seen her. It suited her. Her pale, lightly freckled face was already made up, hair already tied back in a neat, high ponytail. Ariana's hair was still her favorite pale-raspberry color; although the natural shade of mousey-brown was showing at the roots. When Ariana wasn't looking, Lucy stole a glance at her friend's arms. There didn't seem to be any new signs of needles. She seemed calm, too. Less jittery than you'd expect for someone who was going through the early days of withdrawal. Her story wasn't adding up. Maybe Ariana had another reason to visit? Something even more personal—something that she'd confess only after the two girls had reestablished their old bond of trust?

Lucy reached for her cell and called school to say she was sick. It would probably get her in trouble long-term, but she hadn't used the tactic for weeks. Sometimes the suckiness of school got ugly. When that happened, she just had to take a day off, no matter what. But at least she didn't have to petition her college president mother for every sick note, so there was that. Anyhow, there were only four days left in the school year. Even the teachers were barely hanging on at this stage.

Ariana waited until Lucy got off the phone to speak. "Why don't I fix breakfast for you. How about pancakes?"

Lucy feigned enthusiasm. "Sounds good. But you should let me cook; you're my guest."

Ariana hugged her briefly. "You've been so nice. I could see your friends weren't too happy about letting me stay. I feel bad, making trouble for you."

"They're just surprised, that's all," Lucy replied, getting out of bed. "I hadn't told anyone about you. I don't talk about my life back in Claremont, at least, no more than I have to. And they didn't know I'd been in rehab."

Ariana followed her out of the bedroom and down the stairs. "I kind of totally ratted you out to your roomies, didn't I?"

"Yeah and by the way, thanks for that," Lucy replied snarkily. As they arrived in the living room, she noted with approval that the futon had been folded back up into a sofa. The bed linen was gone and Ariana's suitcase was neatly tucked between the futon and the sofa.

"Omigod, Lucy. Your face!" Already in the kitchen, Ariana was sweeping toast crumbs from the countertop with her bare hands. She sniggered helplessly. "I'm sorry, but if you could have seen your facial expression, you'd understand. You looked like your mom did that time when she came to visit you in rehab and we snuck out . . . remember?"

Despite herself, Lucy found a grin working its way to her mouth. "Yeah. I remember."

"She may be the dean or president of some snotty college or whatever, but your mom sure knows how to curse."

"I guess I knew how to get under her skin," Lucy admitted ruefully.

"How're you two getting along, now that you don't see her?"

Lucy opened the cupboard and found the pancake mix.

She noticed that Ariana already had eggs and oil standing by. Casually, she reached across her for an egg and broke it into the bowl, pouring in milk afterward. "We don't talk much. I mostly text her a few times every day. Just checking in, letting Mom know what I'm doing, asking about her and Dad. She replies, tells me something about her day. The main thing is, she doesn't get too nosy. It's like I'm away at college or something. It's cool."

Ariana rinsed the cloth she'd been using to wipe down the surface, then poured two glasses of orange juice. "You think it's changed your relationship with her, being out here in LA?"

"I think, yeah, maybe. It's like, out of sight, out of mind. Which, knowing my mom, is a good thing. She's got to have so much of her life under control; if I'm part of that then it's like, I have to fall in with all those other performance measures."

Ariana shook her head in sympathy. "That's no way to live."

"It's just how Mom is. That's why she's so successful. I think, after a while, she didn't even want to be that way, but she just couldn't stop herself."

Lucy whipped up the batter for about one minute, thinking about what she'd just told Ariana. They'd skirted around these types of topics during their phone calls. But it'd been a while since they'd last had a really long talk. And it was nicer to have Ariana actually in her kitchen, sharing past history.

Ariana must have picked up on this, because she gave Lucy a wry smile. "Face it, honey, you've missed me. Get over here, gimme a squeeze."

Lucy endured yet another hug before moving over to the stove to heat up the griddle. Ariana leaned back against the countertop, juice glass in one hand, observing Lucy in her element.

"You know something, you've really grown as a person."

Lucy scowled. "Ugh–can we ditch the rehab talk? You always gave it to me straight, Ariana. C'mon, now, I can take it."

"You want me to call you out on something?"

"No," Lucy replied. "I just don't want any bull. Out here, I got away from all of that. The housemates, they're my friends, *all* of them. I didn't think it would be like that. We're all so different. But you know what? It really is that way. We've been through some stuff and, yeah, okay, I only told them very recently that I was on *Jelly and Pie*. Then you showed up. Which meant that anyone in the house who hadn't already Googled me, found out about me being in rehab, too. I don't want to be defined by my past. I don't want to be that girl anymore."

"It was sorta careless," Ariana admitted. "I'm sorry, hon."

"It's all out in the open now. No one seemed too freaked out about it. Candace isn't running to her mom to tell her that one of her tenants is a raging junkie. It looks like everything is okay."

Ariana didn't speak for a moment, which surprised

Lucy a little. Instead, she took the pancake batter from Lucy's hand and poured a measure onto the hot griddle.

"Yeah," Ariana said eventually, when three pancakes were cooking. "Your only problem now . . . is me."

It was true—almost—but Lucy had tried to conceal it. Either Ariana was being super-sensitive, or Lucy wasn't playing the role of "hospitable friend" very well.

"You're not a problem."

Ariana nodded without looking at Lucy. Softly she said, "Oh, yes I am. Lucy, I'm four days clean. Today makes five, if you help me get through. Tomorrow is six. It just keeps getting better from there. Meantime, you're still smoking the ol' ganja, am I right?"

Lucy flushed with resentment. "My parents threw me out because they caught me smoking. And they gave up on me. They refused to send me back to rehab. Now I'm supposed to get clean *all by myself*? Hey, I'm trying. All I've done is a little weed, one time, and that was at a party."

Ariana was immediately contrite. "I've absolutely got no right to lecture. Of the two of us, Lucy, I'm the one who started using hard drugs again."

A little mollified, Lucy said, "Well, I did smoke weed. But like I said, it was a party."

"Then you need to learn how to enjoy a party without being high. I bet you did, once."

Lucy shrugged. She had a dim memory, probably from when she'd been about thirteen.

"Maybe if you threw a party here, I could be, like,

your sponsor, watch over you."

"Oh *sure*," said Lucy with a loud guffaw. "Someone five days clean from cocaine is offering to sponsor a party? That'll work."

"Not the party. Just *you*. Let other people smoke. You and me and probably a few other people, we stay clean, we have a good time anyhow. You and me, we take care of each other. The way we always have."

Lucy picked up the spatula and flipped a pancake. "Get clean, huh?"

"One hundred percent raw."

Thoughtfully, Lucy said, "I guess I could be one of those 'straight-edge' punks, like Ruben."

"Who's he?"

"Guy I know," Lucy said carelessly. "Plays the drums. Yeah," she added after a few seconds. "A party. I guess we probably should. I mean, school's out on Friday. We've survived to the end of the school year—six months of official emancipation. That calls for a celebration."

Ariana plucked at the top pancake on the stack and popped the fragment into her mouth. "Gotta mark the occasion." She grinned. "Hand me the syrup. Let's start talking about how we're going to throw you your first drug-free party. And sweetie, I wanna hear more about this *Ruben*."

JOHN-MICHAEL
BALCONY, VENICE BEACH HOUSE,
SATURDAY, JUNE 13

The idea of a "school's out" party turned out to be popular with the housemates. They had a house meeting, where Lucy officially welcomed Ariana. John-Michael went along with the smiles and niceties even though he'd much rather be ignoring Ariana. It sucked to have a new person in the house—now more than ever. Lucy knew that he and Grace were going through difficult times. Didn't it even occur to her to respect their privacy? For the first time in memory, John-Michael found himself feeling distinctly cool toward his former rock-camp buddy.

John-Michael had planned to cook at the party, but as things got under way, he found himself squeezed out of the kitchen by the gum-cracking, loud-talking southern redhead. She'd been in the house almost a week and was already beginning to act like she was in charge.

"Sweetheart, allow me," Ariana insisted when he tried to object. "You gotta at least let me earn my keep."

Candace saw the whole thing and took John-Michael by the elbow, leading him upstairs to the balcony. "Take no notice of the Wicked Witch of Claremont. We need to talk."

The balcony had been designated a "chill-out" zone, no drugs or music. Which made it, as far as John-Michael could tell, a "make-out" zone, because no one at the party was interested in engaging in deep and meaningful conversation. At least, not without some chemical aid.

John-Michael pushed his way past the couple making out on one of two rattan chairs. He vaguely recognized the girl who sat in the boy's lap. "Hey, John-Michael," he heard the girl say, blearily, between kisses.

"Hey, hey, focus," said Candace, grabbing his chin in her hand. "Can we talk about *me*?" She shot a final, annoyed glance at the couple.

"Or they could maybe leave?" John-Michael said pointedly.

"No more space," the boy said as he came up for air.

"Could you please dial it down a notch?" John-Michael replied. "Seriously, I'm gonna vomit."

Reluctantly, the couple stopped kissing. The blond guy made a show of displaying his right hand, which he proceeded to lay on the girl's left wrist.

Candace stepped past them and snuggled next to John-Michael on the sole remaining rattan chair. He wrapped a welcoming arm around her and planted a gentle kiss on her forehead. "All right, tell Johnny what's up." For the next few seconds, John-Michael allowed himself to enjoy the closeness.

"So listen," Candace began. "I think I may have a crush."

"You?" He pushed her away so that he could stare at her. "Shut the front door!"

"Mmm, John-Michael," she murmured, grumbling. "I don't know what to do. I think he has a girlfriend."

"Who is this *Romeo* and what has he done to you?"

She shook his arm, giving a warning growl. "Don't make fun of me! This is serious. His name's Yoandy Santiago. He's an actor on the TV show I auditioned for last week."

John-Michael started. He sat up, facing her, their heads almost level. "Yoandy Santiago? The singer?"

Candace pouted. "He's a singer?"

"Uh–yeah! He's a Latin music artist. Reggaeton. His father is Beny Santiago, who is like a rock star in the world of salsa music."

"How do you know all this?"

"I went through a Latin music phase back when I was staying with Felipe at his boyfriend's place in Santa Monica," John-Michael reminded her. "They were both crazy for Beny Santiago. He's like royalty in Cuba. He can barely walk down the street in Havana without getting mobbed!"

"But his family lives here?" Candace said, suddenly anxious. If Yoandy lived in Cuba *and* was dating a movie star's sister there were just too many obstacles.

"I'm pretty sure that Beny Santiago defected to the US, like, more than ten years ago. Yoandy Santiago is gonna be on your TV show?" John-Michael shook his head, not bothering to disguise his envy. "Jeez. I hate you. He's completely gorgeous."

"He *is* pretty hot," agreed Candace. "But from the way he was acting, I'm gonna guess that he's straight."

"Just because a celebrity has a girlfriend doesn't mean he's straight."

"She's a whey-faced trollop," she muttered sulkily. John-Michael had to stifle a grin. He loved it when Candace lapsed into Shakespearean curses. "Also, she's the sister of that British movie star from the *Macbeth* movie."

"Latin music royalty dating Hollywood royalty? Good luck getting between all that." John-Michael tapped his phone into life and did a Google search for Yoandy Santiago.

"Quit whining," Candace said, "and let's watch a video of Yoandy dancing."

She leaned close to John-Michael and they both stared intently at a YouTube video of Yoandy rhythmically flexing and grinding beside two ridiculously attractive female dancers. Somehow he managed to exude a boyish enthusiasm through the undeniably sexy routine, singing and rapping between soulful, doe-eyed gazes into the camera.

"You get to work with *him*?" John-Michael murmured longingly. "Candace, I'm not sure we can be friends anymore."

Next to them, the couple making out had become suddenly still. "Dude . . . do you smell fried chicken?" The boy began to shift beneath the girl, sniffing the air.

Now John-Michael could smell it, too. "I guess Ariana's world-famous fried chicken is ready," he said sullenly.

"Fooooooood!" said the boy in the chair in his best caveman voice. "We gotta get some of that chicken."

Candace spoke curtly. "Better hurry."

After a minute the couple was gone, leaving John-Michael and Candace alone on the balcony. "I guess you don't like Ariana?" she said.

"I'm not even totally sure Lucy likes her," John-Michael replied, deflecting the question. "I mean, if they were such amazing friends and all, why didn't Lucy mention her before?"

Candace returned John-Michael's phone to his shirt pocket and carefully stood up, moving to lean against the rail of the balcony. "Lucy forgot to mention quite a few things."

"True," John-Michael agreed fervently. Candace didn't even know the half of it.

"We didn't ask for a live-in housekeeper. My mom didn't authorize that. And Ariana's not paying any rent."

"Totally."

Candace pouted. "Does that make me sound too territorial?"

"I don't think so."

"Do you think Paolo's into her?"

"Paolo?" John-Michael picked his words carefully, throwing a quick glance toward the pathway below the balcony, where Paolo had gathered with a few school friends. Staying on the edges of a party was odd, for Paolo. John-Michael wondered if any other housemates had noticed yet that Paolo's behavior had shifted. Whatever happened out there in Malibu Canyon, John-Michael wasn't going to spill a single bean. "Paolo has his own problems."

"So," Candace said, prodding his upper arm with a finger. "Ariana. Do we trust her? Should I kick her out?"

"Well, the girl *can* cook. . . ."

John-Michael was finding it tough to *officially* complain about their new houseguest. She was far from a freeloader–she cooked and cleaned for everyone. She was also super-polite whenever any of them wanted to watch TV. Yet even so, beneath the southern charm, John-Michael thought he could detect a whiff of his father's greedy ex-girlfriend.

She claimed to be newly clean of drugs, but John-Michael had been around addicts enough to know that someone with Ariana's skin tone and healthy sheen hadn't used for *months*, not seriously. There didn't seem to be another reason behind her sudden desire to move from Claremont to LA, and John-Michael wasn't sure he was buying that story.

There was more to it, something that went beyond words and actions. Like Judy Aherne, Ariana had the keen, wary look of someone up to no good. In the case of Judy and John-Michael's father, it had been easy to connect the dots and draw the outline of a gold-digging lowlife.

But what was there for Ariana, here in Venice?

Still, the fried chicken did smell pretty great.

"You wanna get some chicken?" he said reluctantly, noting how Candace was fidgeting with the rail.

"Oh man, do I!" she replied. "Let's go taste ol' Ariana's southern fried."

GRACE
LIVING ROOM, VENICE BEACH HOUSE,
SATURDAY, JUNE 13

The smell of frying chicken had driven most everyone toward the kitchen and living room. A snaking line had formed of people waiting for a bite. John-Michael had given up his spot on the balcony to the first bunch of party guests who were looking for somewhere to enjoy the hot food.

Grace followed him downstairs, where the stereo was blasting some grating music. John-Michael had compiled three playlists, "nostalgia," "punk," and "zone out." They were somewhere in the middle of "punk" and it was giving Grace a headache. She switched to "nostalgia" and an orchestral sound track swelled. It sounded like the sound track to some kind of action-adventure movie. She was about to switch again when cries of "Yeah, the music from Zelda, awesome!" erupted from at least four kids in the chicken line.

Grace locked eyes with Candace. Her stepsister was leaning on the threshold of the French doors, watching her. They both smiled. "Video game geeks," she said, a Sea Breeze in one hand. "Just leave it on."

Grace felt a stab of guilt as she watched Maya squeeze past Candace on her way in from the tiny backyard, which had been designated as the "smoking" area. Only a few months ago they'd taken great pains to protect Maya from the weed and alcohol at their first party. At fifteen, Maya was the baby of the house and back then they thought she needed their protection. Now, no one seemed to care. They'd told her *once*, right?

"I hope you didn't let anyone out there tempt you into smoking," Grace teased, drawing up alongside her step-sister.

Resentment flicked in Maya's eyes. Candace caught the vibe and joined in. "Let it go, Gracie. You wanna call Aunt Marilu over to bust up the party?"

Maya tipped her head toward the long gray sofa, on which six kids were perched, laughing and smoking. "Maybe we should worry more about the fact that people are smoking *cigarettes* inside. Didn't Candace's mom forbid that?"

Candace turned, apparently unaware. "You guys! Put those cigarettes out or get out."

Luckily, no one seemed to take issue with this. Hands were waved in apology and the burning cigarettes dropped into a discarded Coke can.

Candace turned her attention back to Maya. "How's your app going?"

Maya seemed surprised by the question. "Oh–Cheetr? Actually, I'm kind of moving on to something else."

Grace gave a nod of vague enthusiasm. She suspected that Candace, like her, had very little to say on the subject and was just trying to show polite interest. Maya might have noticed, or maybe not. She seemed to get tunnel vision around her coding.

"How about you?" Maya asked Candace. "You hear back from that TV show you auditioned for?"

Candace's grin became broad. "It was the weirdest thing. Not like going through an open audition, at all. I got invited to the audition a little over a week ago and this morning my agent called to tell me they're sending over the contracts. Somehow I missed the actual 'yes.'"

"Wow," Maya said. "That's *literally* insane. Things are gonna start to change pretty fast for you," she observed. "Next it's going to be magazine interviews and photo shoots. Then premieres. The red carpet treatment."

Candace broke off from sipping her drink to chuckle. "Ha–I guess. To all the C-list events."

"Maybe that's how it begins," Maya said. "Then before you know it you'll forget your friends on the beach, hitting the Hollywood party scene, up in the hills, Mulholland Drive, all of that. You'll be able to ask Lucy for advice–although she probably won't want to talk about it. She must not have the best memories from her days as a child star."

Grace froze. Could Maya possibly know how totally right she was? She was acting as if it was no biggie, as though all three girls knew to what she referred. Yet, it was pretty obvious that Candace wasn't entirely sure what Maya was getting at. "Why would she have bad memories?" Candace asked. "She was a kid and she got to be on TV."

Maya replied calmly and with confidence, "I mean because of the murder."

Grace pressed her lips together. Maya *did* know. Cautiously, she glanced at both girls. Candace stared at Maya in bafflement. Maya's attention, however, was divided equally between Grace and Candace.

"What murder?" Candace said.

Maya seemed bemused. "The Tyson Drew murder."

Candace sounded puzzled. "You keep saying 'murder' like I'm supposed to know what you're talking about."

For a couple of seconds, Grace held her breath. How much did Maya know—and more importantly, *how did she find out?*

Grace couldn't imagine Lucy talking about it. Everything Grace had observed about Lucy screamed total and absolute denial of what she might have seen that night, eight years ago.

Not Lucy, then. Her stomach lurched. Which meant that John-Michael must have talked to Maya. But why?

What exactly had he told Maya about their conversation on the Pacific Coast Highway?

Grace searched her stepsister's face for any sign of recognition. She seemed genuinely surprised. Grace reminded herself that Candace was an actor. She was either giving the performance of her life, or her absolute shock and puzzlement were the real thing. Maya, in contrast, was cool and measured, as if she knew the likely impact of her words. She was drip-feeding the information, watching each girl for their reaction.

Grace felt as though a chilly breeze had just swept across her. She sensed, quite suddenly, that Maya knew a lot more about Lucy's past than she was letting on.

But how much?

"Lucy was at a party on Mulholland Drive. A lot of TV people were there," began Maya. "At this point she'd be, oh, I'm guessing nine or ten years old."

Maya seemed to make an executive decision that their discussion would move outdoors. The backyard had emptied as word got out about Ariana's chicken.

Grace hesitated for a second and then followed Candace and Maya into the backyard. She couldn't feign disinterest. At any moment, she was expecting Maya to reveal that she'd heard all this from John-Michael. Grace had to bury the tide of resentment she could already feel building toward him. How could he have revealed her secret? With everything he'd shared with her—how dare he risk it?

Outside, the air smelled thickly of cannabis smoke. A lanky boy wearing only board shorts lay sprawled, asleep on the edge of the lawn. Aside from him, the girls were alone.

Maya continued, fully conspiratorial, "Another kid from *Jelly and Pie* was at the party, too, plus three other child stars. I think the party was for their agent."

"Are you saying someone got killed at the party?" Candace said. She was clearly still puzzled, as though this was idle gossip about someone they didn't know. Grace guessed that it was the alcohol dulling her senses.

"You don't remember the Tyson Drew murder?" Maya seemed surprised. "It was a big deal in Hollywood. Tyson Drew was an up-and-coming movie star. And he was drowned in the pool, at a party on Mulholland Drive."

Grace said nothing. She watched Maya very closely now. She hadn't mentioned Grace's father yet. If she'd gotten this from John-Michael, it would be just plain aggressive to talk this way in front of Grace, without acknowledging that she knew Grace's father had been sentenced to death row for the murder of Tyson Drew.

It really was not like Maya to be so mean. Was it possible that Maya hadn't found out from John-Michael, after all? Grace's curiosity spiked. "How do you know all this?"

"Weird that Lucy never talks about it," Candace interrupted, with a sudden sharpness that grabbed Grace's attention. "Murder? Rehab? She sure has kept a lot of secrets. If I had stories like those you couldn't keep me quiet."

"Maybe we could," Maya remarked, "if what you knew was dangerous."

Candace just stared. Grace watched and thought, *Finally, she gets it.*

Candace repeated Grace's question. "Seriously, where'd

you get this? I Googled Lucy when she first told us about the show. I bet we all did. None of this comes up."

"The *Jelly and Pie* fan forum," Maya replied with sudden authority. "You gotta search deep, 'cause it's behind a child-protection firewall. And the thread has gone pretty cold. There's some interesting speculation, though. They got a guy on death row for the murder. Of course, he says he's innocent. From the beginning, he's said that one of the kids must have seen the real murderer. But the guy they convicted, he was wasted. He couldn't say which one it was. And all the kids denied it."

"So you think Lucy was a *witness*?" Candace was beyond fascinated. "Holy shit. Maybe that's the real reason why she didn't want us to know about *Jelly and Pie*."

Maya's attention moved to Grace. "Could be," she said, deadpan. There was a momentary pause. "Candace, you think you could get us some sodas? I don't want to get into that chicken-crush."

To Grace's astonishment, Candace simply nodded and disappeared back into the house. It was like some kind of magic trick—no one ever told Candace to do anything. But it seemed as though Maya's bombshell had turned Candace into a willing supplicant.

And once they were alone, Maya dropped a second payload.

"Why don't you tell her?"

Grace took a breath. "Tell her . . . ?"

"That Alex Vesper, the man on death row for murdering

a movie star, is your father," Maya said. She spoke quietly but the veneer of calm had vanished. "You told John-Michael, that day you drove back from San Quentin with him—the day he totaled his dad's car."

Grace shook her head as though she'd been slapped. "How can you possibly . . . Did John-Michael say?"

"Our call was still connected. I heard you guys talking."

The breath caught in her throat. "You . . . heard?" Grace's eyes strayed toward the kitchen where Candace was starting to return, carrying three sodas.

"You have to tell your sister, Grace," Maya said. Her words spilled out, the confidence gone, replaced by an urgency that was unnerving. "Lucy has to speak up, too. It's not safe to keep secrets like this. We're all safer if you—"

As Candace rejoined them, Maya's mouth snapped shut. Candace handed her a Sprite Zero.

"You were saying?"

Maya spoke reluctantly. "Oh. Yeah. The Tyson Drew conspiracy theory."

"Okay so—if the guy they got on death row didn't do it, then who?" asked Candace. The shock had faded, apparently, and she was back to the business of serious gossip.

Maya paused. Expectantly, she glanced at Grace. Grace stayed silent. Maya took a breath. Before she could reply, all three became aware of a commotion in the living room, around the sofa. It looked as though a fight had broken out, with a sudden explosion of activity centered on the sofa. One boy was flung from the group's core. He landed hard against the wall, stumbled, teetered, and fell through the gap between the French doors, landing partway on the grass.

"Get out," he gasped. "The sofa's on fire!"

CANDACE

"You're being too obvious." Candace paused. "Okay, look now."

This time, only Grace's eyes moved. Then they darted back toward Candace. "The guy over by the main set with the Lakers hat?"

"What do you think?"

A pause. "*Very* nice. Did you say he's from Cuba?"

"He was born there, but his family has lived here a while now."

"No accent?"

"An unbelievably hot one."

Candace glanced over her shoulder. Ricardo Adams, whose fame had just exploded across the globe following the dramatic ending of the TV series *Deadbeat*, was the star of the new show. He was standing beside a table piled high with fruit and muffins. At one point, he looked right through her. "Oh and look," she muttered, "Mr. Big."

"Not as cute as on TV," Grace remarked. "You were

right." She pointed at the breakfast buffet. "Can you grab me a peach? Then I'm gonna head off to meet John-Michael at IKEA."

"Please. How many people does it take to pick out a sofa?"

"You know how it is. He doesn't want to stay home alone with Ariana."

Candace frowned. "We gotta do something about that girl."

"I know, but how do you throw out the perfect house-guest?"

"The perfect housemate splits the rent. We'll figure something out." Candace moved sideways and approached the snack table obliquely, with a polite smile at Ricardo. She returned with a large, ripe peach, which she handed to Grace. "Just pick out the couch you guys like and my mom will pay for it online. Make sure that someone's home for the delivery."

"Ariana offered to wait around for it."

"Oh, sure, Ariana is all about the helpful."

Grace sniffed the peach with blissfully closed eyes. "Anyway, what scene are you filming today?"

"Annika and Sebastian meet for the first time, rescue some kid, then fight. It should be pretty intense. My char-acter has been walking all night, through the ruined city, to the bug-out location."

"'Bug-out' location?"

"It's what doomsday preppers call their secret go-to

location where they've hidden all their prepper crap, in case of the apocalypse."

Grace grinned. "Good thing my mom made you take those tae kwon do classes."

Candace couldn't help but smile at the memory of herself as a little thirteen-year-old learning to kick ass in an old gym hall that smelled like a Goodwill store. She'd loathed the experience with a passion and swapped it for riding lessons as soon as her stepmother was convinced that she'd covered the basics. "I guess it wasn't a total waste of time. But who knew I would someday fight hot guys for a living?"

"I take it Yoandy is playing Sebastian?" Grace teased.

Candace had a hard time hiding her smile. "Come on," she said. "I'll walk you to your car."

Candace locked arms with Grace and walked her to the front of the lot, which was open to a narrow walkway outside. When she returned to the set of *Prepped*, Candace recognized only Yoandy and Ricardo. Ignoring her, Ricardo went over lines with Yoandy, who took a moment to give her a little smile. Her agent had promised to stop by to say hello, but so far there was no sign of him. She began to regret letting Grace leave so soon.

It sucked to look like such an obvious clueless newbie. However confident Candace managed to act around people her own age, being on a studio lot in Hollywood was still a very big deal. She wasn't sure of the protocol. On the set of *Downtowners* there'd been a strict hierarchy, depending on how big a star you were. As a total newcomer and the youngest person on set, Candace had been virtually ignored at first.

On the whole, she'd found that it was best not to share any insecurities about her acting. Her stepmother, Tina, had drummed that much into her, those first few years of going to auditions. Now that she wasn't stitched to Candace's side, Tina insisted on lengthy postmortem phone calls after each audition. After the audition for *Prepped*, Tina had reiterated a favorite piece of advice: "Someone asks you if you can do something? You say yes. Someone asks you if you're worried about anything? You say no. You gotta fake it till you make it, Candace. Anyone tells you otherwise is just trying to find your weak spot. Don't let them."

Once, it had seemed like crazy advice. The opposite of all the teachers who told her to be truthful, honest, to share any worries.

"I should lie about what I can and can't do?"

"That's right," Tina had snapped. "The entertainment business is all about illusion, Candace. If you can make someone believe something then it might as well be true. Relax. No one's going to ask you to design a vaccine, or anything."

The assistant director arrived on set, rapped his knuckles twice against the snack table, and then announced, "Change of plans, people. The bug-out location isn't finished yet, so we're just going to record the later scenes, not the fight. Let's have first positions for scene six in five minutes."

Yoandy strolled over to Candace. "Too bad, *nena linda*. Looks like we won't get to practice the fight. And I was looking forward to another dance."

"Well, I was looking forward to kicking your ass," Candace returned teasingly.

Yoandy seemed delighted by the riposte. "Oh, were you?"

Fake it till you make it.

"Yeah, I think Annika could take Sebastian out. Easy."

He warmed to their banter. "We'll never know. He's not serious about this first fight; he's only trying to keep things from escalating."

"Sure, but Annika means it. I'm not going to hold back."

Yoandy smiled. "I'll try to remember that."

Candace paused, then asked, "What does *nena linda* mean?"

He looked startled for a moment, then blinked twice, nonplussed. "It means 'pretty baby,'" he answered in a soft voice. "You don't like?"

"It depends," she said hesitantly. "I mean . . . I guess you say that to all the girls?"

"Sometimes," he agreed with utmost sincerity. "But I can call you *Señorita* Candace, if you prefer."

"Now you're making fun."

"Of you?" He stepped closer, touched a hand to his

heart in mock disappointment. "*Ay, mi madre*. No way, *nena*."

"Hmm," Candace said. "What would Kay Alexander think?"

"Kay?" He seemed surprised at the mention of Kay. "It wouldn't matter what she thinks. She's just a friend."

"I thought you two were dating."

"We've been on a few dates but it's not serious."

"Hmm." Candace was unconvinced. "You sound like my housemate, Paolo. He goes on dates all the time and says it never means anything."

Yoandy shook his head. "With *you* in the same house? He's crazy. But I like this Paolo already, since he's keeping away from you." He paused. "What made you think me and Kay were dating?"

"You said that you and Ricardo were practically family," she pointed out.

Yoandy's jaw went slack. Either he was a terrific actor or he was telling the truth. "That? Kay and I hung out at the Latin Grammys with Dana and Ricardo. I was making a joke."

Candace wanted to believe him, but this was getting surreal. "But . . . there are pictures of you with Kay, in *Deadline*."

Yoandy clicked his tongue. She could see a muscle twitching in his jaw. He was visibly upset. "I promise you, Candace, Kay is not my girlfriend."

She raised an eyebrow, on the edge of flirting. "Does Kay know that?"

"Ladies and gentlemen, positions please!" the director announced. "We're ready for the next scene." Candace reluctantly turned away.

Ninety minutes later the recording was finished. They'd shot about two minutes' worth of action, of which maybe one minute would end up on screen. Other members of the cast were already helping themselves to coffee, water, and juice. Candace was opening a bottle of sparkling mineral water when she heard a voice.

It sounded familiar but didn't register for several seconds. It was probably the sexiest female voice she'd ever heard. Slowly, Candace turned around. About five yards away, Ricardo Adams was talking to someone more famous than anyone she'd ever met in person. A jolt went through her as she stared at the woman.

Starstruck. Candace had never really understood what that meant, hadn't appreciated the physical excitement of seeing someone so strikingly familiar, whose face she was used to seeing magnified to impossible proportions on the silver screen.

Dana Alexander, Academy Award winner, three-time Oscar nominee and, in her day, one of the world's most beautiful women. Even now, in her early forties, she still possessed an absolutely magnetic quality.

She wasn't even dressed particularly fancy; a crisp white shirt, a navy-blue trouser suit of impeccable cut, sleek Charles Jourdan heels that clicked against the sidewalk. Slung over her shoulder was a bloodred Mulberry bag. She wore her hair longer than Candace had seen in the movies; a rich mahogany color with a twist and bounce in the tresses that fell to her shoulders. A complex, oriental floral scent hung in the air as the woman turned toward Ricardo, who rose from his chair to greet his wife with a chaste kiss.

"I'll be out in about ten minutes," Candace heard him say. "Why don't you wait in the car?"

Candace watched Dana Alexander leave, accompanied by a second brunette woman who was wearing a black pantsuit. Candace couldn't see her face. Even from behind and at a distance, she could spot which was the movie star and which was the regular person. With Dana Alexander, everything was dialed to the max: haircut, makeup, shoes, right down to the sashay of her step. The other woman might as well have been a shadow.

"How'd you like Dana Alexander?" Yoandy murmured, startling her with his sudden proximity.

Candace turned to him but took a step back. When she stood too close she had a disconcerting urge to lean against his chest. "She's stunning," she said frankly. "So is Kay. But they don't look much like each other, do they?" That was putting it kindly. From the photos Candace had seen, Kay dressed in grungy, urban fashions and went out of her way to look nothing like her elegant older sister.

"Actually, a little bit, she does. But Kay dresses pretty differently," Yoandy said, tenderly wrapping his fingers around Candace's wrist. "And I wish you'd stop talking about her, *preciosa*. I prefer to talk about you."

"Stop it," she said. But the words got somehow stalled and came out at less than half the intensity that Candace had intended. Things were moving breathtakingly fast. She had to take a moment, to think through what might actually be happening here. Yet somehow she couldn't slow the racing of her heart.

JOHN-MICHAEL

"I can't believe you thought I told Maya that your father was on death row for murdering Tyson Drew."

Grace answered John-Michael with a measure of defensiveness. "It was honestly for, like, only ten seconds."

John-Michael rounded the corner, into the living room area of the giant IKEA store. Six rooms had been mocked up, three on either side of a winding pathway. He kept his focus on the furnishings and away from Grace. Her assumption, even if had been momentary, was surprisingly hurtful.

He wandered into a room that felt similar to their own living area: a maple wood floor, beech shelving units, and white, colonial-style wooden folding tables. The space was dominated by a stylish three-seater sofa in pewter gray. He stood back from it for a moment and then looked at Grace.

"Gray?" she said with a doubtful frown. "We don't have to replace the couch with an exact copy." Grace turned slowly, staring off at other examples. She pointed at a traditional red sofa. "How about that one?"

They made their way over to the other room setup. The entire design consisted of three colors: red, white, and black. A black-stained wood veneer floor, tubular metallic shelving with white shelves, and a large red sofa resting on a white, faux sheepskin rug.

Grace tossed aside two silver-white chenille throw cushions and dropped herself onto the sofa. He could see her watching him, long enough to notice the tension that he almost certainly showed on his face. She pouted. "C'mon, John-Michael. Don't be mad at me."

John-Michael shook his head very slightly. He was angry, but not about Grace thinking he'd spilled her secret. It was just that Grace seemed to have forgotten *his* problem, the gravity of what he'd told her about his father. And that anger was much harder to deal with.

I killed my father. I smothered him to death. He asked me to do it. He was checking out of life. But I'm the one who remembers what it felt like to have him struggle beneath a pillow held over his head, and then give up the fight.

He sighed and sat down at the other end, testing the sofa. It felt fine. In his current mood, one couch was as good as another.

Not a day went by when John-Michael didn't think about his father's death. Grace knew what he'd done—he'd confided in her after they'd driven to San Quentin to visit her father in prison. If she told anyone, he was finished.

How could she think he would tell *her* secrets? What planet was she on?

"Do you like the sofa?" she asked.

John-Michael settled back into the thick, textured upholstery. "It's fine." He leaned over, tugging at the price tag. "Six-ninety-nine."

"Perfect, it's within the budget."

They were both quiet for a moment. John-Michael picked up a catalog from a small pile on the nearby folding table and began to flip through it. Grace stood and strolled over to the shelving unit, pulling out a drawer. Then, as if a thought had just occurred to her, she said, "Do you think Lucy would ever come forward and talk to the cops?"

"After all this time? Doubtful. Also, we still don't know for sure that Lucy saw anything that night at the pool."

"My dad thinks she did. But who even cares what he says?" Grace ran a hand through her hair, clenching a fist in her tresses. "Only Lucy knows if she actually saw something."

He heard the frustration in her voice. "If Alex Vesper was my dad, I'd be putting maximum pressure on Lucy to talk," he said bluntly.

"Easy for you to say."

He sighed. Grace had a point. She'd lived with her secret for a long time. Whereas he'd only found out that her father was on death row a month ago. When they'd visited Grace's father, John-Michael had confronted his worst fear—the inside of a maximum-security prison. Exactly the kind of place where he could end up, if anyone ever managed to make charges stick about his own father.

"For what it's worth, Lucy and I have always been close—ever since rock camp," he said. "We can talk about all kinds of stuff. But in all that time, she's *never* even hinted that she saw anything like what you're suggesting."

"I'm not saying Lucy even knows what she saw. Maybe she has post-traumatic stress."

"That's a possibility." John-Michael's eyelashes flickered. "I mean she does have all the signs."

Grace nodded in agreement. "She needed rehab for a reason."

"I always assumed her drug problem was standard child-star stuff. I feel guilty I never realized there could be more to it than that."

"You shouldn't beat yourself up about it. The thing is, Lucasta Jordan-Long has been a huge deal for me, most of my life. All the child actors at that party the night of the murder—I've followed their careers. When we came to live here in Venice, I sort of expected some of you to remember that she'd been on TV." She looked at him expectantly.

"Well, I knew."

"Yes, John-Michael, and when it all came out about Lucy and *Jelly and Pie*, you admitted it right away. Maya didn't."

He paused. "You think she knew all along?"

"Maya's very good at hoarding information."

"She's not the only one," he said. "Honestly, Grace, take a look in the mirror."

Her sapphire-blue eyes flashed with sudden sharpness. "But *you* know why I'm being secretive. I've admitted everything to you. The question is, what is Maya hiding?"

"Maybe she didn't out Lucy for being a child star because she didn't want to make her feel uncomfortable? She's cautious about our feelings."

Grace regarded him cynically. "Seriously? Maya's not cautious, John-Michael. You know what Maya told me at the party the other night? She told me—no *begged* me—to tell Lucy and Candace about my dad."

John-Michael shifted on the sofa. So Maya *had* been talking—that explained Grace's unusually petulant attitude. Another couple had entered the mocked-up living room and were trying not to stare at them. He stood up and offered a hand to Grace.

As they made their way through the store toward the exit, Grace admitted, "The thing is, I saw her eyes. She's scared, John-Michael. I need to know why." She broke off, reaching for the cell phone that had just started to buzz with activity in her purse.

John-Michael watched her look at the caller's name, then take the call, holding up a single digit to him as if to say "one minute." He watched her listen, saying nothing. Her expression went from quiet shock to breathless horror within seconds. By the time she finally nodded and managed to croak out, "I understand" in a tiny voice, Grace was trembling. The phone slipped from her fingers. John-Michael bent swiftly to retrieve it. Just before the screen faded to black he saw the caller's name: *Mom*.

They'd stalled next to a table of kitchen implements and she was leaning against it for support. He took Grace's right hand in his. "Gracie, did you get bad news? I promise, we'll all be there for you. Is someone sick?"

Grace took a shaky breath and slowly pulled her hand away from John-Michael's. She straightened up and shook her head steadily, as though trying to summon up some resolve.

"No. It's something I've been expecting to hear. It's just that . . ." She gave a sudden, rueful laugh. "Just that actually hearing it is so much harder than I expected."

To his astonishment, he saw a shiny film of tears appear in her eyes. Softly, John-Michael said, "What is it?"

Grace's lips pulled tight. She spoke in a forced, hesitant manner. "My dad. The execution. They set a date. July fourteenth. Four weeks, John-Michael. Four weeks from now, they kill my father."

MAYA
TRIPLE BEDROOM, VENICE BEACH HOUSE,
MONDAY, JUNE 22

Jack Cato was waiting with Grace at the bottom of the spiral staircase. Maya could guess why she hadn't invited him inside the house. The smell of smoke from the couch fire still hung over the ground floor. Without the replacement, which was due to be delivered the following day, the living space looked sparse. Or as Candace preferred, "minimalist."

"Morning," Jack said, beaming. "Beautiful day, isn't it?"

Maya grinned. "It is on the outside. Inside, it's kind of smoky."

He looked puzzled. "Did something happen?"

"A fire," Grace commented. "RIP sofa. So, you're taking Maya to a business brunch?"

"It's more of an entrepreneurs' breakfast," Jack said with a chuckle that brought an instant smile to Maya's lips. "But broadly speaking, yes."

"Jack was a finalist in some big-deal entrepreneur

competition for schoolkids in England," Maya told Grace. "And he got to meet lots of famous people and investors who started successful companies. He found out how all that stuff works, so he's taking me along to this thing at Caltech."

"We're just having a go at rustling up some interest," Jack said with self-effacing modesty. Maya doubted that he could be more adorable if he tried.

Three hours later, Maya was collapsing against the wall at the conference center at Caltech. On the other side of the wall was a room full of rich geeks, some barely out of college, who'd just witnessed her first-ever tech presentation. Her heart was still pounding loudly and steady in her own ears as it had throughout the longest five minutes of her life.

"That was bloody brilliant!" Jack said, breathless. She felt his hand, tentatively reaching for her shoulder and then pulling back at the last moment.

Maya couldn't stop a radiant smile.

"I can't believe it!" she said. He was gazing at her so intently that she wanted to look away but she couldn't seem to do it. "Two of them! *Two* of those guys want to invest in my app! Actual backers. This is unreal."

"You did it, champ," he said, straining to sound humorous. He gave her a playful punch on the shoulder. Their eyes caught for a second and she sensed an undercurrent of tension. This was either more adorable British reticence or he really, really wanted to touch her and didn't know how.

The whole event had been pretty casual, like an

open-mike type thing. Jack had put Maya forward to do a five-minute "bit" about her new Promisr app, and Maya had stood there pitching her social-bartering app in front of everyone, her voice shaking a little bit. It was like some terrifying kind of entrepreneur comedy club.

Halfway through, she'd decided the best thing was simply to demonstrate her app. A cluster of potential investors had gathered the instant she'd finished; all of them young men, none older than thirty.

"I've never seen investors jump like that," Jack marveled, running one hand through his unruly fair hair as he struggled to absorb what had just happened. "You don't get it! Mostly they're kind of bored, actually. You really made those nerds light up!"

"I did, didn't I?" Maya said, equally dazed. "It's incredible to think that some people can just drop that kind of money after a five-minute presentation."

"Well, they did get to grill you for a good hour or so afterward. They can drop a lot more, too. They *will* drop a lot more. You'll see. A hundred K is nothing to these guys. It's not just the tech, it's you. Maya, you wowed them."

"But why?" she asked, bemused.

"Because you're young, brilliant, gorgeous, and, as a girl, you stand out! These guys are dreaming of the day that your photo is on the cover of *Wired* magazine. Or even *Time*!"

Maya beamed, and then shoved him lightly in the chest. "Oh, please. Now you're exaggerating."

Jack caught both her hands in his. She could feel her knees buckling slightly, unable to concentrate on anything but the sensation of his fingers intertwining with hers.

"Are you okay?" he said as she closed her eyes, suddenly leaning against him for support.

Maya was experiencing an exhilarating jumble of emotions. Relief and excitement, but also fear. "Jack, what if I screw this up? I can write code, but what do I know about running a business of any kind?"

"Oh, you shouldn't worry about that. They're counting on you to write the code. You're the brains, the creativity. The business side of things, that's their end."

Her eyes fluttered open. Now she really did feel scared. "You think—you think there's any chance I could get ripped off? It happens."

He raised a finger to her cheek and stroked her skin lightly. "Hey," he said very softly. "I'm the one who got you into this. You think I'd stand by and watch you get ripped off?"

She felt an overwhelming surge of gratitude toward him. "If it wasn't for you, I'd still be fixing bugs in Cheetr, just watching downloads mount up. This is a whole other league. It's major."

"What nonsense," he murmured, his fingers still caressing her cheek. "You'd already started work on Promisr when you first talked to me."

They were standing very close now, enough that she could feel the whisper of his breath, which smelled sweet, of orange juice. She shivered in anticipation of more but instead he pulled away a little, before letting his hand fall to his side. Maya realized with a start that she'd been willing him to kiss her. She released a held breath when he turned away.

"Um, so we'd better get back in time for the next round of presentations. It'd look rude to miss them," he said with obvious effort.

Why won't he kiss me?

Maya thought Jack was cute the first time she saw him but now it was as though some kind of filter had lifted away and she could finally see him. The longer she stared, the sexier he became.

"Jack," she said quietly, not moving from where he'd left her, by the wall. Jack stalled on his way to the door and turned. Frustration clouded his expression.

In that moment, Jack stopped being her tutor, a chemistry genius, a business coach. All Maya could think about was a cute guy with the sexiest accent ever, and everything he'd done for her. At that moment, all *she* wanted to do was kiss *him*.

Maya strode across to Jack and grabbed him by the arms.

She drew him closer, until he was no more than a slight lean of her head away. She sensed that he was still waiting for her to make the first move. A feeling of euphoria went through her and her skin buzzed all over. Then Maya leaned in, no tentativeness now, pushing herself against him, challenging him to resist. The softness of his lips surprised her, something that she'd think about many hours later when the shock of the initial contact had passed.

This time, he didn't hold still. Their mouths seemed to melt together and she reached her arms around his neck, clinging on to him while they kissed.

"Good Lord," he murmured faintly, pulling away.

Maya released her fingers from his hair and stepped away. "Your first kiss?" she said, trying to sound innocent. Who was she kidding? She'd never kissed a boy like that.

"Might as well be," he said with a nervous laugh. "Look, Maya, I . . ."

"Is it because you're my tutor?"

"No! I mean, yeah, a bit, but that wouldn't stop me. I mean if that were an issue I'd ask them to find you another . . . it's just that . . ." His lips twisted in a grimace. "Clarissa," he concluded bitterly.

"Your ex-girlfriend?" Maya could barely contain her disappointment. "You told me it was over. I thought she'd gone back to England."

"And it is, but she's going to be here a bit longer, as it turns out," he said, more than a little guiltily. "She's found some wretched course she wants to do at UCLA. Now she's waiting to see if her uni will let her onto an exchange program."

"Okay but—what's that to you?"

"Maya, I'm the only person she knows in LA. I can't just abandon her. Clarissa is from a tiny village in Suffolk.

LA is bloody terrifying to a girl like her."

Maya couldn't speak. A hundred arguments and insults lined up in her mind.

"Hey," she said, drawing herself up with effort. "It was only a thank-you kiss. If you want to keep this strictly business, then just say so."

"I didn't say that, Maya," Jack said unhappily. But she'd already turned to leave.

PAOLO
THE GETTY VILLA, MALIBU, MONDAY, JUNE 22

"Man, I'd sure like to dive into that pool."

Paolo eyed the broad stripe of blue that stretched through the Outer Peristyle garden, toward the Doric pillars at the far end of the fake Roman villa. Maybe if he could immerse himself in that glassy, turquoise water, he'd be able to shift the anxiety that seemed to have settled on him since that horrible night in Malibu Canyon.

He fumbled with the leaflet they'd been handed at the start of Van Buren High School's tour. It was the first activity of a summer school program he'd promised his parents he'd join. They didn't want their son to spend 100 percent of his time training for the tennis tournaments in July, and while Paolo still had ambitions aside from being a tennis pro, he had to go along with what they wanted. Or else his parents might stop funding his emancipated lifestyle—the last thing he wanted them to do.

John-Michael had gamely agreed to join him in a college-prep course enticingly titled "Art History—Beauty Meets

Brutality." He wasn't obligated by any kind of parental edict—John-Michael's funds came directly from an inherited trust fund that was set up to pay for his education and living costs until he was twenty-five. In fact, JM had chosen the course.

The two boys split away from the rest of the class, who went inside the gallery for a lecture on Byzantine art.

"Even for a guy with boatloads of cash, it's pretty weird to re-create a burned-out Roman villa," John-Michael said. He glanced at Paolo, who seemed just as out of it as when he'd left that morning for his daily training session at the tennis club. "So are you on some new diet?"

"Just don't feel like eating." Paolo reeled a little, taken aback by the sudden switch in conversation. "Why the interest in my diet?"

"Because now that I look at you," John-Michael said, suddenly earnest, "you've lost some weight. Your cheekbones are more prominent. Also, your clavicle."

"My *clavicle*?"

John-Michael touched a wary finger to Paolo's skin, just below his throat. "You're hardly eating these days."

"I am a little preoccupied," Paolo confessed.

"It's *starve-yourself* bad? What'd you do? Kill someone?"

Paolo glowered at him but said nothing.

"The suspense is killing me." John-Michael leaned against one of the pillars of the peristyle and faced his friend squarely. "You ever gonna tell me what went down that night in Malibu Canyon?"

Paolo couldn't look him in the eye. "You said you preferred not to know."

John-Michael gave a nod. "I changed my mind. I've never seen you like this. Walking around like you're on eggshells, skipping out on some of your tennis training. Something has gotten into you."

Carefully, Paolo replied. "If you don't know, you'll never have to lie."

"Jeez, dude, who would I have to lie to?"

Paolo said nothing.

John-Michael continued, "Paolo, listen, I was happy to help out. There's nothing illegal about putting gas in your car and driving it home. If anyone asks, it was you. I don't have to say anything about it ever. That's always my preferred strategy when it comes to the cops anyway, but really, I deserve to know."

Paolo gave a quick nod, glanced around. This wasn't a conversation he could risk having overheard. His skin prickled from the sensation that he was being observed. With every day that passed, one quiet reminder sounded more insistently in his mind:

Somebody knows. It's all going to come out.

"The thing is, Paolo, let's say it comes to it. Who'd I be keeping quiet from? The cops? Or someone else?"

Paolo turned away without bothering to respond.

But John-Michael circled him until he could look him in the eye. "Did you piss off someone important? Some rich guy with his own private army?"

Paolo was confused. "What are you talking about?"

"You seem scared, Paolo. Which makes me think this is really serious. I thought you were just trying to get out of a situation at the country club, maybe with someone who you shouldn't be seen with."

"That's fine—keep believing that." Paolo allowed a little hostility into his voice. Is this the only reason John-Michael had suggested coming out into the garden—so he could interrogate him?

"You can trust me. I'm involved now. If I'm going to be committed I need to know what the deal is, so I can stick to the story and cover my own ass."

Paolo glared, disbelieving. "You really want this?"

Slowly, John-Michael nodded. "Yeah. Lay it on me. I can handle it."

Paolo took a couple of quick breaths and exhaled rapidly, as though warming up for a race. After a moment, he began to recap what happened that night in the hills—the older woman, the hit-and-run, the borrowed cell phone, everything.

And John-Michael held his breath for a long moment, finally gasping, "Seriously? Are you kidding me?"

"I wish I was. Meredith was wasted. I got out of there, man. There was no way they were gonna find the guy who killed her. But there'd be questions about me. Why I was with her, all that."

John-Michael made a clicking noise with his cheeks. "This isn't Saudi Arabia, dude. Adultery isn't a crime. I mean it's frowned upon, but . . ."

"It was more complicated than that."

"In what way?"

Paolo sighed. "I prefer not to say."

John-Michael seemed to consider. "You see any other witnesses?"

"You think I'd have risked walking away if I had?"

"You figure the cops will think she was alone?"

Paolo nodded and said despondently, "That's the general idea." He started to walk along the terra-cotta tiles around the central reflecting pool. After a second, John-Michael followed.

In a low voice Paolo said, "The problem is, the security camera at the country club might have spotted me getting into her beamer."

"Ah. It's making sense now. Hence getting me to supply your alibi."

"Meredith didn't turn on the GPS," Paolo said, "in case her husband checked the car to find out where she'd been. She was pretty careful about who saw us talking. But the parking lot is a potential blind spot."

"Anything you can do about it? I mean, you work there, don't you?"

"I thought of that," Paolo said, nodding. "I tried to get into the security room when I was training yesterday. But there was never a moment when it wasn't occupied."

"If you've got a chance to steal that tape, or erase the hard drive or whatever system they use, you've got to do that, Paolo," John-Michael said. "If the cops are wondering if anyone was with her, they'll probably ask at the country club."

"I didn't sign into the club that day. I didn't have a lesson. Neither did she, so there's no reason the cops would think she'd done anything but drive down from Montecito and head for her cabin in Malibu Creek."

"Alone? Who does that?"

Paolo shrugged. "Why would the cops care? They'd probably just figure she was meeting someone at the cabin."

"And that 'someone' will never come forward," John-Michael concluded. "Meanwhile, if anyone does look at the footage from the parking lot at the club, they'll see someone who looks like you coming back in the taxi, putting gas in the tank, and then driving away."

Mechanically, Paolo said, "Exactly. If anyone asks, I just say I ran out of gas."

John-Michael couldn't stop a note of admiration from entering his voice. "You brilliant bastard. You figured out that whole alibi, made it happen using a stolen cell phone, just after you'd seen your girlfriend killed by a hit-and-run driver, all on the slim possibility that someone's gonna check the security footage at a tennis club that no one even knows she was at?"

"She was *not* my girlfriend, man," Paolo said resentfully. "Of *course* I thought about the security footage! The first thing I thought about was who might have seen me with her. That's basic self-preservation! I did the only thing I could think of fast. Something that gives me a legitimate reason to be getting in that BMW and getting out of it before Meredith heads for the hills."

"Man, that's stone-cold."

This time, Paolo remained silent. Was it obvious to John-Michael that he was glad this woman was dead? Maybe not with the way it had happened, but he was relieved she was out of his life. Relieved enough to feel guilty, to wonder when the day was coming that a detective would knock on the front door, walk in to find Paolo in the kitchen, whipping up a strawberry-flavored protein shake and believing his problems were behind him. Thus far Paolo had failed to find any follow-up to the initial, one-line report of Meredith's death on the internet. But maybe it was too soon?

"Try not to worry, Paolo. You've got to take each day as it happens. I know how you must feel. But think of this: every day they don't come looking for you is a bonus. The more time goes by, the less likely it is that they'll connect you to the accident." John-Michael knelt down, tugged at a bay laurel leaf on a neatly trimmed shrub near the water's edge. He pulled it off the branch, twisted it, and crushed the leaf, raising it to his nose to inhale the fragrance. "Mmm. Makes me want to cook some chicken Parmesan."

Paolo struggled to summon an expression of hope or relief, anything to give John-Michael the impression that his words had taken effect. But he couldn't.

The afternoon hadn't taken Paolo's mind off anything.

Confession was supposed to lighten a burden, wasn't it? Yet all Paolo felt now was a faint, queasy sensation.

Would today's admission someday come back to haunt him?

MAYA

Maya arrived home before Paolo and John-Michael returned from the Getty. When she saw that Grace was alone in the room they both shared with John-Michael, she closed the door. Grace stopped reading Junot Díaz's *Drown* to look up at Maya, who paced a little and let her jacket and books fall where she dropped them.

"You're gonna pick those up, right?"

"Oh. Yeah." Maya made a halfhearted attempt to scoop up a discarded book. Then she turned to Grace. On her face was a deepening blush. "Can I get some advice?"

Grace closed her paperback on a bookmark. "Oh, you want my advice now? Does that mean you're done giving advice to me?"

Maya flushed. Her voice dropped to a whisper. "Gracie, that wasn't anything personal. I'm sorry about your father, really I am. But it's not something you should keep a secret from your own sister. I don't even understand how you've managed to keep it quiet this long."

Grace sat up, sweeping Maya with a calculating look. "It's not my secret, though, Maya, is it? There are other people involved. My mom, for one. Candace's dad."

"Oh," Maya said. She hadn't thought about that. "God, I'm an idiot, aren't I? I bet it wasn't even your idea to keep it a secret."

Grace shrugged a little. Maya's admission seemed to have relaxed her. "No. But I'm part of it now. I don't like it, either."

"You will tell her, though, won't you?"

"Candace is so busy with the TV show now, I don't see much of her. I will tell her, Maya. I'll have to, soon."

"Why?"

Grace blinked a couple of times, as though she was holding back tears. She smiled a wan smile and swallowed hard. "The universe has a way of getting its own way."

"That's BS," Maya said. "Don't believe in the 'universe.' You make your own fate."

"You believe that?"

"Of course," Maya said. She sat on the floor between their beds. "I'm trying to take control back over my own life. You remember Jack Cato, my tutor?"

"British guy, I passed him in the hallway," Grace said. "You went to a business breakfast or something."

Despite the residual annoyance at Jack's announcement about his ex, Maya was slowly returning to her original feelings of disbelief and euphoria at the result of her presentation. She found herself smiling. "Yep."

"How'd that go?"

"Extremely, amazingly well," Maya said, her smile widening.

"Seriously?"

Blithely, Maya replied, "Yeah, I basically ruled. Two investors want to back me. Oh, and I kissed Jack."

Grace said, "Pardon me?"

"I totally kissed my tutor. But take it easy, turns out he's not into the idea of a high school girlfriend."

Before Grace could ask what happened, the door behind Maya opened. She turned, ready to snap at the interruption, but held her tongue when she saw it was Ariana.

"Oh, hey, guys. Say, d'y'all know when Lucy might be home?"

Ariana was everywhere, all the time, and Maya and Grace exchanged looks of irritation. Things were getting tense inside the house.

At least, that's how it seemed to Maya.

She wanted to say something to Lucy about it. But Lucy maintained a quiet, taciturn edge that made it difficult to broach any subject that Lucy herself hadn't raised. Throw in the fact that Maya had spent part of the last six months spying on her housemates, reporting back their every move—especially Lucy's—and the guilt made it impossible. That's if she and Lucy even crossed paths. Ever since school finished, all Lucy seemed to do was stay in bed until around two in the afternoon and then leave for some kind of appointment–Maya assumed it was something musical.

Her other option was to encourage her housemates' frustration with Ariana's extended stay. Like when Candace had asked bluntly, "So Ari, you get a job yet?"

It was like water off a duck's back, though. Ariana would just reply with a snake-eyed smile and give a throaty chuckle. "Honey, this town isn't ready for ol' Ariana, not yet."

The excitement of meeting those investors fueled another long night of coding. Around two in the morning she fell asleep, but woke too early–7:10. Her mind wouldn't stop spinning, mentally solving coding glitches in Promisr, until she knew that only food, caffeine, and her laptop would do the job.

On the stairs outside the front door, she heard voices from the kitchen. The window had to be open. A tinny voice, distorted by the speakerphone of someone's cell, was saying, "Bloody well make friends with them! How hard is it, honestly? You're only a couple of years older than them."

The accent was undeniably British. It sounded familiar but Maya couldn't place it.

"I'm doing my best," Ariana managed to reply.

"Find that bottle of nail polish," the woman said firmly. "Or make damn sure she didn't keep it. Do that, and then get out of there."

Ariana gasped. There was silence. Maya guessed that whoever Ariana had been talking to had hung up.

On the spiral staircase, Maya stalled. She didn't dare

take another step, either toward the kitchen or back to the second floor.

That voice. It had sounded almost exactly like . . . no.

It couldn't be.

Dana Alexander?

Maya gripped the handrail tightly and held her breath until she couldn't anymore.

She strained to hear any further sounds from Ariana in the kitchen. She heard the tap run, water slapping against the metal sink. Then she heard a chair being shifted, movement back toward the living room.

The muscles of Maya's legs tensed. If Ariana headed upstairs to the bathroom, she'd definitely catch her on the stairs. Ariana would know that someone had heard the conversation, or at least part of it.

She heard the front door opening and made her decision. Maya bolted back into her room, slipped under the quilt, and buried her face in the pillow, pretending to be asleep. She held still as Ariana's footfall sounded on the landing outside the door. Was she listening? Would she dare to open the door and confront the three sleeping roommates?

Maya's heart pounded, ricocheting inside her rib cage.

Ariana was in the house to spy on Lucy. Which meant that Dana Alexander wanted more than Maya was able to provide—someone to directly interrogate and maybe even provoke Lucy.

Or that Dana no longer trusted Maya.

CANDACE

KITCHEN, VENICE BEACH HOUSE,
TUESDAY, JUNE 23

"Grace already left to play beach volleyball. So she won't be able to wait in for the IKEA delivery." Candace helped John-Michael set the dining table, carrying over steaming plates of scrambled eggs, crispy bacon, and hash browns.

Lucy collected three different bottles of hot sauce from the cabinet and set them on the table. "Oh, it's fine, Ariana said she'd do that."

"Oh, well, that's just lovely," Candace said, her tone flat. Dryly she added, "Are we expecting Ariana to eat with us?"

"She's taking a hot bath," Lucy replied. "She said her back hurt from sleeping on the futon."

Candace said nothing, but locked eyes with John-Michael for a moment. He shook his head very slightly, amazed. "How about Maya?" she asked.

"Still in bed. She's nocturnal, that girl."

John-Michael laughed. "So are we. Breakfast at two thirty in the afternoon?"

"Dude, it's summer vacation," Lucy replied. "Maya's probably asleep because she worked until dawn."

"It's that app," Candace said. "'Gotta keep moving, like a shark.' Isn't that what she always says? Well, you know what they say about all work and no play . . ."

"Says the girl who spends all her free time working on a TV show," Lucy commented. "Or can we presume you have an ulterior motive there? 'Cause I've been hearing rumors."

Candace arched a single, perfectly shaped eyebrow at Lucy as she helped herself to bacon and eggs. "Guys, I'm *dreaming* about Yoandy now."

Lucy poured out three glasses of ice water. "Do tell. Or are we talkin' R-rated dreams here?"

"Those'd be the only kind of dreams I'd have about Yoandy Santiago," John-Michael admitted.

Candace gave a wicked smile. "We were totally doing it, if you must know."

"Goddamn dream-hussy, I knew it!" John-Michael said, pointing an accusing finger.

"Hmm," Candace responded lightly, "look who's talking. *He* calls me *nena linda*," she added with a softness to her voice that surprised even her.

Lucy's interest perked up. "In real life? Or was that in your dream?"

"In real life, of course."

John-Michael clutched a hand to his heart and said passionately, *"¡Nena linda, te quiero, cuanto te quiero!"*

Lucy sniggered, but Candace merely flicked a lump of

scrambled egg at her. "*Silencio*! I've decided it's romantic."

"*Nena linda* isn't bad," John-Michael added. "I've heard Maya's aunt call her that."

"But I think he has a girlfriend . . ." Candace said, sighing.

"A guy that hot probably has more than one," Lucy agreed.

Candace continued, somewhat reluctant, "I mean, he says they're not together, but . . ."

"You suspect you're being lined up as number two," chuckled John-Michael. "Although I gotta tell you. Kay Alexander doesn't seem like his type. She's one of those weird Hollywood enigmas. Famous for being Dana Alexander's sister, and not much else."

"She did a reality TV show," observed Candace. She'd researched Kay quite a bit since learning of her connection to Yoandy. None of it made her feel any more secure.

Lucy stopped in mid-reach for the SunnyD. She seemed a little shocked. "Yoandy Santiago is dating *Dana Alexander's sister*? I did not know that."

"Oh, you've been taking an interest?" Candace said flatly.

"In Kay Alexander? Not particularly," Lucy said, a little cautiously. "But Yoandy Santiago I've heard of. I didn't know he could act."

"He's great at stage combat," Candace admitted. "Acting—I guess I'll find out later today, at the table read. *Prepped* is meant to be his big break."

After their spectacularly late breakfast, Candace showered and brushed her teeth with careful precision. She held her own gaze in the mirror and remembered the dream.

She hadn't been totally honest with her housemates. She and Yoandy hadn't been having sex—or at least, they hadn't gotten to that part before she'd woken up. In her dream, he'd been removing her clothes, slowly, staring into her eyes as he did so, and she'd simply waited, trembling at his every touch.

Who knew that a few softly spoken words could have such an effect on her subconscious?

Maybe it was because he spoke in Spanish. In English, she'd probably have laughed at him. But the Spanish lent him a sincerity that was hard to deny.

She drove her newly serviced Prius to the studio and parked, swaying her hips as she strolled through the lot, conscious of the fact that at any moment, Yoandy might appear. She wanted to appear gracious, feminine, *hot*. But she didn't see him until they'd already taken their places at the table, because once again, he was the last to arrive for the late-afternoon rehearsal.

When the pages were handed out, Candace scoured them for scenes where her character, Annika, appeared with Yoandy's character, Sebastian. When she found a scene, she pored over the lines, for any hint of sexual tension. The production team was keeping any future developments under wraps, so she had no idea whether a relationship between Annika and Sebastian might be explored. But she could hope. Hope fueled her fantasy.

Prepped was going to be screened on cable. She'd already seen that the language they used was fairly adult. It wasn't beyond the realms of possibility that she'd have to record a bedroom scene with Yoandy. Even with the "no nudity" clause in her contract, Candace knew she could be asked to push boundaries. She imagined the tension from acting such a scene. Would it spill over into their real lives?

For some reason, boys her own age didn't interest Candace. She'd certainly gotten their attention, especially in the past two years. Her curves gave her a whole new look, away from the skinny athleticism of her childhood. She'd even had a couple of boyfriends. Hooking up with a high school boy, though—it wasn't all that.

Yoandy was twenty-one, and those few extra years made all the difference.

She was positioned almost directly opposite Yoandy at the table, on a very slight diagonal. When they read their scenes together, he'd obviously memorized his lines. And he looked her straight in the eye as Sebastian spoke to Annika: *If you were mine, you wouldn't have been alone.*

"What makes you so sure I was alone?"

The intensity of his attention was unnerving. It took her by surprise. Fumbling her own line, Candace flipped the pages back and forth, her cheeks burning hot as she realized that she'd somehow missed this exchange in the preparation. Or at least she'd missed the potential for romantic tension.

"Annika," the director said wearily, "could you maybe try that with a little more *pizzazz*?"

Candace stared at the line. She turned to the director, keenly aware of Yoandy's eyes on her. "You want me to say that kinda flirtily?"

"Would it be too much trouble?" the director replied, politely sarcastic.

She cleared her throat and faced Yoandy. The combination of lust and tenderness she saw in his eyes shook her to the core. "If you were mine, you wouldn't have been alone," she said.

"Which is a very nice delivery, Miss Deering," sneered the director, "of Sebastian's line."

There was a general snickering from the rest of the cast, apart from Ricardo Adams, who, Candace noticed, looked positively frosty. For a moment, she caught Yoandy's reaction—a hopeful smile.

"Shall we take five? I could use a cigarette," the director said, pushing back his chair.

Everyone but Candace rose to their feet. She remained in place, unsure if her legs could be trusted to carry her. It was as though she'd been poisoned. Her pulse was racing, palms sweating. She'd embarrassed herself in front of the entire cast of a brand-new TV show, possibly her best chance to get her career off to a decent start.

When she looked up, however, there was Yoandy, offering a hand.

"It happened to me," he confessed, "the first time I had

to sing in public. I forgot the lyrics."

She allowed him to help her to her feet. When he didn't release her hand right away, she tried to relax. "Okay, so we're holding hands now, are we?" she mumbled nervously.

"*Nena*, it's all right. Breathe."

She tried to laugh and pulled her fingers away, leaning against the table for support. "You're the newbie," she murmured. "I shouldn't be the one making mistakes like this."

"Newbie? Me?" He shook his head, smiling. "Candace, I've been singing and dancing in front of people since I was thirteen. You have any idea how vulnerable some of my lyrics make me feel? It's like reaching into my chest, pulling out my heart, and slapping it down on a plate for everyone to eat."

Candace didn't know what to say. She had no idea what his songs were about, but she could guess. He looked at her for a moment, as though coming to a decision. Then with a brief grin, he turned and took off toward the recording equipment. She watched, baffled, as he moved between the technical crew until one of them nodded and handed something to him.

Yoandy turned to her, microphone in hand. When he spoke, his voice echoed in the studio space. "Candace, this is for you."

"Oh God," she whispered, clutching the edge of the table. "Don't *sing* to me . . ."

"Jigg-a-lypuff. Jigg-a-lypuff!" he sang, loud, his voice a perfect, soulful tenor. He didn't break eye contact with

Candace, despite peals of amazed laughter in the studio. He continued, "Jigg-a-ly–puff–Jigg-a-ly . . ."

"Oh good grief," Candace muttered. Her nervousness vanished, like smoke.

Yoandy couldn't finish the song; he was overwhelmed by uproarious laughter from the cast and crew. From outside where he'd been smoking, the director yelled at them. A few minutes later, Yoandy was back at the table, guiding her back to her seat and beaming with glee.

"Jigglypuff." She smirked. "Really?"

"I was eight years old when I came to this country. Pokémon became *my life*," he answered earnestly. "Someday I'm gonna show you my collection."

Candace propped up an elbow, rested her chin on her hands. "Pokémon? That's actually hilarious," she drawled. "Your favorite thing about America is actually Japanese."

"Everyone gets nervous, *nena*," he told her, tenderly, taking her right hand in both of his and massaging just beneath her thumb. "One day you'll look back at this and you'll laugh."

"One day?" she said, trying desperately to take her mind off what he was making her feel with his touch. "I'm thinking of you singing the Jigglypuff song and I'm laughing *right now*."

MAYA
TRIPLE BEDROOM, VENICE BEACH HOUSE,
TUESDAY, JUNE 23

Maya dug her fingers into the pillow, trying to calm her thoughts, trying to focus on what she'd actually heard Dana Alexander say on the phone to Ariana earlier that morning. It was a blood-freezing notion.

"Bloody well make friends with them."

Ariana was obviously well aware of the fact that she wasn't getting along with the rest of the housemates. She'd retreated into the bathroom to take a nice long bath, precisely when they were about to eat breakfast together. Their irritation was finally getting to her.

"Find that bottle of nail polish."

What nail polish? For Maya, this was an entirely new element to the whole mystery. What if something about nail polish featured in some unpublished clue, something that hadn't been raised at the murder trial? Something that only the real killer would know? Could something as seemingly insignificant as a bottle of nail polish link Dana

Alexander to the murder of Tyson Drew?

Maya sat up on her bed, opened her computer, and scoured her collection of data from the Hollywood murder of which Grace's father had been convicted. Nail polish hadn't been mentioned in any of the articles she'd dredged up. Given that Tyson Drew was supposedly drowned by Alex Vesper—a guy—it seemed like a stretch.

But she simply couldn't think of any other reason why Dana would go to such lengths to plant someone else in their home. Why she'd make such a big deal over some nail polish.

Or why she'd plant Ariana in Lucy's life from the start.

With a mounting sense of helplessness, Maya faced up to the fact that Ariana hadn't been brought in as a stranger to the house, not like Maya. Ariana had been friends with Lucy for *years*. They'd been rehab buddies.

Had Dana Alexander arranged all of that, too?

Maya twisted in the bedclothes, listening for the flush of the toilet to signal Ariana getting ready to leave the bathroom.

Just how powerful was Dana Alexander?

Maya had to stall for time to think things through. If she blew Ariana's cover now, Maya would need to come clean about her own role as a spy.

Any trust in Maya would be gone. Her housemates might even throw her out. Then Dana would find out that she wasn't cooperating. The woman might even make good on her threat to tell immigration that Maya and her mom were in the United States illegally. Then it would be back to Mexico City.

No more Venice Beach house. No more introductions to Silicon Valley business angels. *No more kissing Jack.*

On the other hand, Maya didn't want to do a single thing that might actually help Dana Alexander. She'd eventually have to expose Ariana to her housemates. Before Maya made her move, though, she had to at least try to mediate the blowback. Maybe get some evidence against Dana Alexander herself, something that Maya could use as leverage?

Rat me out to immigration and you'll have to deal with me, Alexander.

It was a lot to think about.

Maya heard a creak in the floorboards and became aware that she was not alone in the bedroom.

She stared up at the open door to the triple bedroom, feeling woozy.

Ariana stood there in her bathrobe, looking inquisitive. Naturally.

Maya was about to rearrange her scowl into a sweet smile, when it struck her that Ariana might get suspicious if Maya suddenly altered her behavior toward her. Of all the housemates, Maya was the one most inconvenienced by Ariana's arrival. Maya's habit of coding on the sofa, or at the kitchen table, long after everyone else had gone to bed, had set the two in competition for the same space. If anyone was allowed to be snarky about Ariana, Maya figured it could be her.

With the same friendly grin that she used each day to greet the housemates, Ariana said, "Hey, Maya. Can I get you a coffee?"

Maya emitted something like a snarl and rolled over, facing away.

"How's the app coming along?" Ariana asked lightly.

Maya grunted. "Not great. I'm supposed to show an alpha version soon. I'm gonna have to work all day and night to get it done. Where is everyone?"

"Work," Ariana replied vaguely. "The beach."

Maya forced her voice to remain even, casual. "So, you're staying home today?"

"I'm waiting for that delivery from IKEA."

Maya's eyes registered surprise. "That's today? Oh, I'm here all day. You can go out, if you have something you need to do. I'll stay in for the delivery."

Ariana smiled slightly. "It's okay," she began quietly, but was interrupted by a knock on the front door.

Maya checked her watch: 3:27 p.m. Jack! She'd forgotten all about her meeting with him. She leapt to her feet, dressed quickly, grabbed a pair of beach shoes from beneath her mattress. She was dragging a brush through her hair and checking her makeup as Ariana made her way downstairs to let him in.

A few moments later she was in the living room and

letting Jack kiss her on both cheeks, super-polite as ever, barely any indication that they'd ever taken it further. Before Jack could say anything to betray either of them, Maya called out, "This is my tutor, Jack Cato." She made an informal gesture in Ariana's direction. "Jack, Ariana."

"Hello, Jack." Ariana smiled, appearing at the edge of the kitchen. "Can I get you a coffee? Juice? Milk?"

"Actually, a tea would be brilliant if you've got it—milk, no sugar," he replied. To Maya's relief, Ariana disappeared back into the kitchen.

Maya led Jack to the green futon.

"You guys have a hugely privileged situation, you know that?" Jack said. "What I'd give to live on this beach, be able to walk down to the ocean for a swim. Or a run."

Maya smiled at him mischievously. "Just hypothetically— what *would* you give?"

Jack seemed to have some difficulty framing his reply. Minutes later, Ariana reappeared. She handed Jack a mug of tea, then sidled away. Maya turned and watched Ariana pop two earbuds into her ears before she made herself something to eat.

"How's your tea?" Maya asked.

"Hot," he said, blowing across the surface of the tea. "It'll do. Lord knows I could use it after that traffic. The state of the roads in this city is nobody's business!"

Maya wrinkled her nose. "It's a long drive from Pasadena, huh?"

"It's not exactly around the corner," he agreed. "But

today I've come from the airport."

Maya couldn't stop her eyes lighting up. "Your ex . . . ? What happened to doing a course at UCLA?"

He grinned, delighted. "Her uni emailed last night and said it's a no-go. So this morning, off she popped, back to the UK."

"Oh," Maya said, a little deflated. All that getting annoyed, for nothing. Or–had it just been an excuse? "So you're really not into her anymore?"

Patiently he said, "Maya, she booked the flight months ago, when we were still together. It would have been pretty mean to abandon her in LA."

"I guess that's true." Hesitating slightly, Maya said, "About the drive from Pasadena, if you ever need a place to crash one weekend, there's a bed here. Don't look so shocked–I didn't mean my bed. I meant this futon. Ariana's only supposed to be staying for a few more days."

A slow smile touched the corners of his mouth. "You certainly managed to crowbar 'bed' into the conversation."

"Oh please," Maya said with a gentle slap of the back of her hand to the thigh that was almost touching hers. "It was written all over your face."

He laughed and leaned closer, until she realized that he was going to kiss her. Maya pulled her face away from his lips and whispered, "Not here. Ariana is watching." Before he turned to look, she hissed. "Don't look!"

Disappointment clouded Jack's features. It was a cute look for him, she decided. Puppy-dog-like, very sweet.

"Not a fan of the PDA?" he asked.

Maya produced a small smile. With a sigh, Jack leaned over to pick up his brown leather messenger bag and withdrew a MacBook. He flipped it open and began to talk once again, the playful tone now banished.

"Okay, so the news is that one of the angels has dropped out. But not to worry—we do have an offer on the table: Kyle Joseph, who used to work at Google. I've had a bit of a chat with some of the guys in the entrepreneur society. They reckon the offer isn't bad—pretty much in line with what he mentioned at the presentation. He's offering a hundred K for twenty percent—subject to due diligence."

Maya shook her head in wonder. "Wow. One hundred thousand dollars!"

Jack smiled, pale blue eyes like a wading pool. He leaned closer and whispered into her ear, "Sweetheart, you are seriously smart. And I for one am going to do my utmost to see to it that you go a very, *very* long way."

PAOLO
VENICE BEACH, FRIDAY, JUNE 26

MEREDITH ERIKSSON, 42, WAS HIGH WHEN HIT-AND-RUN DRIVER STRUCK

Paolo focused on the headline on his cell phone. A mixture of emotions assailed him. Mostly, relief.

Meredith had been reported dead, killed outright by a hit-and-run driver, up in Malibu Canyon. At the Malibu Lawn Tennis Club, Paolo had been too cautious to ask a single question that related to her. He'd even been too scared to set up a news alert on the internet—didn't the NSA monitor searches? Instead, he'd checked the local news every day. This latest headline confirmed it—he was in the clear.

Climbing directly up the spiral staircase from the boardwalk outside, Paolo put his phone in his desk drawer and changed quickly into the short wet suit he'd just bought; black with turquoise trim. Then he took his keys, some cash, and skipped back down the stairs. Maya and her tutor, Jack, were outside now, on the ground floor, by the front door.

"Just popping out for a spot of kitesurfing, old bean," Paolo said in his best English accent, grinning at Jack.

"Kitesurfing, are you out of your mind?" Maya folded both arms across her chest, swept her eyes up and down Paolo, examining his short wet suit.

"You're taking lessons?" Jack said, impressed.

"I've taken *a* lesson," Paolo confirmed. Now he was eager to fly solo.

"You got it after one lesson?" Maya asked.

He hadn't. But what was the point paying a tutor to tell him the same thing over and over? Paolo knew what to practice, he just needed water, wind, a board, and a sail.

Jack said, "I did a bit of that myself, on Eton Dorney. It's an artificial lake, at school."

"Your high school had its own lake for kitesurfing?"

"Mostly for rowing eights."

"You ever take him surfing?" Paolo asked Maya.

Jack looked curiously at Maya. "You surf?"

"Not very well," Maya admitted. "But I can catch a wave, once in a while."

"You're a woman of many talents, Miss Soto," marveled Jack. "And I would absolutely love to go surfing with you, one of these days when we're not both up to our eyeballs in work."

"Don't hold your breath," she said dolefully. "Promisr is eating up all my time. But I bet you're pretty good at surfing."

"I'm a Cornish lad," he said, "so I'm not totally inept. I, too, can catch a wave, once in a while. Anyway, Maya, I'd best be off. I'll keep you posted, all right?" With a light kiss to her cheek, he was gone.

"So," Paolo said, hooking a thumb at the tutor's retreating form. "You and the Brit?"

"So?" Maya said with a quiet smile, closing the front door on him slowly. "You and Lucy?"

"You're way behind," he called after her. "That's old news."

Left on the outside, Paolo headed for the surf rental store. Most places wouldn't rent equipment unless you were taking classes or already had some kind of badge. But John-Michael knew a guy who knew a guy. Paolo felt pretty sure he'd be allowed to rent some gear today.

Along the crowded boardwalk, he saw Lucy sitting cross-legged on a bench. *Of course, after just talking about her.* Next to her was a guy with shoulder-length black hair. One arm was entirely covered in colorful tattoos from shoulder to wrists. Around him were abstract paintings made from some kind of rubbery streaks of paint. When she saw Paolo she waved. "Hey, King, you know my boy Luisito, right?"

Paolo gave a short nod in Luisito's direction. "Hey, man."

"Where're you headed?" Lucy said. "Surfing?"

He stopped in front of the paintings. "Yup. Not waves, though, I prefer to stand up, right from the beginning. Gonna get me a kite."

She frowned. "Isn't that super-dangerous?"

"Nah, it's cool."

Lucy sprang to her feet. "Okay if I walk with you a little?"

Paolo shrugged. Ever since the Meredith incident, he'd almost stopped thinking about Lucy. She hadn't sought him out, either, but then that was normal. Could it be that she was actually feeling guilty? It was over a month since their little moment of misunderstanding. It had really stung at first but now . . . compared to what had happened to Paolo since, a fumbled romantic situation with Lucy barely registered.

"That'd be nice," he said with an easy smile.

Lucy fell into step beside him, and he soon picked up the faint trace of her perfume—Flowerbomb. He'd noticed it on her nightstand about six weeks before, had made a mental note to buy her some at the next gift-buying opportunity. That was when he'd still hoped to get into the gift-giving zone with Lucy. Paolo was only faintly surprised to realize that this thought didn't sadden him.

"I've been meaning to talk to you about something," Lucy said. "Somehow, you're always busy . . . or avoiding me."

"Me? No way," Paolo said, holding up both hands. But she was right and he knew it. Meredith's death had preyed on his mind almost constantly. If he stayed home too long he became anxious. It was better to be out, to be distracted.

"Well," she said, and her fingers took his elbow in a sudden grip, hard enough to halt his progress. "This is important, so listen up."

Paolo stared at her curiously. Lucy looked serious and he had no clue what else she might be about to say. For a moment, he wondered if Lucy somehow knew about Meredith. It was beyond comprehension that John-Michael would betray that confidence—not when he'd made himself an accessory to whatever crime Paolo may have committed.

It took a few seconds before Lucy was able to form the words. "Grace . . ." she began with difficulty, "I get the impression from John-Michael that Gracie's having a hard time lately."

Gently, Paolo pulled his elbow from her grasp. "Okay? What does that have to do with me?" Lucy was steering him toward another girl in the house? This, he really could not believe.

"You haven't noticed at all?" Lucy said with an almost-smile.

"Have I noticed Grace?" he said candidly. "Of course; she's beautiful."

"But you don't . . . y'know, *like* her?"

"I try to limit my interest to one girl at a time," he said, more sharply than he'd intended. Evidently, Lucy had expected more of a flirty response and was taken aback by his brusqueness. "Why're you telling me this, Luce?"

Lucy's eyelashes fluttered for a second before her jaw clenched. "No, sugar," she said, her voice taut. "I thought I'd tell you because honestly, I don't know what's going on with you these past few weeks but there's somethin'. I thought maybe another girl? And I wanted you to be aware that Grace, for all she tries to hide it, is into you, Mr. King, whether or not you deserve it, which by the way you do not."

"Grace is a nice girl," Paolo said with a smirk. "Too nice for me."

"I just thought that maybe if you knew she liked you, you'd be sweet to her."

"You think I should let her down nicely? That's what you're saying? Like you did with me?"

Lucy broke into an amazed chuckle and pulled away from him. "Man, you're uptight right now. What's going on with you?"

"I'm uptight? Ever stop to think that maybe you broke my heart?"

"Did I?"

"No."

Annoyance flashed across Lucy's face. "Stop playing games, Paolo. And don't play games with Grace." She backed off some more, staring Paolo hard in the eye. Then she turned, began to stroll back toward Luisito and his paintings.

Paolo watched her go, then shrugged. He could feel a

pleasant afterburn from their tense exchange. Grace liked him? Interesting. She hid it well.

She really was beautiful. Not as stereotypically pretty as her stepsister, Candace, for sure. Grace had a whole different vibe—brains and a quiet, understated beauty. She still had a girlish quality, a sort of adorable cuteness. That was probably why he hadn't thought of her that way, Paolo reflected.

He'd assumed that Grace found him kind of skeezy. It wasn't at all disappointing to know that she liked him. Once he opened up his mind to the possibility, imagined Grace in any romantic situation, he found himself responding with a pleasant warmth.

He was on the verge of catching up to Lucy to ask how she knew, but thought better of it. That certainly wouldn't look too smooth. After a few more moments, Paolo pushed the idea out of his mind. Kitesurfing was more dangerous than he'd let on to Lucy; enough to require total mental focus. Danger was what his body called for—he needed that pure rush of adrenaline—to feel alive, invincible. No more hiding and waiting, no more praying that what happened in Malibu Canyon would stop haunting his nights and crowding his days with omnipresent anxiety.

The sun was warm, heating up his wet suit enough that he longed for the chill of the ocean. Ahead, he spotted two bright blue and red kites on display at the surf rental shop. He picked up his pace a little, smiling.

He had to stop worrying, accept that the whole Meredith

situation was over. He was home free. Nothing could touch him. And now, he had the chance to be with someone he could laugh and hang out with. Someone who really liked him, not just for the way he looked or played tennis. Someone real.

Grace.

MAYA
TRIPLE BEDROOM, VENICE BEACH HOUSE,
SATURDAY, JUNE 27

"Wake up, Maya. Time to start the rest of your life."

The cell phone was on the pillow next to her head, the voice coming out of it was Jack Cato's. But even he couldn't make her a morning person, especially with how exhausted she'd been lately.

"But it's Saturday," she grumbled, then peered more closely at the time on her phone. "And it's only seven thirty!"

She could actually hear a smile in his voice. "Ah, that'll be why I'm at a breakfast meeting. Come and meet me when it's over. I promise the waffles will be worth your while."

She rubbed her eyes. "Jack. What are you talking about?"

"That café on the boardwalk, say, two hours from now. How does that grab you? My treat."

Maya rolled away from the wall and glanced at the other two beds, where John-Michael and Grace were dozing. Like a slap in the face, she suddenly remembered the phone call she'd overheard between Ariana and Dana Alexander. A groan escaped her. She'd have to do something about it. But not right now. Jack obviously had something important to tell her about her app project. Whatever she decided to do about Dana and Ariana, it would have to wait.

"Sounds good," Maya said as she drew her feet up beneath her and curled up into a ball. She resisted the urge to fall back asleep. "I'll be there."

She hauled herself out of bed and into the shower, dressed, and applied makeup to a degree that would have delighted her mother, who often despaired of Maya's perfunctory concession to all things girly. An hour later in the boardwalk café a little down the beach, she and Jack split a plate of waffles with strawberries and cream.

Jack told her he'd spent Friday night drinking with Kyle Joseph and some of the guy's investment banker buddies at a fund-raising seminar on campus. This morning they'd "done" breakfast. A good sign, apparently. "These blokes don't even crack their eyes in the morning unless there's a deal on the table," Jack assured her.

Maya tried to focus her mind on what really mattered—the potential investment in her app. "Jack, can you bottom line it for me?"

"Ha-ha. I love it when you talk business."

"I'm serious."

"I was getting to that," he said with a grin. "Kyle Joseph posted the link to the alpha version of your app on some private tech-investor network, who forwarded it all over the bloody planet, and the downloads are insane. We're talking a thing of epic proportions."

"You mean it's gone viral? How many downloads?"

"It's not about the numbers," Jack said breathlessly. "It's about who's seen it. Half of this game is about visibility. If your app is seen by enough people, it has a better chance of being seen by the people who count. And Promisr just happens to have been seen, used, and frigging *loved* by one of the people who count."

Maya was perfectly still, fully awake now. "Who? Zuckerberg?"

"Alexa Nyborg."

"The woman who started Kilowant?"

"The very same."

For a few seconds, Maya was speechless. Against her silence, Jack continued, "There we were, eating croissants together, Maya, and the woman is *stoked*. She's working on some megasecret, multiplatform social networking app thingy. She wants to embed Promisr. Says it's just at the right stage, development-wise. She wants to meet you."

"No kidding . . . Alexa Nyborg? She's amazing. I read her book. It's all about how women have to 'leverage their network' to get ahead."

"And now she wants to get ahead with *you*. Alexa and Kyle reckon that together, they want to put in another hundred K each to get to fifty-one percent between them. They'll do some of that as an equity swap to you for shares in Nyborg's new thing. When she sells that, your shares should easily be worth between two and five million."

The numbers were beginning to swim around in Maya's head. She picked up a napkin and asked a waitress to lend her a ballpoint pen. She made Jack repeat himself and listened carefully, jotting down figures.

"You think there'll be enough cash for the additional development we need to do?"

"No problem at all."

Maya peered in amazement at the numbers she'd written down. Now that Jack had explained them, they didn't seem totally insane. Within twelve to eighteen months, Maya could be a multimillionaire.

"I need to process this," she said.

"By all means," Jack said, calmer now. He freshened up her coffee cup. "Let's both think about it and have another chat later today."

They fell silent as both began to work on the waffles, which were delicious. A glow of wonder was slowly sweeping through her. She felt light-headed with disbelief.

The initial offer of a hundred thousand dollars had blown her mind—for about five seconds. Then she'd realized they'd need to spend the entire amount on paying extra programmers. There wouldn't have been a spare nickel for Maya. But for someone like Alexa Nyborg to put Promisr inside a more substantial social networking app, for Maya to get entry-level equity in something that big . . . It could be like getting in on a ground-floor investment like Instagram.

Maya's family had never had much money. Her dad worked as a fermentation technician in a pharmaceutical plant, something that required a lot of specialization but didn't pay all that well. No one in her extended family was rich. She'd hardly been anyplace other than Mexico City or California. Just once, the family had blown some savings on a trip to Acapulco and stayed at a fancy hotel. The next trip they'd dreamed of taking as a family was to Disneyland.

Maya was still waiting on that one.

To be rich. More money than the mere cushion needed to make life bearable. Enough never to have to worry again. She hadn't even imagined that. It just didn't happen to people like Maya and her family.

The real American dream. Maya put her fork down for a moment, wrapped her arms around herself, as though trying to hold on to some semblance of reality.

She glanced up to find Jack's eyes on her. He smiled then, warm and comforting. "It's so good to see you this happy."

"Thank you," she whispered. "You did this. You made this happen."

Jack reached across the table. He teased one hand free from where it was clasped to her upper arm, and intertwined his fingers with hers. "Nonsense," he chided softly. "Maya, this is happening because of you. You're the one who worked hard at your app, who kept improving it. You're the one who came up with this amazing new idea.

I'm the one along for the ride, not you. Frankly you could ditch me now and never look back." Jack gave a hopeful grin. "Obviously, I'm hoping you don't."

"Why's that?"

"Well, I'm pretty much in this for the kissing, that's pretty obvious . . ." He smiled, squeezing her hand so she knew he was joking. "Clearly, I'm hanging out for more of that."

"Sounds doable," Maya replied, blushing.

Jack's cell phone began to buzz once again. He shrugged in puzzlement when he saw the number, picked up the call, and mouthed at Maya with pantomime gestures, *Alexa Nyborg!*

He listened for a moment, punctuating the silence with the occasional "Ah-ha. Mm-hm. Great. What about the equity split? Interesting. I'll certainly ask her." When he finally ended the call, Jack's eyes looked like they were about to catch fire.

"Maya." He sounded ready to burst. "Guess what she said. *Alexa Nyborg*, Maya! Go on, try."

Maya shook her head with a cynical smile. "'*Too late, loser*'?"

"No, Maya. Dead wrong. She said, and I quote, 'Maybe she'd like to talk it over in Napa, soon?'"

Maya was momentarily speechless. Then, "Alexa Nyborg wants *me* to go to Napa Valley?"

His delight was infectious. "Alexa's got a property there, nice and private, swimming pool, tennis court, great walks.

She suggested that we fly up there on Friday and join her for lunch. Asked if there's any food you don't like and . . . let me see, let's be sure I'm not forgetting something. Oh yes, and *casually* mentioned that if you do agree to partner up, she'd be happy for you to stay there whenever you like. '*I'm hardly ever there, so I kinda like to share the place with my friends.*'"

Maya gasped. "Friday? You gotta be kidding. I got a ton of coding to do before I show the beta version of Promisr."

"*I know!*"

"Does this kind of stuff really happen?"

Jack said, "I guess this is what happens when an investor really, really wants your technology."

Maya gave a tiny shrug of her narrow shoulders. "But why? I mean, the whole thing only took me a few weeks to build. She could easily rip it off and start over."

"First off, no," he said. "It took more than a couple of weeks. You started with the basic code from Cheetr, which took you months to develop. Second, that's not how people like Nyborg do things. It's not just your tech she wants; it's you. Your mind, Maya. She likes the way you think. She wants you on board." He pushed away from the table and rose to his feet, approaching.

The sensation of lightness returned. Maya could swear that the soles of her feet were no longer in contact with the ground. Ariana was forgotten, Dana Alexander, too, as Maya allowed Jack to enfold her in a tight, blissful hug.

JOHN-MICHAEL
VAN BUREN HIGH, WEDNESDAY, JULY 1

"JM, could you try that part one more time?"

John-Michael picked up his guitar pick and tried again. From her expression, he could tell that Lucy hated having to direct. She probably hadn't been the bossy one in her previous band, Whatnot. When she'd been kicked out, she'd asked John-Michael to start a new band with her. He liked Lucy too much to turn her down.

But now, he wasn't so sure. It had been weeks since Grace had told him the truth about Lucy being in the house when Tyson Drew was murdered. And Lucy herself, supposedly his best friend in the house, still hadn't offered up a single word on the subject.

John-Michael was pretty sure that the only reason he was in the band was because of his access to Van Buren High's summer Rock Challenge program, which guaranteed rehearsal space and time in the recording suite. He watched Ruben, who sat calmly behind his drum kit, one stick lightly resting on the high-hat, teasing it. He'd changed his haircut since John-Michael had last seen him. It was more self-consciously spiky; the blue dip-dye had been freshened up, too. The sleeve of one T-shirt was rolled right to the shoulder, exposing what John-Michael could see was a new tattoo. It might have been his imagination, but was that lip piercing also new?

He caught Ruben's eye for a second, at which point John-Michael fluffed the chord. Instead of the irritation he expected to find, there was nothing but a wry smile, as if to say *Now you're gonna get it* . . .

"JM, is something wrong?"

"Mr. Ruben got a new tattoo," John-Michael said petulantly. He didn't dare to confront Lucy openly about what was really bothering him. Damned if he was going to play nice, though. "It's distracting me."

"Good eye," Ruben said, looking directly at John-Michael. His smile widened as he followed John-Michael's eyes, which were staring at his upper arm, just above the older Sex Pistols tattoo.

Lucy shook her head, her face drawn tight. John-Michael instantly felt a shred of remorse over his quip. "Sorry, Luce. This song is a little difficult for me," he confessed, putting both hands on the neck of his sea-green Fender Stratocaster. "I'm having a hard time making all those changes so fast."

"It's okay, JM." She spoke calmly, very reassuring. "What if I take over most of the rhythm section there and you just bring in a walking bass line?"

He gave a hopeful shrug. "Sure. I mean, if that isn't a pain for you."

Ruben stopped drumming and got up. "While you figure it out, I'm gonna get some air. I'll be over by the bleachers."

John-Michael turned to watch, surprised and disappointed, as Ruben left the room. "I may have mentioned that there's a girls' beach volleyball match," he admitted to Lucy. "I bet you a dollar he's going to watch."

"Yeah." Lucy began to play some chord transitions. "Puerto Rican dudes with tattoos, piercings, dyed black and blue hair. That's exactly the kind of look 'those girls' go for." She stopped strumming, looked thoughtful for a moment, then tried the chords again, playing a variation on the initial sequence.

"Maybe sporty girls are his secret vice," John-Michael suggested. He hoped not. A horrible cliché for a pretty hot guy. Even if Ruben was straight, he could at least not be *that* straight.

"More secrets," Lucy said, half to herself, listening to the chords. "Just what we need."

"Not you," John-Michael said absently, examining the strings of his instrument. "You're the last person that needs another secret."

Lucy stopped playing. "Meaning what, exactly?"

"You know," John-Michael said. He tried the first few notes of the sequence she'd shown him. "*Jelly and Pie*, rehab, Tyson Drew."

There was a painful silence. John-Michael stopped playing and looked up, gauging her reaction.

Eventually, Lucy seemed to find her voice. "Tyson Drew?"

"Yeah," murmured John-Michael, turning red as he realized what he'd said.

It wasn't easy to stay calm, but Lucy was clearly trying. "John-Michael, what are you talking about? *What* about Tyson Drew?"

He struggled for words for a few seconds and then finally exploded, "Why'd you never tell me, Lucy? Why?"

Lucy mouth fell open. "Tell you what?"

John-Michael faltered slightly. He'd been meaning to avoid this, but still, it had slipped out. Now that it was out there, he couldn't resist digging further. "That you were *there*, Lucy. That you were at the party where Tyson Drew was murdered? All those conversations we had at rock camp. All the things *I* told you about *my* life. About my mom dying. About my dad and his skank-girlfriends. About coming out, about the first time I kissed a guy. But you—you told me hardly anything."

"I'm not big on sharing, JM," Lucy mumbled. "You know that."

"I do, I totally get that, but it can't all go one way. Then a few weeks back, when I told you Grace's dad was on death row for Tyson Drew's murder. Even then, not a word. You didn't mention that you were at the party where that guy's murder took place? That it was the reason you got dropped from your TV show? Dude, how could you not tell me about that?"

They were close enough now that their guitars were almost touching. Lucy seemed to be struggling to process her emotions. When she finally spoke, it was obvious that *anger* had won.

"*How did you know?*" she said, her voice raised. "What, are you stalking me online now?" Lucy faced him with sudden clarity. "You couldn't have known, back in rock camp. Tell me *you* haven't been keeping this from me, all these years."

Her eyes flashed with danger. John-Michael immediately shrunk back. "Of course I didn't cyberstalk you," he said resentfully. He pulled away, removed the guitar from around his neck, returned it to its case, which was leaning up against the wall. After a moment, Lucy did the same with her Telecaster.

Lucy popped the Telecaster case shut. "So where's this coming from?" she fired back. "'Cause I know it's new."

A shadow of guilt crossed John-Michael's face. "Grace told me."

"Grace?"

"I told you we visited her dad in San Quentin." He was indignant. "Did you really think Grace wouldn't find out, of all people? She's known about you since she was little. Her dad's on death row for Tyson Drew's murder—she's been keeping that in for a long time. You can't blame Grace for finally cracking and telling *one lousy person*. Not everyone can be an Easter Island statue like you."

Lucy visibly reeled. "Grace's father . . . told you I was at the party where Tyson Drew was killed?"

John-Michael's feelings of guilt vanished in a wave of righteous anger. "Grace's father is Alex Vesper, Lucy. He's on death row for the murder of Tyson Drew. But he didn't do it. And now they've set a date for his execution–July fourteenth."

Lucy sucked in a long, deep breath, trying to steady herself. "Wow. Grace is handling it awfully well, I'll give her that."

"It's not like she has much choice," he snapped. "Since she's not allowed to tell us about it."

"How long have you known about the execution, John-Michael?"

"Since we went to pick out a couch at IKEA–that's when Grace found out."

"Looks like I'm not the only one keeping secrets from my best friend," she finished scornfully. "Not only that but you've known for a *month* that I was at the party where Tyson Drew was killed."

"A month, Luce. I kept quiet for a month. *You* kept quiet about this for *years*. I didn't tell you I knew 'cause I wanted to give you the chance to say something on your own."

"Oh, I get it," she said, now indignant. "You were testing me." Lucy backed toward one of the two chairs in the small rehearsal space. Finding the back of one with an outstretched hand, she slid into it. "Grace has been living with me this whole time . . . and she never said a word to me about all this."

"You're overreacting. She respects your privacy. Grace hasn't even told Candace. Not yet."

A hint of a smile touched Lucy's otherwise tense features. "*Candace* doesn't know? Her own *sister*? Huh. I'd buy a ticket to be there when that particular piece of information leaks out."

"Lucy," he said earnestly, "Grace has been waiting all these months, hoping you'll give her some tiny bit of hope, some clue that maybe you remember what happened that night. She won't ask you herself. I don't understand why. If Vesper was my dad I'd be doing everything I could to get you to talk."

"*Get me to talk?*" She looked at him with disgust. "JM, you seriously think that I would let an innocent man be executed, if I knew something that could help him?"

John-Michael looked crushed. "You really didn't see anything that night?"

"I saw Tyson Drew's dead body in the pool," she admitted hesitantly. "But other people saw that, too. And—oh, John-Michael . . ." For the first time, he noticed a hint of shame in Lucy's voice. "I *used* so much, in the years that came after," she added in a dejected voice. "I had dreams, I had hallucinations. That stuff, it messes with your mind, twists memories. It warps them until you don't know what's real anymore."

Lucy went silent, so John-Michael continued in a more

conciliatory tone, "Grace's dad said that when he left the party he saw the silhouette of a little kid on the balcony that overlooks the pool. One of the kids at the house that night had to have seen something."

"There were four kids at the house that night," Lucy said. "Why do you assume it was me?" Then, as though the thought was only just occurring to her, Lucy asked, "Did . . . did Grace have something to do with you asking me to move in? *Did they use you to get to me?*"

John-Michael was stunned. "Who's 'they'? Candace's mom found Paolo, *he* found me, remember? There was no way to predict Paolo would know that I knew you. That's insane."

Lucy's attitude puzzled him. For a moment it had seemed as though she might be on the brink of admitting something and now she was back to being confused. John-Michael wanted to help Grace, wanted to get these secrets out in the open where they wouldn't fester. In the end, though, it wasn't his business, as Lucy seemed eager to point out.

The *Death Note* anime theme broke the silence. John-Michael's ringtone. He turned away from Lucy as he looked at the new text on his phone.

Dude, how much more obvious do I have to be? Make an excuse. Leave Lucy to arrange some music. Wanna get a burger or something?

Amazed, John-Michael texted back, Ruben?

Who else? Now get over here, I miss you.

John-Michael returned his cell phone to his pocket, mind racing. Ruben wanted *him*? This was huge. He hadn't even suspected because he thought Ruben was into Lucy, but maybe Ruben was bi? Although in retrospect it was starting to make sense. Lucy did nothing but throw out hints that she liked Ruben and he all but ignored them.

"I . . . Uh, I gotta bounce," John-Michael mumbled. "We were done anyway, right?" He hoped so. Ruben had brightened up the day about a thousand percent. The situation with him, Lucy, and Grace would have to be put on hold.

Lucy just nodded. She looked unhappy, seemed to be mulling over her thoughts. "Yeah, I think we're definitely done for today."

GRACE

"I'm just saying–what's the point busting in on her? Can't it wait?"

Grace heard the tension in John-Michael's voice on the staircase outside their bedroom.

The door to the bedroom Grace shared flew open. From her desk at the foot of her bed, she turned slowly in her chair until she was facing Lucy, who stood framed in the doorway.

Lucy looked angry. Instinctively, Grace knew what she was going to say.

"John-Michael told you about my dad," Grace began softly, with compassion. It was a sincere expression of how she felt. After months of living with Lucy, Grace had come to accept that Lucy was probably not *consciously* hiding the truth. For whatever reason, it seemed that Lucy didn't even understand what she'd seen that night, eight years ago.

John-Michael arrived, slightly out of breath, behind Lucy.

"I did tell Lucy that your dad is on death row for the murder of Tyson Drew," John-Michael admitted. "But Grace, you two have to start talking about it. I know you don't want to be reminded but, seriously? Time is not on your side, here. It's insane, keeping all this quiet. What if Lucy does know something?"

His words brought instant tears to Grace's eyes. But she quickly wiped them away when she heard a third set of footsteps on the spiral staircase. Both Lucy and John-Michael turned to see who it was.

"Ariana, would you mind? This is kind of private," Lucy said.

There was a faintly embarrassed pause. Grace dried tear-covered fingertips on her shirt as Ariana stood awkwardly behind Lucy and John-Michael, apparently sizing up the situation. "Hey, no problem," Ariana said. "I heard raised voices. I thought maybe something was wrong. Totally don't want to butt in on your business. I'm just gonna finish up in the kitchen and head out for some air." Ariana hesitated a moment before turning for the stairs.

"Thank you, Ari," Lucy called after her friend. She sounded more than a little embarrassed. That embarrassment continued as she turned back to Grace. The anger had all but vanished.

"I have to ask," Lucy said. "How long have *you* known that I was at the party?"

Grace took a calming breath. "I recognized your name from the moment I heard you were moving in with us. Then

John-Michael told us that your dad was in the government. 'Lucy Long' isn't a million miles away from 'Lucasta Jordan-Long,' the child actress. I looked you up on the internet and—bingo. Found out about *Jelly and Pie*. Saw the names of the other kids who were at the house that night."

Lucy glanced at John-Michael. "Could you give us a few minutes?"

"Actually, Lucy, would you mind?" interjected Grace. "I'd prefer it if John-Michael sat in. It's kind of a delicate discussion."

John-Michael hovered close to his own bed, as if waiting for the girls to agree whether he should stay or go. Lucy was clearly taken aback but she didn't object. "If I'd seen anything, Grace, I'd have told."

Grace didn't reply for a minute. When she did, she spoke carefully, avoiding any accusation in her tone. "I know that if you could have talked, you would have. I'm just . . . I'm just wondering," she continued, "in fact I always have . . . if maybe someone got to you. Tried to shut you up. When you were a little kid?"

Lucy shifted her weight from one foot to the other. Warily, she asked, "Got to me—how?"

John-Michael turned to face Lucy, his eyes registering anxiety.

Grace struggled to contain the emotions that were bubbling up inside. She had to persuade Lucy to tell them everything she could remember. Even an apparently stupid detail might be crucial. John-Michael was right—they were running out of time to act. "There are lots of ways to get to a kid. Think about it Lucy, you were little. It was late, you were half asleep. Whatever you saw, maybe you buried the memory. Maybe someone *made* you bury it."

"Like who?"

Grace replied simply, "I don't know." She looked over at John-Michael, who had finally settled uneasily onto the edge of his own bed. He was regarding Lucy with a mixture of curiosity and pensiveness.

Lucy paused. "But if I don't remember anything?"

"There are ways to help you remember," Grace said cautiously. She didn't want to frighten Lucy off, didn't want her to realize just how much thought she'd put into this over the last few months. "Hypnosis. Recovered memory therapy."

"That actually works?" John-Michael sounded hopeful.

Grace didn't take her eyes off Lucy, who seemed to be considering their words. "It can."

Eventually, Lucy asked Grace, "And you think it would be enough to get your dad off the hook? If I remember something under hypnosis?"

"Maybe," she replied. "The evidence that convicted him was circumstantial. That's why he got all the stays of execution. Each time it was like, another chance to find some better evidence for the defense. So far, they haven't found it. He had a motive, he was at the party, and he doesn't have an alibi. They connected his DNA to Tyson Drew's body, but my dad says it's because they got into a fight earlier in the evening over something stupid like money. But Lucy—my dad was nowhere near the pool that night. He got up to use the bathroom and he saw someone little up on the balcony, looking down. He couldn't see what the kid was looking at, but that balcony overlooks the pool. That little kid saw the murderer, Lucy. My dad is sure of it."

They all shared a lengthy pause. Then John-Michael said, "Why're you so sure it's Lucy?"

"Think about how you behaved afterward, Lucy," Grace said gently. "You went into a tailspin. That didn't happen to any of the other kids at the party. You're the only one who acted like they'd been through some kind of trauma."

"That's not true, Tyger Watanabe was messed up, too."

"Maybe later, when he hit fourteen, fifteen, but right after the murder, Tyger kept doing the show for another season, whereas you, they dropped. You said it was because you were acting out, Lucy. In one of your interviews, *you* said it."

To Grace's immense relief, Lucy didn't deny it.

"I . . ." Lucy seemed to be struggling to get the words out. "I have wondered. From time to time. Recently, maybe more." She seemed reluctant to continue.

"Please, Lucy."

Lucy was about to speak and then stopped. She tilted her head toward the door. Grace listened for a moment, but heard nothing.

Lucy stood, went to the door, and opened it wider. Grace watched her push open the bathroom door, too.

"What's up?"

Lucy turned back, closing the bedroom door behind her. "Coulda sworn I heard someone on the landing outside."

"I didn't hear anything," John-Michael said, shrugging.

"Gotta say, this whole conversation is making me a little jumpy," Lucy said, sitting down next to John-Michael. He shifted toward his pillows, making space.

Impatiently, Grace got out of the chair and sat between the two of them. She placed a tentative hand on Lucy's bare arm, suddenly painfully aware of how frosty Lucy could appear.

"I know it can't be easy for you to think about that night. If you really did see Tyson Drew being murdered, that would have been a seriously traumatic moment. Just to see it, I mean. I remember the only time I saw a guy throw a real, honest-to-goodness punch at another guy. It happened right in front of me, outside school. And I was physically shaking, Lucy. I can only imagine what it could do to a kid to watch a grown man strangled and drowned. It's no wonder your mind closed it down."

"I . . . Grace. I really don't know if I wanna . . ."

"All I'm asking is that you try. Lucy, please. If there's something there, something your mind has been trying to suppress . . . it could seriously help my father."

"It's not going to overturn the conviction, though," Lucy said doubtfully. "I mean, Grace, I'm real sorry that your dad's in that situation. But I'm not the one who put him there. The jury won't convict him without evidence."

"It's all circumstantial, though!" Grace cried, rising to her feet.

John-Michael half rose, as if to steady her in case she toppled over. He put a soothing hand on hers, saying, "Gracie, it's okay . . ."

"It's circumstantial evidence," she reiterated, this time calmly. "A high-profile case—the cops were under a lot of pressure to get a conviction. And the district attorney did a great job with the jury, I have to say. I've looked at the trial records and even though I'm no lawyer, Lucy, I can see that."

John-Michael stared curiously. "You've looked at the trial records?"

"I'm an expert on the Tyson Drew murder case," Grace said. "My dad taught me that."

"If you're such an expert," Lucy began insistently, "then I guess you must have some idea of who did it."

Grace allowed herself a tiny nod.

Lucy pressed on. "Who?"

But all Grace could say was, "I can't tell you. I'm sorry, but that might seem like I was leading you. If you're going to try the recovered-memory therapy, you need to go into it with no preconceptions. It won't help us if you and I discuss the case beforehand." She tipped her head toward

John-Michael. "That's why I asked him to stay. John-Michael's a witness that you and I never talked about who you might have seen."

"But you have a specific person in mind?" Lucy asked.

Grace turned to John-Michael. "Have I ever said anything?"

He shook his head, emphatic. "No way." To Grace, he said, "Dude, I had no idea you had any clue who might have committed the murder."

Lucy sat on her hands now, rocking back and forth very slightly on the edge of the bed. It was like watching her regress from a confident sophomore to an anxious child.

"Is it dangerous, this memory-therapy thing?"

Grace said, "It's a kind of hypnosis."

Lucy shook her head. "Not what I asked."

Grace found herself releasing a shaky breath. "I don't know for sure, Lucy. It's kind of like letting out some buried demon, I guess. Not literally, of course. But once that memory is out . . . well."

"It's probably buried for a reason," John-Michael said. Grace could hear a slight strain in his voice. "You don't know what kind of crap you're going to dig up. Stirring and stirring. It's sure to release a stink."

"John-Michael's right," Grace said a tad cautiously. "Uncovering a repressed memory can be traumatic. Lucy, I'm begging you. This is the fourth time they've set a date for his execution. The *fourth*. His lawyer will appeal—she always does. It might even work out, again. Even if it does, the fear—it's sapping his strength. Being in prison has changed him. If this goes on much longer, I think he might give in, just to end it all. And then I'd lose my father, forever."

"A bad odor, I can handle," Lucy said. But she sounded reluctant.

Grace felt hope like a pressure against her chest. "So you'll try it?"

Lucy nodded, once. "Okay."

CANDACE

The cast and crew of *Prepped* had been at Leo Carrillo beach all afternoon. Most had left around five, along with Ricardo Adams. Only three actors stuck around to shoot the final two night scenes.

Candace had elected to spend the day in Malibu to minimize on driving. She'd met her mother for lunch at her home on Malibu Beach. Later, she'd agreed to return there to spend the night.

One of the final three, Candace sighed as she watched the crew setting up. "Why bother to shoot at night if they're gonna light us up like a Christmas tree?"

Out of the corner of her eye, she saw Yoandy beaming at her comment. She'd watched him wander off to smoke a cigarette, and followed him. Now they leaned against the rocks at one end of the beach, waiting while the crew finished prepping the scene. At least five minutes had passed. So far, hers was the only comment that either had made. Yoandy seemed comfortably silent. Meanwhile, Candace was itching with tension and half-formed sentences that never made it to her lips.

She closed her eyes for a second and then jumped in. "Should we talk about this kiss?"

Yoandy didn't turn his head, but she heard a smile in his voice. "You think maybe we should rehearse?"

"He'll probably wind up choosing the first take anyway," Candace grumbled. "Directors usually do. But they like to have the choice. And the feeling of power."

"I would like very much to kiss you right here, *nena*," he said warmly. "But it's Sebastian's first time kissing Annika. Maybe better if we wait. Try to capture some of that 'first time' energy on camera. What do you think?"

Candace said nothing, feeling her skin buzz. He wanted their first kiss to be recorded.

"And then after we kiss, you hit me," Yoandy added cheerily.

"What?"

"You didn't see the new pages?"

"Ah, no!" Candace looked toward the director, feeling somewhat thrown.

"Oh!" Yoandy turned to her, finally engaging with energetic enthusiasm. "It's a little different from before. We start in the water, we head for the beach. Once we clear the water, count two beats. Then you fall. I grab you when you fall, kiss you, you hit me, and we keep running."

"I fall? I *hit* you?"

"It's dark. There are lots of rocks and seaweed."

"A kiss . . . and then I pop you one." Candace let the statement settle, solidify into a concrete truth. "Why?"

"I guess you don't like being kissed!" he said with a shrug.

"Yeah, that'll do it," Candace said disdainfully. "I guess 'feisty' is what passes for character on this show."

If it were up to Candace, she'd have written a kiss that Annika initiated, not Sebastian.

"Tension!" Yoandy said, smiling widely. His hand steered near her waist but stopped just short of touching her. Candace couldn't help but feel a pulse of excitement—within minutes she'd be in his arms. "The director wants it to be a will-they-get-together kind of thing," Yoandy told her. "We can practice that, if you like."

"I should look at the new pages," she mumbled.

"Or you could trust me?" he offered, looking hopeful.

Candace glanced at the director. She'd already gotten a couple of dark looks from him when she'd caused delays. It wasn't worth the risk—but she *did* trust Yoandy. She'd just have to wing it.

Soon the director yelled for Candace and Yoandy to move into position. Yoandy began to step over the rocks. He held a hand out to her. After a moment's hesitation, Candace took it. They shared a tender smile, both surprisingly nervous.

A minute later they were both thigh-deep in the chilly waters of the Pacific. The tide was stronger than she'd expected. Fronds of knotted seaweed brushed against her legs and hands.

Candace peered toward the beach. But with the dazzling lights streaming directly at them, it was impossible to see any of the crew. Through a megaphone she heard the director yell, "Action!"

Candace ran headlong toward the sand. Beside her, Yoandy sloshed ahead. When they reached the beach, she counted to two. She stumbled and fell. Yoandy reached out and yanked her to her feet. He pulled her close. In the last second before their bodies touched, he slowed it down. He stroked strands of hair from her cheek.

Candace stared deep into his eyes, which were meltingly deep, chocolate brown, before he closed them and leaned in for a kiss.

Then his lips were on hers. They tasted of salt. His hands tightened on her waist. She could feel the tip of his tongue, trying to coax her lips farther apart. She wanted to relax into his arms, to open her mouth to him. But she didn't dare, not for a second. Each movement was deliberate. She pulled her right hand back. She formed a fist. She swung it toward his head. Yoandy yanked his head back as though he'd been struck. His left hand shot up to his cheek. He stared at her in shock and disappointment.

Candace felt an immediate surge of regret.

"Cut!"

Yoandy held back for a moment, and then grinned, delighted. "Pretty good, *nena*! I barely got out of the way in time!"

"Go again," called the director. "This time, Candace, let *him* kiss *you*. And could you look less upset about hitting him? We need more anger, more gravitas. Remember the virus has reversed the aging progress. You're an experienced woman in the body of a teenage girl. Before the apocalypse, you were a contender for the Nobel Prize. Sebastian is just some schlub whose ass you already had to save from that gambling den. He's not worthy of you. 'Kay?"

They waded back into their water to their first positions. They played the scene again. This time Candace's lips were closed when he kissed her. The director called a halt partway through. "Go again," he said grimly.

They played the scene a third time. This time Yoandy didn't pull his head back fast enough and her fist actually made contact with his jaw. Ironically, though, it appeared to be a much weaker punch. So they went again.

By the time the director was happy, they'd recorded another five takes. Soaking wet and with the cold onset of the night sea breeze, all Candace could think about was when she could kiss Yoandy again. His lips were soft, his touch warm against her cold ocean-kissed skin—but the most potent memory was the fleeting sensation of being pressed to his chest. She'd felt the heat of his body, even through the soaking-wet shirt. He made her feel sexier than she could ever remember feeling. From the way he was looking at her, Candace could see that Yoandy was eager for more, too.

"You wanna go dancing sometime?" he asked as they toweled their hair and shoulders dry.

"Latin dancing? I—ah—I don't know how."

"Don't worry about it," he said, obviously amused by her uncharacteristic skittishness. "I will be very, very gentle. You won't even notice it's a lesson. How about Saturday night?"

"The Fourth?" Candace stalled. "You're not with your family?"

Yoandy shrugged. "Sure, we can go to the family if you prefer. There'll be dancing there, also. Dancing is everywhere when you're with me." He smiled.

"I think maybe my housemates have plans," she said, making a decision. "But you know what? Sure, okay, I'll come out with you. But not right now. My mom, she, ah, she's picking me up soon." Candace finished with a wan smile. She hated to disappoint him.

But Yoandy didn't appear disappointed at all. *"Excelente."*

She looked at him expectantly until Yoandy finally chuckled and leaned closer, reaching for her waist with both hands. "Which kiss did you like best?" he whispered, close to her ear.

"This one," she murmured, turning her face to his so

that their mouths met. She sucked gently on his lower lip before releasing him with a tiny nip of her teeth against his chin.

"Ay, mi madre," he groaned as Candace pushed him away, smirking. "You're gonna kill me, *preciosa.*"

"Don't worry," she replied. "I'll be very, very gentle."

JOHN-MICHAEL
SANTA MONICA, THURSDAY, JULY 2

"Lucy, let's go back to when you were nine years old."

"I was Charlie back then," murmured Lucy. "On *Jelly and Pie*."

In a plush, Santa Monica consulting room of the psychiatrist, Dr. Barney Kessler, John-Michael watched the therapist remove a small, dark gray electronic device from the breast pocket of his sports coat. He touched a finger to the tiny screen and then placed it carefully on the desk to record the session. He pushed it along with the tips of his fingers until it was closer to Lucy, who sat in a leather easy chair, half reclined. The cream-colored damask curtains were drawn, reducing the midday glare from the oceanfront to a mild, cool glow. From compact speakers on the nearby birch wood bookcase, faint music played. It took John-Michael a few moments to realize that the music was the rather whimsical theme from *Jelly and Pie*. Nervously, he allowed his eyes to settle on Lucy. Her eyelids were half closed and she swayed ever so slightly in her chair, as if she were on the deck of a boat. It was the first time he'd ever seen someone hypnotized. The whole thing creeped him out a little.

"Did you go to a party on Mulholland Drive?"

"Yes," Lucy said. "Where Tyson Drew was killed." She sounded weary, as though having to relate the story for the thousandth time. John-Michael noticed that Dr. Kessler made a note before moving on.

"Tell me about that night, Lucy."

There was a long silence. Then, very softly, Lucy said, "I don't want to."

The therapist didn't react. "Can you tell me who you were with at the party?"

"Tyger was there. Alexis, Marc."

"That's great, Lucy. So your costars from *Jelly and Pie* were there. Can you remember anyone else you saw at that party?"

"I guess I saw Tyson Drew," she said resentfully. "He was dead."

"Where did you see him?" asked Kessler. He used a calm, kind voice.

"In a swimming pool."

"Was anyone with him?"

"Huh?"

John-Michael watched Lucy's face closely. She sounded lost, like a little girl clutching a teddy bear. Her eyes moved rapidly under eyelids that were shut tight. There was a very long silence. Kessler didn't move, his expression didn't change.

"Lucy, was anyone near the pool when you saw Tyson Drew?"

When she spoke Lucy's voice sounded hoarse. "It's a bad, *bad* dream."

"That's fine, Lucy," Kessler said. He set down his yellow pad, folded his hands across his lap. "It's okay to tell me about the dream."

"I'm not supposed to," Lucy blurted. The force of the comment jerked John-Michael upright.

Kessler just nodded. "You can tell me, Lucy. I'm here to help you. Your friend John-Michael is here, too. You're safe."

"Bad girls tell tales," Lucy said, moaning. "Bad girls make up stories from their dreams."

Finally, Kessler began to react. He leaned forward, toward Lucy. "Did someone tell you that?"

"It's a secret," was all Lucy would say. John-Michael could see the stress in Lucy's entire body. Her hands gripped the edge of the chair so tight he could see the bones through Lucy's skin.

"Who told you not to tell?"

Lucy made a tiny, whimpering sound. "I'm not bad, miss."

"Did 'miss' tell you not to talk about the party?"

Fretfully, Lucy nodded, eyes still firmly closed.

Kessler's gaze strayed for just a second, catching John-Michael's eye. He held up a single finger to his lips. John-Michael nodded in response.

"Secrets can be like a prison, Lucy. But you're the one with the key. You can let yourself out of the prison, any time."

He waited for a response, but Lucy made none. Kessler continued, "Would it be possible for me to talk to *Charlie?* Charlie from *Jelly and Pie?*"

Lucy mumbled something incoherent.

"Maybe *Lucy* didn't see anything at the party," Kessler said. "Maybe Charlie is allowed to talk about what she saw?"

"Charlie don't care about her," Lucy said abruptly. John-Michael immediately recognized the slightly exaggerated accent. It was working. Lucy had slipped into her character from *Jelly and Pie.*

"She dug her nails into his neck. Pretty nails, all shiny. Like peaches. On fire. His eyes bugged out when it happened. He tried to get away, but she had something around his neck—a tie. I saw her shoe on his shoulder, holding him under. It took him a *long* time to die. Bobbing up and down for air, but he wasn't getting any."

John-Michael couldn't move. Kessler let Lucy's words resonate in the following silence. "Did you recognize the lady you saw, Charlie? Do you know her name?"

"Pretty lady, nice shoes."

Kessler kept his voice level. "Charlie, can you tell me her name?"

John-Michael realized that he was holding his breath. Grace was outside in the waiting room, probably nervous as hell, praying to hear the words that might finally spell hope for her father.

There was a tiny sob in Lucy's reply. "Lady doesn't want anyone to know."

The therapist said, "Did she threaten you?"

"Bad girls tell tales."

"But I'm asking Charlie."

"Charlie's bad," Lucy said suddenly, adding in a sing-song voice, "bad, bad, bad."

"The lady's name, Charlie. Can you remember?"

"Dana said I shouldn't tell," Lucy said, practically whispering. "I was crying 'cause I wet my pants. She cleaned me, put me to bed. She sang to me, gave me a bottle of nail polish from her purse when she saw how much I liked the color of her nails. Dana said it was a bad dream, is all."

Kessler hesitated. "Where did Dana find you?"

"Around," replied Lucy in a small voice.

"Did you like Dana?"

Lucy's eyes opened slowly. She turned and stared at John-Michael as though he were a complete stranger.

"Lucy, this is Dr. Kessler," said the therapist in a voice of sudden authority. "Lucy—are you awake?"

Lucy's expression didn't change for a moment. "I remember. Damn, John-Michael. I *remember.*"

She rose, unsteadily, to her feet, catching the arm that John-Michael offered for support. When he felt the shake in her muscles, he pulled her close.

"It's okay, Lucy," he breathed against her neck. "It's gonna be okay. Let's go out and . . . and tell Grace."

"Grace!" sobbed Lucy, tightening her grip around his neck. She sounded distraught. "What am I gonna tell her? What have I done?"

"You didn't do anything wrong, Luce, you didn't know." John-Michael tilted her chin up so that he could look into her eyes. "I'm with you, all right? We'll tell Gracie together."

He steered her toward the waiting room, with a final glance at Dr. Kessler, who stood aside to let them pass. "Come see me in a few days," he said. "You need some aftercare."

Grace stood up as they entered the waiting room. Her arms were by her sides, both hands clenched tightly. Eyes wide with hope, she said, "And . . . ?"

John-Michael gave a quick nod.

Grace could barely speak. "Lucy, did you remember something?"

"I remembered," Lucy said shortly, her voice suddenly curt. "There was someone else there. That woman from the *Macbeth* movie, Dana Alexander."

"Did she . . . ?" Grace stopped, placed a hand just above her breastbone, as if to steady her breath. "Did Dana see who did it?"

Lucy made the tiniest suggestion of a shrug. "Maybe. Or maybe . . . maybe she even did it."

Grace gasped. Tears sprung to her eyes almost immediately. Gulping now, she asked, "Do you think my dad . . . ?"

"Can I get your dad free?" Lucy said, almost snapping. "Who knows? Maybe. Can we go now?"

Grace hesitated. "Lucy, are you mad at me?"

"Of course not," Lucy replied, too quickly. "It's just . . ." John-Michael edged around so that he could look at her. Her sudden shift in mood had taken him by surprise, too. "I'm not angry," she managed to say after a couple of deep breaths. "But this . . . this is a shock."

"We understand that, of course," Grace said. John-Michael echoed the sentiment with a vague mumble and then asked Lucy, "You wanna get a taxi?"

Lucy just shook her head. She pulled the door open and stepped out onto Santa Monica Boulevard. "I'll walk. I need to think."

Grace grabbed Lucy's arm. Lucy stopped walking and stared at Grace's hand with a kind of appalled inertia. "Lucy, you're in shock. And I know it's kind of my fault. Do you want to talk about it?"

Lucy's lips moved in silence for a moment, as though she were rehearsing a line. Then: "Talk about it? No. This is messed up, Grace."

Anger threatened to explode within Grace. "In two weeks my father is going to be put to death, Lucy, executed for what that woman did," she blurted. "You've got to tell the cops what you remember. You have to!"

"Hey, hey," John-Michael said, getting between them.

"Cool it, Gracie, I know you're upset, too."

"What I remember?" Lucy stared at Grace, ignoring John-Michael. "It's all flashes. Nothing that will convince the cops that Dana Alexander killed him. I *need* to think about this."

"You think *Dana Alexander* killed Tyson Drew?" Grace asked.

"Of course," Lucy fired back. "She's the one who made me keep quiet about it."

"Whoa," John-Michael said. "That's going to be tough to prove. An A-list actress like Dana Alexander—not exactly an easy takedown."

"You don't need to convince the cops that she actually did it," Grace pleaded, gripping Lucy's arm even tighter as her friend tried to pull away. John-Michael sidelined a couple of passersby who'd noticed their altercation, made sure they gave the two girls a wide berth as they walked past. "You just need to plant reasonable doubt that my father *didn't* do it," Grace continued in a lower voice.

Lucy said forcefully, "There is no way that Alexander is going down for this, Grace. She's too smart. Too powerful."

"She wouldn't even have to actually be convicted. Even the suspicion would be enough to set my father free."

"Listen to me," John-Michael interrupted reasonably. "It looks like Dana Alexander was only too eager to suppress Lucy's testimony from the very beginning. Maybe she knows that if they start up the murder investigation all over again, they might find something."

"But that was eight years ago," Lucy said. "If she cared so much about keeping me quiet, why haven't I heard *word one* from the woman since that night?"

"Too risky?" John-Michael suggested.

Grace became quiet, thoughtful. "On the other hand, it would have made sense to keep tabs on you, somehow."

Lucy became very still. "Tabs? Like, how?"

"Like, I don't know . . ." Grace shrugged. "Maybe make friends with someone *close* to you. Your parents, maybe? Get them to keep her posted, in case you started to talk."

Lucy's expression flattened. The energy seemed to be visibly draining from her frame. "Oh no."

John-Michael steadied her with a touch to her shoulder. "What is it?"

Lucy stared from Grace to John-Michael beseechingly. She began to shake her head. "It can't be. She wouldn't do that to me. We were rehab buddies! She wouldn't betray me."

"Lucy, who are you talking about?" John-Michael asked.

"No, not Ariana." Lucy shook her head, confused.

John-Michael took in Grace's expression, watched her go from stunned to bitter resolution. Grace took two breaths in quick succession. She put both hands on Lucy's shoulders.

"If it's Ariana, Lucy, then you have to accept . . ."

"No," Lucy said in a low moan, her voice trembling. "Not Ari . . . She knows everything, Gracie. About Charlie, about my dream, what I saw that night when Tyson Drew was killed; Ariana knows everything!"

"And she was listening on the landing," Grace said, her voice clear as cut glass in the warm, balmy air. "When we were talking yesterday."

"She probably even heard you talking about getting the regression therapy," John-Michael pointed out. From the sudden gasp that Lucy gave then, he realized how shattering this had to be.

"Then she's already warned Dana Alexander. And now she's at home, waiting for me to come back and spill the beans," Lucy snarled, bitterness dripping from every word. "Well, those two lying witches are gonna deal with *me* now."

"And me," Grace said.

"And me," John-Michael added fiercely. "Whatever happens now, Luce, we've got your back."

LUCY
KITCHEN, VENICE BEACH HOUSE,
THURSDAY, JULY 2

John-Michael, Grace, and Lucy returned from Santa Monica and retreated to the second-floor bedroom to discuss their next move. Paolo and Candace had gone for groceries, and Maya was running errands with her aunt Marilu, so they were less likely to be disturbed. Only Ariana was in the house, cooking. They left the door wide open this time, so that they'd easily see if someone approached.

"Better do it quick," Grace had advised, "like pulling off a Band-Aid."

The trouble was, Ariana was stuck to Lucy a whole lot harder than a Band-Aid. The years they'd shared. The tears, the pain. Things they'd told each other that no one else knew. And yet through it all, Lucy realized that she'd never truly considered Ariana to be a *friend*. The relationship was too complicated for that. Friends shared tiny intimacies, meaningless banter, food, philosophical conversations, the quotidian *nothing* of life. Lucy and Ariana shared little but their sadness, and had done so from the very beginning.

The second that Grace had said the words, *with someone close to you*, it had been as though a blindfold had been lifted from Lucy's eyes. Ariana. So simple, yet so unthinkable. What kind of person would intrude on the privacy of a damaged teenager? What kind of monster would use another damaged kid to accomplish that?

Her rational mind tried to brush away the cold, hollow feeling that had warned Lucy that Ariana was just too perfect. The girl had appeared in Lucy's life at just the right time. What did people do in rehab? They talked. It was the new confessional.

It flashed through Lucy's mind that maybe Ariana wasn't actually damaged. That maybe it had all been an act. But the memories from their Claremont days piled in pretty quickly to dismiss that thought. Ariana passed out drunk at her hostel. Ariana calling Lucy to pick her up from outside a bar where she'd fallen down, half blind from whatever drug she'd taken. Hours at her side, watching her go cold turkey. No actor would be so committed.

Lucy couldn't figure out how Ariana could possibly know someone like Dana Alexander. Ariana came from Louisiana, where as far as Lucy could make out, she'd been a nobody. It struck Lucy that she hadn't bothered to find out many concrete details about Ariana's background. The accent sounded genuine, and Ariana had some airs and graces that matched her story of faded elegance, a once well-to-do family fallen on poverty. But nothing that could connect Ariana to a Hollywood movie star from England. Lucy just couldn't see it.

This was the detail that almost persuaded Lucy that she was wrong. After she and John-Michael returned from the psychiatrist's office in Santa Monica, Lucy couldn't stop mulling it over. Maybe they were jumping to conclusions?

But then Lucy recalled, with a stab of anguish, how she'd told Ariana about the dream that wasn't. They'd talked about it recently, right here in the house, in Lucy's room. But now that Lucy *really* thought about it, she remembered that it hadn't been the first time she'd mentioned that dream to Ariana. The subject had come up several times over the years. And each time, Lucy realized, Ariana had soothed her, calmed her, reassured Lucy that it was just a dream.

And probably gone straight back to Alexander with the news.

Lucy still thinks it was all a dream.

Ariana had to go, and now, before Lucy's mind could be changed.

"There's not one person in the house who won't be glad to see her go," Grace had admitted when Lucy first mentioned it. "You didn't like her . . . ?" Lucy said, bemused. "Why didn't you say so?"

"She was your friend. But now that we know she's not I'll be honest—she's a creeper for sure," Grace said. "The way she hovers, always trying to listen in on conversations, not really contributing."

"Ariana can be shy in groups," Lucy said. Defending Ariana was a reflex, even now. "Like Maya. Remember how quiet Maya was, too, at first?"

Reflex or not, Lucy had to override her own impulse to look out for Ariana. No one could ask her to leave but Lucy. It had to be done, and it had to be done today.

"We're behind you, Lucy, whatever you decide," John-Michael told her. Lucy went directly downstairs and into the kitchen, where Ariana was chopping onions for dinner. "Ariana," Lucy began, her stomach lurching. "We have to talk."

Ariana placed the knife neatly to one side of the chopping board. "What's up, hon?"

"Ari, I'm really sorry. But it's been over three weeks. You said you'd only be staying here for a few days. And, the thing is, we're not really allowed to have more than six of us here. The insurance, Candace's mom. We've been skating around issues here, but it can't go on."

To Lucy's astonishment, Ariana began to smile. It was a sad smile, filled with compassion.

"Your friends don't like me."

"This isn't about you. It's about how the house is set up."

Ariana gave a slight shake of her head. Her smile had become ironic, verging on cynical. "I tried real hard to get them to like me, Lucy, but they're not easy. You ever get the feeling that something messed up is going on with all of them?"

Lucy hesitated. She didn't like the sound of where this was going.

But Ariana was hitting her stride. With her back to the kitchen sideboard, she tossed the knife aside. Nervously, Lucy watched it clatter toward the sink.

"Candace, she's totally focused on her career. She'll want this whole place for herself soon enough. Wait and see. Paolo, I don't even know what that boy's deal is. John-Michael, well, okay, he's a sweetheart but what he did to his car? No normal guy drives a Mercedes-Benz off a cliff. Take my word for it; he's got a screw loose."

"Ari," Lucy began, half smiling in utter astonishment at the tirade that was flowing from Ariana's mouth.

"Maya's a nice kid, I got nothing against her. I mean, who wouldn't want to get rich from some dumb piece of software?"

"Are you done?" said Lucy. Their smiles had vanished now.

"Almost," Ariana said with a touch of vehemence. She walked around the dining table until she was standing half a yard away, staring Lucy right in the eye. "Grace is the one, isn't she? She's the one who told you to kick me out."

"She's not—"

Ariana interrupted, musing. "Grace—so nice and so quiet. She wants to be the housemother. Girl got nothing else goin' for her. She's not talented or brilliant, like the rest of you. Not tortured and angsty, like you, or John-Michael. Just plain, ordinary, dull Grace. And I threaten her. It's as simple as that."

"Grace is none of those things," came a voice from behind Lucy. She turned to see Candace standing in the open door. Paolo stood beside her, and behind them both, Grace and John-Michael. Together they presented a firm, resolute front.

"Grace is amazing," John-Michael said, pushing forward until he was shoulder to shoulder with Lucy. "I wouldn't have got through some of the worse parts of my life without her."

"It's true," Paolo said. "Grace is awesome."

Lucy's eyes met Grace's. She was trembling, very slightly, but looked right back. Lucy turned slowly to Ariana. "They're right. Grace is the one who binds us together. And no one asked me to get you to leave, Ari. But you can bet your ass that they want you to go now."

"My bag," Ariana muttered through gritted teeth, "is always packed."

They watched, uncomfortably silent, as Ariana made a point of flinging the freshly chopped onions into the sink, then flounced off into the living room. She reached for the suitcase that was tucked neatly in the space between the futon and the new three-seater sofa. Within five minutes she was ready to go.

Lucy pulled away slowly. Out of the corner of her eye, through the French windows to the rear of the living room and beyond the small backyard, she glimpsed a white Cadillac. Maya's aunt was pulling into a parking space behind the house.

Ariana dropped the suitcase to the floor. She faced Lucy, seemed to consider for a moment, and then, almost reluctantly, she put one arm around Lucy's neck.

With her mouth close to Lucy's ear, Ariana whispered, "Watch out for these people, Lucy. They don't know you the way I do."

JOHN-MICHAEL
KITCHEN, VENICE BEACH HOUSE,
THURSDAY, JULY 2

"You're going to the movies?" John-Michael said. He watched Lucy wrap the cheese she'd been slicing and put it back in the fridge. She arranged a few slices on a plate around some cherry tomatoes and began to eat, leaning against the kitchen sideboard.

"Are you sure?" he said. "Wouldn't you prefer to hang out with us? Although, now that I think about it, Maya probably won't want to do anything–she's totally obsessed by her app these days. I don't know when Paolo will get back from the tennis club. And I'm kind of going out . . ."

John-Michael's voice trailed off. He hadn't mentioned yet to Lucy that Ruben and he might be kind of seeing each other. He probably should.

Lucy chewed for a few seconds, then shrugged, a little sadly. "Today has been intense. I think I need to be out of the house, out of my head."

"Want me to go with you?" John-Michael offered. "I'd be happy to break my date."

The beginnings of a smile appeared in Lucy's eyes. "A date?"

"Ruben." He felt a blush steal over his neck and cheeks.

The smile vanished. "Ruben is gay?"

"Bi," corrected John-Michael.

Lucy put down her plate, eyes downcast; she wouldn't look at him.

"You're upset," he said sympathetically. "I'm sorry–Ruben said you might be."

She shook her head for a moment, blinking back tears, and then tried to smile. "I should have guessed. Now that I think about it, he was always asking me to get you to play guitar again. It was all an excuse."

"It may have been," John-Michael said nervously. "I'm not that good."

Tentatively, she asked. "Have you guys . . . you know?"

John-Michael grinned, more confident this time. "Hey, none of your beeswax, Long!"

She crossed her arms. "No fair stealing a bandmate's guy, Weller."

"Well, technically, he was never yours . . ."

"Seriously, how long has this been a thing?"

John-Michael picked a cherry tomato from Lucy's plate and popped it into his mouth. "A day. After we rehearsed yesterday, at school, we went for burgers and shakes, then made out on the beach."

"Ugh, that's so high school."

"I know!" John-Michael said happily. "It was awesome. Like being sixteen again. Ah, sweet sixteen!"

"Sweet sixteen?" Candace said, sailing into the kitchen with an empty plate, which she placed in the sink. "Who's sweet sixteen?"

"John-Michael kissed a boy on the beach," Lucy said, pouting.

Candace said, "Oooh, spill. I want details."

"Ruben, the drummer from Whatnot. They met at Grace's benefit concert."

"That band you were in for all of five minutes?" Candace asked, taking a dining table chair and turning it to face them. "Is it still going?"

Lucy shrugged. "I guess they found a replacement for me."

"So we both like *los latinos*, eh, John-Michael?" Candace said, nudging him.

"Is that actually happening then?" John-Michael asked, a little surprised. "You and Yoandy Santiago?"

Candace beamed. "Maybe."

"But—doesn't he have a girlfriend?"

Candace rolled her eyes. "No! You can't believe the gossip. He's music-famous and she's reality-TV famous, so they get the paparazzi treatment once in a while."

"He actually told you he's not with Kay Alexander?" insisted John-Michael.

"Yes," Candace said, annoyed. "Yoandy doesn't have a

girlfriend. Yet," she added with a wink.

Shaking his head, John-Michael said, "I hope you're right. I don't want to see you getting hurt."

The amusement dropped from Candace's face. "Man, you sure changed your tune."

"Dude, I am *one hundred percent* Team Yoandace. Just be careful. Those stories about him dating Kay gotta come from somewhere."

"Anyway . . ." Lucy interrupted, "I should go. I'm meeting Luisito. We're seeing *The Death of Caesar.*"

"The one based on the Shakespeare play? Oh man, I totally want to see that," John-Michael said. "The guy who plays Antony is brutally hot."

"Me too," Candace said. "We did *Julius Caesar* in my youth theater company. 'Friends, Romans, countrymen, lend me your ears.'"

The kitchen went silent as Grace strolled in, her head on her chest, arms lightly folded in front of her. She looked up, first at John-Michael, then at Lucy with an awkward "hey." Finally, she turned to Candace and reached out to touch her sister's shoulder. "Hey, Candace? We need to talk."

Candace did a comic half frown, glancing at John-Michael before she looked back at Grace. "Sounds serious. You breaking up with me, sis?"

Lucy shot him a look that confirmed John-Michael's guess. Grace was about to tell Candace the truth about her father. Hurriedly, he took Lucy's plate and added it to the pile in the sink. "That's our cue to leave."

"No," Grace said in a very clear voice. "No. Lucy, John-Michael, I'd like you to be here for this. I need help explaining everything."

Lucy's expression turned sickly, as though she would prefer to be just about anyplace else. In fascination, John-Michael watched Grace turn to her stepsister and take her hand. "I've been keeping something from you, Candace. It wasn't my idea to do it, but anyway, I did."

Candace gave an embarrassed laugh. "Jeez, Gracie, what's going on?"

Grace took a long breath and released it through pursed lips. "Wow. This isn't easy."

Candace tugged at her hand and gently pulled her step-sister toward another chair. "Sit. Okay, sis, hit me with it. Whatever it is, we'll be cool. Unless you're Yoandy's other secret crush. Then we definitely are not and you, my dear, are an onion-eyed wretch."

John-Michael smiled to himself. Despite her joking, Candace was a loyal sister.

Grace took another breath. "So you know how you've never met my dad, Alex? Well, his name isn't really Alex Grant. He doesn't live in Canada. His real name is Alex Vesper." She paused for a few moments, then in a quieter voice added, "Candace, do you know who that is?"

Candace shook her head. She looked baffled. "Should

I? Although the name sounds familiar."

"He's the man they convicted for the murder of Tyson Drew." Grace paused and took a deep breath. John-Michael could see tears welling up in her eyes. "Candace, my dad's on death row."

Candace clasped a hand to her mouth, then looked first at Lucy, then John-Michael. "Did you guys know?"

Lucy nodded gravely. "Yeah," she whispered. "Grace told me a little while ago. John-Michael too. I . . ." She hesitated and settled a meaningful look on Grace before continuing. "I was at the party where Tyson Drew was murdered. I was just a kid, but I think I may have seen something. Something that could maybe get the conviction overturned."

Grace's eyes shone with the hint of tears, her voice shook, but only slightly. "My dad is innocent, Candace, I know it. I'm absolutely certain. But the evidence just didn't fall the right way. They've set a date for his execution. It's happened before. This time, it's in about two weeks."

"Oh, Grace, no, I'm so sorry, baby!" Suddenly, Candace was pulling her stepsister into her arms and squeezing, her head pressed to Grace's shoulder, her eyes tightly shut. "You poor thing," she said. "That's so horrible!" She pulled away. "Lucy, why haven't you testified yet, if you know something?"

Lucy sighed wearily. "It's complicated."

"It really is," said Grace. "Please, Candace, Lucy's been through a lot. But she's going to do the right thing now, aren't you, Lucy?"

Lucy nodded. "Yeah," she said quietly. "I am."

Wonderingly, Candace shook her head. "All these years . . . Why didn't you tell me? I would have been there for you. Did you ever visit him? I'd have gone with you. Oh!" Her eyes widened as realization struck. "Dead Man Walking!" For a moment she sounded almost joyful. "He's your dad! Although—God—that totally sucks for you. Oh, I'm sorry!" Once again, Candace fell on Grace's neck and hugged her stepsister.

John-Michael nodded at Lucy. "I think maybe we should go."

"How come John-Michael and Lucy knew before me?" Candace pulled away, puzzled. For the first time, a note of hurt entered her voice. "And your mom and my dad. They—you—were all lying to me all those years?" Now the tears were shining in Candace's eyes as well. "Why—? I mean, Gracie, didn't you trust me?"

"Yeah, we should definitely go," John-Michael said. He reached for Lucy's hand.

As they left the kitchen, he heard Grace saying, "Of course we trust you, Candace. Please—let me explain?"

CANDACE

By 7:30 a.m. Candace was strolling along the beach path as the joggers and dog walkers enjoyed the soft, milky light of Venice Beach in the morning. She watched them as she made her way to her Prius for another early start. As Candace pulled out her keys, she heard a car approach. A white Cadillac pulled into the parking spot next to hers.

"Hey, Marilu." Candace smiled as Maya's aunt emerged.

"Hola, linda," Marilu replied affectionately. She looked almost exactly like Maya. Light, olive-colored complexion, five five, probably a size ten rather than a six or eight like Maya, but proportionately very similar. The aunt's hair, like Maya's, was a glossy, dark chestnut brown and worn straight, down past the shoulders. She was dressed in smart indigo jeans, unremarkable black heels, and a black blazer over a fitted white blouse. Her look was basic yet professional. Her eyes were hidden behind black Ray-Bans.

Suddenly, Candace felt like something was off. It wasn't

déjà vu but a very distinct feeling that she'd seen Marilu before, but in a completely different context.

"Maya's still in bed," Candace volunteered.

Aunt Marilu's jaw hardened for a moment. She lifted her face briefly toward the house. "Really? But I'm taking her to the airport. Today is her big lunch in Napa with the investor."

"Maya's got a meeting in Napa?" Candace had heard something about this from Grace, but no details. The truth was, she hadn't completely believed everything Maya had been saying about her app recently. Maya would get to chatting, breathlessly, using techy language Candace didn't understand and didn't care to have explained, or else she spent her time buried in a stack of geek books and tapping away on her laptop. "She was up super-late, working on her code, I guess."

"Aha," Marilu said. "I guess I better go wake her."

"Okay, well, so long." Candace got into her Prius for the leisurely drive to the studio. At least that was one advantage of early-morning starts—less traffic. Her thoughts turned to her last kiss with Yoandy, and Candace daydreamed about their promised first date the following day.

When Candace arrived at the Culver City lot, Ricardo Adams was buying coffee from a cart outside the studio. As she stepped out of her car, he headed in her direction. He stopped in front of Candace before she made it to the studio doors. Ricardo looked tense, possibly even angry. She waited for him to speak first.

Ricardo cleared his throat. "You and Yoandy. It's got to stop."

Candace gasped. "What . . . business is it of yours?"

"It's a family affair. His girlfriend is my wife's sister. Or have you forgotten about Kay?"

"What? Yoandy says they're just friends."

Ricardo's upper lip was drawn back in a cynical sneer. "You believe that?"

Candace gulped but stood her ground. "Yes."

"Kay is *very* important to my wife," Ricardo said, his voice lowered, the tone darker. "And you of all people should know better than to bite the hand that feeds you."

"Bite the hand . . . ? What the hell are you talking about?"

He cocked his head to one side. "Who'd you think suggested you for the part of Annika?"

This was getting a little surreal. "It wasn't you? Or Yoandy?"

"It was Dana. She saw your pilot, that *Downtowners* thing. She's the one who put me in touch with you."

Candace didn't know what to say. Grace had mentioned Lucy's suspicions, but they'd both agreed that it was an odd coincidence that she'd ended up working on a production with the British woman's husband. But to find out that Alexander had actually picked her? That was creepy. "Oh."

"Oh? Is that all?"

"I'm, ah, um, grateful," she replied. "O-obviously."

If not for the connection to Lucy, Candace would have

been excited to know that a movie star of Dana Alexander's stature even knew she existed. But that the woman had been the one to suggest her for a big-break TV role? And kept quiet about it? That was a total surprise. Not at all the way Hollywood people usually behaved from what Candace knew. But then again, Dana Alexander wasn't the kind of person who'd be reluctant to call in a favor, now that she wanted one.

"Kay and Yoandy are together," Ricardo said firmly. "You're not here to meddle; you're here to work. So work."

As Candace watched him walk away, she realized that her skin was tingling, as though she'd been slapped. Just the same, she made herself stroll confidently into the studio, a little way behind Ricardo. When she spotted Yoandy at the breakfast buffet, she turned away, hoping that he hadn't noticed her arrive. Ricardo had reprimanded her as though she'd been having an illicit affair with Yoandy. The only explanation she could imagine was that Kay must be lying about her relationship with Yoandy—talking it up. Even though this meant that Ricardo's accusation was way off base, she felt its sting.

She managed to avoid Yoandy until lunchtime—they had no scenes together that day and she needed some time to figure out how she felt about Ricardo's proclamation. But as she halfheartedly picked at her gluten-free Pad Thai, she saw him approaching her. Casting around for a possible escape route, Candace found none. When she realized that their encounter was inevitable, she straightened up, steeled herself. After all, maybe he'd had the same warning.

Close up, though, she saw that his eyes were full of gentle concern. "Candace, what's happened? You look worried."

Nervously, she glanced over his shoulder. Ricardo was in plain sight, over by the main set. He was looking right at them. "We can't," she whispered. Miserably, she closed her eyes. "And I can't go on a date with you tomorrow."

"Really? I thought you were excited."

"I was," Candace started. Yoandy looked crestfallen but Candace was fully aware of Ricardo's eyes burning into her. "But it was a bad idea. It just has to be this way."

"Give me one reason why it's a bad idea."

"Kay," said Candace, so quietly that it was practically a hiss. "Ricardo keeps saying that Kay Alexander is your girlfriend."

Now he looked seriously upset. "Candace, Kay is not my girlfriend. I'm telling you the truth! Kay . . . she's a little unusual. We had a few dates, and that's all. Now she's texting me and calling me . . . inviting me. And Ricardo is a friend of my family, you know that. So I'm not gonna say no, am I? Okay, maybe Kay still thinks we have something but I haven't replied, I haven't called her back, and we *never* agreed to date."

"Did you call her *nena linda*, too?" Candace said, pursing her lips.

Yoandy pulled back, frowning. "Are you kidding?"

Candace held up a hand. "I'm done."

"Please," he murmured reasonably. "At least let's talk. Come to my dressing room after we finish? Please, Candace?" He reached for her left hand, but she snatched it away, left him looking forlorn. "If you don't come, then I'll know you don't want me. And I promise to leave you alone."

She looked past Yoandy's dejected eyes and saw Ricardo smirking at her. She was giving a convincing performance.

"Look, I'm sorry," she said, backing away. "I've got to go."

Candace didn't know if she should believe Ricardo or Yoandy. But in that moment, she didn't care whether Kay Alexander was Yoandy's girlfriend or some kind of delusional dater. She only knew that Yoandy had been forbidden. And in that moment, nothing and no one had ever seemed quite so irresistible.

In the absence of any scenes playing opposite Yoandy, Candace found herself daydreaming about the two of them together. She'd run through every detail: where he'd be standing when she came into his dressing room, what he'd say (not much), where he'd make her stand, where he'd put his hands, the slight rasp of his stubble on her lower lip, how soft his mouth would feel against her own. Candace knew she would remember almost nothing of what they recorded that day.

At the end of the day, she made her way to Yoandy's dressing room, where she found him buttoning closed a crisp, white linen shirt.

She hesitated, standing in the doorway watching him. But instead of approaching her, touching her, kissing her, Yoandy kept his distance. He regarded her with a tight, pained expression.

"Candace. Why didn't you mention that you're under-age?"

For a moment, Candace balked. It was the last thing she'd expected to hear him say. "That? I'll be eighteen in five months. You're not so much older," she said, finally approaching him. "And anyway, mister, what makes you so sure you're getting any, ever?" She finished with a gentle pinch of his cheek.

To her surprise, when she looked up at his face she saw utter sorrow.

"Ricardo and me," Yoandy began, "we talked."

"Oh, you did, did you?" she said caustically. "What did that tattletale have to say?"

"He warned me. He was very reasonable, actually. Said that I had to let Kay down nice and gentle—even if she's the one who's misunderstood our relationship. He reminded me that you're still in high school, that technically you're still a minor, that it could start a scandal, because I'm more than three years older."

"With you, he's reasonable," she observed. "With me, he makes threats."

"*Amor*, listen." He tried to touch her arm, but held off when she flinched. "The show's about to go on summer hia-tus—we'll get a natural break from each other. Kay will have time to understand the situation. Maybe it's better," he said, looking thoughtful. "Until after your eighteenth birthday."

"Yeah," she said, defiant. "By then, I might like someone else."

Yoandy gave a nod and crossed his arms, gazing at her with amused speculation. "It's possible. I'm pretty ugly."

"Yeah, y'are," she said with a hint of a smile. "But I'm not all that particular."

"*Nena*, don't be cruel," he said teasingly, pouting. "It's my father's fault I'm ugly."

Candace couldn't resist chuckling at this. "But you inherited his musical talent, so there's that."

Yoandy laughed, too. Then, as if he'd only just remembered, he stuck a hand into his jeans pocket and withdrew something that he kept hidden inside a tight fist. He took Candace's left hand and carefully unfurled her fingers, tenderly placing in the center of her palm a coiled necklace made from tiny yellow and ocher beads. "It's for you. From El Cobre, in Cuba; the colors of Our Lady of Charity."

When she accepted it without hesitation, he visibly relaxed. Barely brushing the skin of her cheek with his lips, Yoandy kissed her. "It means we're for each other. I don't give this necklace to just any girl, Candace."

Candace was a little overwhelmed at this. She closed her hand around the beads as she took a moment to recover, trying to appear nonplussed.

"I like you like this," he whispered, bringing his mouth to the curve of her shoulder.

Suppressing a gasp of pleasure, Candace managed to say, "Oh sure, you like it when I'm speechless?"

She felt the flutter of his lips against her skin as he chuckled. Despite herself, she felt arms snaking around his neck, bringing him closer.

"Not speechless," he protested. *"Impressed."*

"You're so full of it," she murmured, bringing her lips against his, shutting him up.

Candace's heart was still racing when she left the corridor leading from Yoandy's dressing room. Across the soundstage she sensed Ricardo's eyes on her, baleful and suspicious, but she ignored him and headed straight for the parking lot. What Candace needed right now was some time alone on the beach, or maybe ice cream with her sister.

As Candace strode to her Prius, a majestic white Cadillac had just slowed to a standstill outside the studio. She recognized it immediately. Not only the car, but the driver. With one elbow poked casually out the window, it was quite clearly Maya's aunt. And in the front passenger seat, dressed in an elegant, short-sleeved white dress with a single vertical red and black stripe, was Dana Alexander.

Maya's aunt worked for Dana Alexander.

Why had Maya never mentioned this?

PAOLO
BALCONY, VENICE BEACH HOUSE,
FRIDAY, JULY 3

It was a baking-hot day, the temperature still rising at eleven thirty, the sun a harsh diamond in a sky devoid of even a wisp of cloud. Beyond the pale expanse of sand, the sea was a mirror. On the balcony of the beach house, Paolo, Lucy, and John-Michael were eating a late, lazy breakfast. Candace and Maya had both left before Paolo had woken; Candace for the studio and Maya for her meeting in Napa.

"*You're* getting a tattoo, Mr. King?" Lucy hadn't bothered to hide her skepticism. "Who's doing it, Luisito's buddy?"

Paolo nodded while munching his toast.

"He does good work," Lucy acknowledged. "Although if they find out he's tattooing under-eighteens they'll have to fire him, so keep it zipped afterward, okay?"

"What about shopping for the Fourth of July?" John-Michael interrupted, looking up from his bowl of Cinnamon Grahams.

"Plus, Paolo, I distinctly remember you promised to clean up the yard," Lucy reminded him. "It's a mess, ever since that goddamn party. Ariana could've done something about that," she observed tartly. "But then, I guess she wouldn't have been able to spy on us inside the house."

"Ariana was *spying* on us?" Paolo said, startled. The spike in his pulse astonished him. Just the idea that anyone might be interested in his secrets was kind of horrifying. "*That's* why you kicked her out yesterday? When were you gonna mention that?"

Paolo had completely assumed that she had finally seen sense and asked a long-overdue houseguest to move on. He'd have done it a week ago, at least. The house was cramped for six tenants, let alone seven.

"Oh, I doubt *you* even made it onto Ariana's radar," Lucy said. Her eyes narrowed briefly. "Although, dude . . . kind of a guilty look you got on your face right now."

Paolo scowled. "I value my privacy, like anyone else. Why would anyone want to spy on us, of all people?"

He watched John-Michael and Lucy exchange a wary look. "How long d'you have?" Lucy groaned. "Look, basically, the girl was in the house to keep an eye on me. She knew stuff about me, from rehab. I saw something when I was a kid—well, *may* have seen something."

"Seen what? Sounds serious," Paolo said. The relief at finding out that this couldn't involve him was instant, and led to immediate curiosity about what it did involve.

x

222

"I may have seen who really killed Tyson Drew," Lucy admitted.

As the words settled into him, Paolo glared at them both. It was obvious that John-Michael knew exactly what Lucy was talking about. "You saw who really killed Tyson Drew? Man, you have to tell the police."

"And it wasn't Grace's father," Lucy added with a guilty tilt of her head.

"Grace's *father* . . . ?" Paolo said, struggling with the implications of yet another bombshell. "Since when was he even involved?"

"You should maybe ask her," Lucy said.

Grace appeared at the top of the staircase, startling Paolo. He hadn't heard her climbing the stairs. In a fragile voice she said, "Ask me what?"

Paolo could only stare, feeling a little stupid to be caught gossiping about something so serious.

"You should go with him to get the tattoo, Grace," Lucy said with a careful glance at Paolo. A signal. "Our boy Mr. Disney Channel here is getting his lily-white skin inked—that's not something you see every day. I'd come too but I'm doing *that thing* I promised you I would do."

"Yeah, Grace, go with," John-Michael chimed in, a little too quickly. "Paolo, leave me your keys and I'll do the shopping."

Paolo took his car keys from his pocket and tossed them over to John-Michael. "Don't forget the fireworks," he mumbled. "It's not the Fourth without something going up in smoke."

Lucy and John-Michael either wanted Grace out of the house—which didn't make any kind of sense. Or else, John-Michael, like Lucy, was in on the "secret" that Grace had a thing for Paolo, and both were trying to make something happen.

Paolo watched as Grace came to an apparently reluctant decision. "Okay," she said. "If you're sure you don't want my help with *the thing*, Lucy."

"I'm fine," Lucy came back. "Like I said, I'll get to it."

As Paolo and Grace made their way along the boardwalk, Grace seemed distracted. He snuck a glance at her face a few times as they walked and it looked like she was in another world. Not what he'd have expected, if she really did like him.

"What's the thing that Lucy has to do today?" Paolo asked to break the tension.

"Oh, something she promised to do," Grace replied.

Paolo added, "Does it have anything to do with your father?"

He waited for her to reply, but nothing.

Great. For a girl who is supposed to be into me, Grace seems pretty reluctant to share.

"You know," she mused. "I don't get why you're getting a tattoo. You want to be a lawyer, or a tennis pro? A pro with tattoos, I can see, but a lawyer?"

"I *am* a tennis pro," Paolo said. "The question is, do I always want to make my living being a tennis pro? Or do I want to be a lawyer?"

She stopped walking and faced him. "Well, do you?"

He shrugged. "Be a lawyer? Yeah, I guess so."

"Then why get a tattoo? Is it for Lucy?" Grace shielded her eyes as she watched him, then shook her head. This time there was no doubt about it—disappointment.

She couldn't meet his gaze. "I know you like Lucy," she began.

She still wouldn't answer his question! He was beginning to feel bad for asking about her dad. Clearly, the subject was too painful to address.

Her voice was small and very slightly broken and he wanted to put both arms around her, in that moment, and tell her that no, he didn't like Lucy so much, not now anyway. But what did he have to offer Grace? It was too early to know how he felt about her. Paolo had a strong sense that with this girl, he couldn't afford to make such a misstep.

"I do like Lucy," Paolo said as he led Grace to the edge of the boardwalk, where they found a place to sit. There was no point in lying. Grace deserved the truth. Might as well engage on the only subject she seemed to want to talk about. "But Lucy, she doesn't like me, anyway, not like that. Nothing happened between us. It's the truth."

Finally, Grace looked up at him. It could have been his imagination but Paolo thought he saw a glisten of moisture in her eyes. "You're over her?"

"Totally," he said softly.

"Then why're you getting the tattoo?"

Surprised, Paolo said, "You really think that's about Lucy?"

"She likes body art, piercing, all that punk stuff. I've heard her say you'd look good that way."

"It's not for Lucy," he told her firmly. He really didn't care how Lucy felt about his tattoo. The thought struck him with a forceful energy, like a ray of sunshine breaking through mist. It wasn't for any girl.

Paolo hadn't analyzed the whole tattoo thing as deeply as Grace. Just that he'd seen the designs at the parlors on the boardwalk and over the past few weeks he'd started to get this feeling, like his skin was calling out to be marked, to be different.

"Then why?" Grace said. He could feel her eyes taking him in, roving across every exposed inch of his upper body. Like the gentlest of breezes, it sent a faint shiver through him.

Grace had a point; why was he about to get his flesh bruised and stabbed, hundreds of times, maybe even a thousand?

"I want . . ." he replied, slowly constructing his answer, "to be different. Not from everyone else—from myself."

She considered this for a moment. "You won't be different. It's not what's on the outside that matters, Paolo. I thought you would understand that."

But I'm not the same, he wanted to say. *That's the lie of all this smooth, unmarked skin. It makes me look the same as I was, no different. And I'm not. Inside, I'm different. Meredith did that to me. I did that to me.*

"I'm . . . I'm not the same person I was six months ago," Paolo ventured cautiously. He wanted to be honest with Grace, he really did, but there were things that he couldn't ever share. Not with any woman in his life. Not with anyone. He shouldn't even have told John-Michael.

Unconsciously, Paolo rubbed his still-untouched left bicep with the thumb and forefinger of his right hand. Sometimes it felt like his guilt had to be written on his face, like everyone knew how he'd left Meredith on that road. Well, now it would be written on his body—for anyone who could understand his code.

"Paolo," Grace said with difficulty. This time, there were definitely tears. "None of us are the same person as six months ago."

Tentatively, he dared to ask what he was dying to know. "Gracie. Is there something going on with your dad?"

"He's . . . my father is . . ." Grace was obviously having a hard time spitting this out. She couldn't meet his eyes.

Paolo took her hand in his lightly. He felt his heart shudder as he waited for her next words. "Gracie, please. Tell me."

"Paolo," she said, looking up with difficulty, "my father . . . is on death row. And they've set a date for his execution. In less than two weeks, they're gonna execute him."

Paolo was still for several seconds as it all came crashing together. Their drive up to San Quentin. Grace's letters to Dead Man Walking. How upset she'd seemed after she and John-Michael had returned from the second trip to the prison. "Grace," he said breathlessly, opening his arms. "I'm so sorry."

He gathered her close then and just held her against his chest, soothingly caressing the soft skin of her shoulders with his thumbs. Grace was quiet, not crying exactly. She released only a muffled sob that quickly abated. But through her shirt, he could feel the thudding of her heart.

GRACE
TRIPLE BEDROOM, VENICE BEACH HOUSE,
FRIDAY, JULY 3

"And then we kissed," Candace said. She was grinning as she took a seat on Grace's bed, forcing her stepsister to move over to make space.

"Who kissed you?" Grace inquired absently. She sat up, a little put out to be interrupted by Candace entering her quiet room. She put down her copy of *Drown*, which she'd been reading since she and Paolo had returned from getting the tattoo, several hours ago. She checked her watch. It was almost five in the afternoon.

Candace rolled her eyes, demanding attention. "Yoandy."

Just the same, Grace barely heard the reply. The day was almost over, and still Lucy hadn't returned from her visit to the police station. That's assuming she'd even gone at all. Grace wouldn't have been surprised if Lucy needed more time to think—the hypnosis had clearly been a traumatic experience. Since her father had been jailed, Grace had been forced to learn significant patience. Part of her understood that one more day couldn't make much difference to a legal process, at least not two weeks from the execution date.

But another part of Grace had been reawakened by a newfound hope. By the evidence—finally—that someone else might know what really happened that night at the party on Mulholland Drive. That side of Grace's personality was suffering an ordeal. Every extra minute of uncertainty felt like agony.

What would she do if Lucy hadn't gone to the police? Grace wasn't sure she'd be able to contain her frustration and rage.

She glanced up at her stepsister, trying to focus on what Candace was saying. "You kissed . . . who again?"

Candace looked faintly annoyed. "Urgh. Yoandy Santiago! Try to listen. We were at the TV studio, earlier on."

"And then what?"

"Not much," conceded Candace. She sounded frustrated. "He's gotten cautious."

"Uh-huh," Grace said, trying to sound interested. "Why's that?"

"I'm gonna take a wild guess that it was the fear of having Kay Alexander shredding his clothes maybe. Scissors supplied by her big sister, Dana."

Grace put down her book slowly. The mention of "Dana" sent a prickle along her spine. "Why . . . would she do that?"

"Who can say?" Candace said. "God only knows what Kay is like." She sighed. "For some reason, the woman thinks that she is Yoandy's girlfriend."

"Candace," Grace said unsteadily. "Are we talking about Dana *Alexander*?"

"Yeah," agreed Candace. "Lady Macbeth is a big deal, it turns out. Which is why I gotta be careful—real, real careful that Dana doesn't find out. Apparently, *Dana* is the one who recommended me for the part of Annika. Now it sounds like she thinks I owe her, big-time. She seems to think I'm gonna take Yoandy from her sister, Kay." She gave a crafty grin. "I tell you, owing Dana—honestly? I don't see it."

Grace couldn't speak for a few moments. Then, struggling to remain calm, she said, "You . . . are connected to *Dana Alexander*, the British movie star? *She's* the one who got you into *Prepped*?"

"I know," Candace said, now thoughtful. "I thought it was odd, too, especially after what you told me yesterday about Lucy kicking out our delightful ol' houseguest, not to mention the whole Tyson Drew thing." As though an idea had just occurred to her, she added, "Hey, did *you* know that Maya's aunt works for Dana Alexander?"

This additional piece of information hit Grace like a slap in the face. "Who—Aunt Marilu?"

"That'd be the one."

"No," Grace murmured. "I did not know that."

Unreal. Impossible. How deeply had Dana Alexander insinuated herself into their lives?

Dana's sister was dating a guy who Candace also liked. She'd recommended Candace for a part on a new TV show. Dana Alexander might be the true killer of Tyson Drew.

And now—it turned out that Maya's aunt actually worked for the woman.

"This is too much," Grace mumbled. "It's—no. This is too many coincidences."

"It really is," mused Candace, "I mean, Hollywood can be kind of incestuous and all, but . . ."

She stopped abruptly when the door flew open and Maya came bounding into the room, throwing her messenger bag onto her bed and flopping down next to it.

"Guess what?" Maya said, her eyes bright with excitement. "Jack and I met with Alexa Nyborg today, up in Napa."

But Candace just groaned. "Give me an actual break! Maya, could you knock first? We're trying to have a private conversation here."

"It's my room, too," Maya said with surprising levity. "If you're having a private conversation about me, maybe include *me*?"

"You clearly don't understand the rules of gossip," Candace said with pronounced irony.

Grace waited for a moment. "And? How did the meeting go?"

Maya drew herself up even straighter, her bare knees pressed almost daintily together against the edge of the quilt on her bed. "*And* she made me an offer."

Both Candace and Grace now faced Maya, managing to keep their sighs of irritation to a minimum. After a moment Candace said impatiently, "Come on, Maya, let's hear it!"

Maya opened her messenger bag, removed the laptop, a sphinxlike grin playing about her lips. As the MacBook started up, she glanced at them in turn and said, "Alexa has this amazing little *casita* up in Napa. It's all mission-style, white adobe walls and arches. The garden is full of tangerine and lemon trees, pink and white hibiscus flowers everywhere and the most beautiful swimming pool I've ever seen."

"Sounds great," Candace said with more than a hint of eye roll. "But what did she actually offer you?"

"I'm telling you about the *casita*," Maya said, her smile ever more mysterious, "because that's part of what she offered me. Alexa hardly ever goes there. These days she's usually flying somewhere every weekend. She said I could stay there whenever I like. Even offered to let me stay this weekend—July Fourth. She was planning to fly out by private jet right after our meeting 'cause she's going to be in Washington at some event with the president."

"She offered to loan you a house in the Napa Valley?" Candace said, her mouth falling open.

Maya grinned, typed something quickly, and said demurely, "I said no, thanks. After all, we're having a barbecue and fireworks here, right? Just the six of us. But Nyborg was actually pretty insistent. Said if I change my mind, the key is with a neighbor."

Candace responded with an amazed grin.

There is something very badly wrong in this house, Grace thought as Maya prattled on about her app. Too many sudden connections to Dana Alexander, to a person who she now realized was not only getting information through Ariana, but who had found a way to keep tabs on the housemates via Maya and Candace, too.

Why?

Grace could understand why Alexander might want to spy on Lucy—a buried memory that threatened to expose the woman's secret, possibly even that she was a murderer.

But Maya? Candace? What possible threat could they be?

A cold, crawling sensation ran through Grace, as though an ice-encrusted spider was walking along her spine. Lucy wasn't back from talking to the cops yet; she'd ignored the two, hopeful texts that Grace had sent: Hey just checking in. How's it going? Any news?

Technically, no news was good news, yet Grace's instincts told her it wasn't good. She felt her chest muscles clench around her ribs, and wondered fleetingly where Paolo had gone. His embrace had been such a comfort to her earlier today. If he was here, she'd feel safer. Grace didn't feel safe around Maya and Candace, not right now. Not until she understood their connection to Dana Alexander.

Maya continued to chat: Alexa Nyborg *this* and Napa

that . . . until Grace simply couldn't tolerate it any longer.

"That's just great, *Maya*," retorted Grace, and her tone was so uncharacteristically sharp that even Candace flinched in response. She paused, waiting until she had Maya's complete attention. "But let me ask you this: why didn't you ever mention that your aunt was Dana Alexander's driver?"

Maya simply froze for several seconds. Guilt was written all over her face: guilt and shame and regret.

LUCY
LIVING ROOM, VENICE BEACH HOUSE,
FRIDAY, JULY 3

Lucy didn't return from the police precinct until almost a little after five in the evening. Barely across the threshold to the house, she stood absolutely still, listening. Just before she'd arrived, she'd heard the front door slamming shut as someone entered the downstairs part of the house. As she turned her key in the lock, she heard voices toward the back of the house, presumably in the yard. Paolo and, if Lucy wasn't mistaken, Grace. Lucy's hand stilled. Grace was the very last person she wanted to face right now. She extracted her key as silently as possible and turned toward the spiral staircase that led to the second floor.

As she approached the landing, she could hear Maya, Grace, and Candace inside the triple bedroom. The name "Dana Alexander" was clearly mentioned, at least twice. Lucy approached quietly, hoping to eavesdrop awhile.

Maya was speaking rapidly, sounded agitated. "Could you stop asking me about Dana Alexander, already? I told you—she's my mom's boss, *that's it*. I don't have anything to do with her, never met her, never so much as talked to her on the phone."

There was a lengthy, tense silence. Then Candace said tentatively, "Your *mom's* boss? Don't you mean your *aunt's*? Doesn't your mom live in Mexico City?"

Lucy had heard enough. She pushed open the door. "What's going on? Why're you giving Maya the third degree?"

But Candace's eyes were fixed on Maya. She looked utterly baffled. "Maya, who *are* you?"

Maya moved to leave. Candace held up a hand. "Not so fast. Maya, you need to answer. Is Marilu your *mom*?"

From behind Lucy came the sounds of footsteps on the stairs. She took a quick look. Paolo was on his way up, too.

"Did I hear correctly?" Paolo said. "Did Candace just say that Maya's aunt is actually her mom?"

Lucy glanced at Grace. She seemed paralyzed with tension, suddenly pale and wan. "Did you go to the police?" Grace asked her, coming straight to the point.

Lucy swallowed. "I tried, G. Really, I did."

Grace whimpered, touched a palm to her head. Paolo responded immediately. He sat down beside her, wrapped an arm around her waist, and drew her close. "Lucy," whispered Grace.

All eyes were now on Lucy. "Where's John-Michael?" she asked, suddenly defensive. The room felt pretty hostile. At least John-Michael might understand.

Paolo said coldly, "He's in the kitchen."

"Look, can we all talk about this downstairs?" Lucy said, pleading.

"I still want to know why Maya's been lying to us about her mom being her aunt!" Candace objected.

"Seriously?" Paolo retorted. "You actually think that's more important than Lucy going to the cops with evidence that might get Grace's father off death row?"

"Obviously not," Candace said hotly. "I'm just sayin' that Maya isn't getting off the hook so easy. Especially since it turns out that her *mom* works for a total Hollywood player who's been meddling in my life."

To Lucy's astonishment, Grace made her way over to Maya, and said gently, "Come on, Maya. I'm sure you had a good reason for telling us Marilu was your aunt, but you need to trust us now. Please. There are things going on in this house that you're not aware of. And Dana Alexander is at the center of too many of them." Grace cleared her throat. When she spoke again, her voice sounded shaky. "Lucy's right. We should go downstairs, where we can all talk this through."

Without another word, the housemates trooped downstairs. In the kitchen, in front of a stunned John-Michael, they arranged themselves around the dining table, and each took a chair. The atmosphere had grown as suddenly chilly as the air outside, now that the clouds obscured the setting sun.

"Um . . . what the heck?" John-Michael said, placing the

large kitchen knife back on the chopping board next to a heap of sliced carrots and celery.

"Lucy's got something to tell us," Paolo said with a reassuring glance at Grace.

"Maya too," Candace added.

Lucy couldn't quite put a finger on it, but she sensed guardedness in almost everyone in the room. Or maybe she was just projecting her own feelings? Her instinct had been to protect Maya from the sisters' questioning. Some people had private stuff going on. Why did everything have to be out in the open? It didn't make things easier, in Lucy's experience. To give away a secret was to give away your freedom.

She couldn't help wishing that people would just mind their own business. But right away, she felt her conscience smack her down. Grace's dad was going to be executed in less than two weeks. *Executed.* How could Lucy's own issues come close to that?

"So, I went to the cops," Lucy said, carefully avoiding Grace's hot, teary gaze. "All kinds of stuff going down in the precinct today, or so they told me. Drunks and drug dealers being chased around, all the detectives out on cases or busy, a major traffic accident on the 405."

"They didn't see you?" concluded Grace. Her disappointment sounded bitter.

"Oh, they saw me but for, like, five minutes," Lucy admitted. "Had to wait a long time before anyone would meet with me. When they finally did, well, they got big eyes, like saucers, and started saying that I had to be interviewed by a detective, but they didn't have anyone available today, it had to be recorded properly and witnessed, that I needed an appointment."

"You need an appointment to give testimony that's going to save someone's life?" Grace said, incredulous.

"That's pretty much what I said," Lucy agreed. "As it turns out, you do. At least when the person whose life you're saving 'isn't in any immediate danger.'"

Grace gasped. "Every extra day puts my dad in immediate danger. It's called *death*!"

Paolo squeezed Grace's knee to calm her down, which seemed to work somewhat as she sat back in her seat. Lucy managed to minimize her surprise. *Well, at least that's moving in the right direction*, she thought.

"I know," Lucy said to Grace. "And I'm sorry. But what with it being the holiday weekend, I could tell that the cops just weren't interested. I got an appointment for Monday. Grace, don't worry, I won't let this go."

"Okay, so that's Lucy dealt with," Candace concluded impatiently. "Now, let's hear from Maya. Girl, explain yourself!"

"Okay, the woman I've been calling 'Marilu' is my mom," began Maya warily. "I didn't tell you because . . . because . . ." At this, Maya dropped her head into her hands. "Oh God, I really don't want to do this."

Grace put one arm around her roommate's shoulders.

"I know this isn't easy. But we need to know we can trust one another."

Lucy, Candace, and John-Michael murmured some bland words of encouragement. But Lucy noticed that Paolo remained quiet, not moving, his eyes fixed on Maya's arms.

Reluctantly, Maya drew herself upright. Her eyes were damp. She wiped one with the back of a hand. "I guess you'd better know. My mom does work for Dana Alexander. If you look up Lupita Soto de Padilla, it's pretty easy to find online that she's connected to Alexander. So I told you she was my aunt, whose name is Marilu Soto."

Firmly, Candace asked, "Why didn't you want us to know about the connection with Dana Alexander?"

Maya looked at each housemate in turn as she replied. "Listen, I didn't know about the setup here, okay? Just what you guys told me when we moved in. But for some reason, Alexander wanted to know what was going on in the house."

There was an audible flinch from Grace and Candace. Lucy herself felt as though a lump of air had solidified in her own throat. "Excuse me?"

Maya's expression had become sorrowful. "She's interested in everything that goes on in the house. But Lucy, I gotta tell you . . . most of all she's interested in you."

"That goddamn witch, of course she is," Lucy said, seething. "That's why she got Ariana to spy on me, too."

Maya seemed taken aback. "Ariana was spying?"

"We were going to tell you," Grace said. "We only found out yesterday. You and Candace have been awfully wrapped up in your work."

"And to be strictly accurate," John-Michael pointed out, "we don't know for sure about Ariana, isn't that right, Luce?"

"Ariana spying," Maya repeated thoughtfully. It could have been Lucy's imagination, but for a brief moment she had the strangest feeling that Maya *wasn't* all that surprised. "But I think that's right," Maya continued, shaking her head. "Listen, I was supposed to send a written report every few days. About a month ago, after I overheard Grace talking to John-Michael about how he crashed his dad's car, I decided to stop telling Alexander anything useful."

"Wait up, wait up," Lucy interrupted, frowning. "You *listened in* on Grace and John-Michael?"

"It was kind of a pocket dial," Maya admitted. "It wasn't intentional. And I already told this to Gracie. I heard her say something that made me wonder about Dana Alexander."

Lucy watched Grace acknowledge this with a slight nod. Suspiciously, Lucy said, "What'd she say?"

Maya said quickly, "Enough to make me worry that Alexander was bad news and to realize that what I was doing could be dangerous to you guys. And since that day, I swear to God, I haven't given her a single useful report."

"Which does not get you off any kind of hook!" Candace bristled.

"But it does explain why Dana sent Ariana," Lucy concluded with bitter understanding. "The second you stopped sending anything useful, Ariana shows up on our doorstep."

Maya nodded, clearly relieved. "Yes. At least I think so. But it only started to make sense recently. Just little things about the way Ariana behaved . . . she was always hovering around where most of us were, not joining in conversations, just listening."

"The way *you* used to?" John-Michael observed dryly.

"Like I said: I realized it was wrong."

"Why'd you do it at all?" Candace said. "It's kind of a skanky thing to do to your friends."

"Guys," Maya said, eyes wide, hopeful, her hands spread wide on the table before her, "Alexander has stuff on me and my family. I'm not exactly sure what, my mom won't give details. But Alexander goes to immigration and my mom gets deported."

"Wait, your mom is here illegally?" Candace asked. "I thought you were a citizen."

"I was born here, yes. But not my mom, obviously. And there's some issue with the documents."

John-Michael broke in, "It's got to be horrible to live that way, trying to stay under the radar."

"Then Alexander had me under observation from the beginning," Lucy said, shaking her head. "She must have gotten to Ariana when we were in rehab. Maybe even put her there with me, for all I know."

Maya leaned toward Lucy. "What I didn't understand

was *why*. Until you told us that you were in *Jelly and Pie* and we figured out your real name. And until I heard Grace talk to John-Michael. Dana Alexander was at the party when Tyson Drew was murdered, wasn't she, Lucy? Is there a chance that she thinks you saw who really killed him?"

"You figured all that out, too, and you didn't tell us?" gasped Paolo.

"Maya, seriously, you wanna consider acting for a living?" chipped in Candace. "'Cause you are one high-end liar."

"I think Alexander knows *for a fact* that Lucy saw who killed him," Grace said grimly, ignoring the other housemates' jabs at Maya. "I think it's pretty obvious that Alexander is the one who scared you into silence, Lucy. But now she knows that you remember the truth and you are going to testify . . . right?"

Lucy felt the slow burn of everyone's attention as they focused on her. She found herself unable to look any one of the housemates in the eye. *Alex Vesper is on death row because of you*, they seemed to be saying. *An innocent man has been in prison because of you. All because of you.* Because little Lucasta was so scared she wet her pants that horrible night on the balcony. She was shaking when a woman took her by the hand, a woman with soft hands with beautiful peach fingernails. They were all Lucasta could see as she led her to the bathroom murmuring gentle words of comfort in her ear.

You're sleepwalking, honey. Dreams grabbing you by the throat. Time to get back to bed, Charlie.

Lucy wanted to cry, yet tears wouldn't come. Instead, she felt her core growing cold. Numb paralysis. Someone's hand reached out to touch hers. But she barely felt it.

PAOLO
KITCHEN, VENICE BEACH HOUSE,
FRIDAY, JULY 3

Another time, another place, it could almost have been entertaining. *Probably would have been*, Paolo thought. He reached behind him, stretching as far as he could from his position at the corner of the dining table, to the refrigerator. He managed to pop the door and felt inside for a can of Diet Dr Pepper. Paolo studied the faces of each housemate as he drank.

Candace, upright and hostile, a contrast to her normal laid-back, jokey demeanor. Grace, struggling to keep her feelings in check. This must be great for her; a moment of intense relief—the most hope she'd had in years: Lucasta Jordan-Long could save Grace's father from execution. And yet, Grace was pale with anxiety. John-Michael, somber and pensive, as he often was, had taken the sixth place at the dining table and was slowly chewing on a piece of celery. Maya's caginess. She seemed fretful, presumably worried about Dana Alexander.

Should I be worried, too? Paolo thought.

It was impossible to drag his own mind too far from the lurking horror of his own recent past. A secret fresher than any of theirs, one that still hovered at the fringes of Paolo's thoughts, every waking minute. The simple pleasures of life were a distraction. Even the tingling burn of his left upper arm, still hot to the touch, took him away for only a minute. Every time he tried to dismiss this memory it felt more and more impossible, grinning like a death mask at every opportunity.

"How much do you think Ariana knew about us?" he asked abruptly.

It wasn't his secret that Ariana was trying to find but could she expose him anyway? What would his own housemates think if they knew, these girls who Paolo realized he was proud to call his closest friends? What if right now he were to stand up and tell them about how he'd hustled Jimmy out of a car, had sex with the idiot's mother, and then left the woman for dead, alone, in the canyon?

"Enough," Lucy replied. "More than enough that we gotta be careful." For a moment, her eyes locked with Maya's. "Too bad that you gave her the goods on every last one of us," she said in bald accusation.

A burning silence followed. Then Maya turned to Candace. "Maybe you shouldn't have made out with Yoandy Santiago. We warned you from the beginning he was Kay Alexander's boyfriend. Now it's just another reason for Dana to get mad."

Paolo watched the expression on Candace's face shift from incredulity to sheer indignation. "Oh, that's *it*, we are so done," she hissed. "I guess you never really stopped spying?"

A deep, beet-colored flush spread across Maya's face. "You were talking in my bedroom, which is where I actually *sleep*. So I stood outside for a few seconds, waiting for a good moment to walk in. I wasn't going to say anything about you and Yoandy. It has nothing to do with me."

"No, you were just gonna write it up in your lousy, stinking report to Alexander," Candace snarled.

Maya raised her voice. "Is there something wrong with your hearing? Didn't I already tell you that I stopped doing that?"

"Oh gee, thanks for saying you wouldn't spy on us anymore, Maya, thanks for rediscovering the meaning of 'friend.'"

"Maybe we should all just chill?" Lucy said. She was making a pretty obvious effort to remain calm herself. "Sugar, you're in no place to accuse anyone of *anything*. Okay, so you were forced into it by your mom's boss. We get the picture. You still spied on us. *Own* it."

"Look, Maya," John-Michael followed up, reasonably, "not one of us here is gonna win any kind of prize for how we've handled everything difficult that's happened in our lives. But it turns out that out of all of us, you're the one who's still taking orders from Mommy. The rest of us, y'know, we're trying to be responsible, like adults."

"But we're *not* adults," Maya said emphatically. "And driving a car, cooking and shopping and cleaning and paying the rent—that doesn't make you one. Making good decisions, the kind you make with *actual* freedom—that's what makes you an adult. And as you've cleverly pointed out, John-Michael, unlike the rest of you, I do *not* have freedom."

"We're supposed to take life coaching from a liar and a spy?" Candace said. Her voice was laced with sarcasm. She tilted her chair back so violently that it tumbled to the floor with a crash, and Candace narrowly managed to avoid toppling over with it.

Paolo stood up, blocking her route out of the kitchen. "Candace," he began. But she pushed him aside with surprising force, shoving hard against his left arm. The tattooed skin burst with a hundred hot stings. "Oww, dammit, Candace, what gives?"

Grace stood, too. "I agree with Lucy—we need to calm down. Maybe take a time-out. This is getting intense."

"You got that right," Candace said, fuming. "I'm out of here. Grace, you coming with me?"

It was a pointedly exclusive invitation. Reluctantly, Paolo stood aside, watching Grace depart with her stepsister. He placed three cool fingers across his burning tattoo and turned to Lucy. But Lucy's eyes were on Maya, who was next to stand up. "I could use some air, too."

"You want some company?" John-Michael asked Maya.

"At least as far as the Starbucks," she replied. She'd turned pale in the last few moments, yet Paolo noticed that she seemed surprisingly calm given that John-Michael had just called her a child. Yet there she was, chewing thoughtfully on a fingernail. "I'm gonna get a Frappuccino," she said to no one in particular.

Maya and John-Michael were walking out a minute later. Finally, Lucy faced him. Paolo's hesitant smile became awkward. "Just us then," he said.

Lucy hadn't shifted from her position at the table. She looked very tired, but managed a halfhearted grin. "Yup." She went to the sink and turned on the hot tap. "I guess I'll clean up some dishes. Since none of you lazy-ass jerks seem to know how."

"In that case," Paolo countered, "I guess I'll go dig up some weeds in the yard. Since none of you lazy-ass jerks seem to know how."

Storage space in the house was precious, so the three garden tools that he'd picked up at the hardware store more or less lived in Paolo's Chevy Malibu. He trudged out through the front door and around back. Since the house faced the beach, the road where Paolo parked his car was in the rear. John-Michael had left his car there earlier on, some ways down the road since most evenings it could be difficult to find a spot close to the beach.

Paolo popped the trunk and grabbed the shovel and the long-handled lawn weeder.

As he returned, he approached the house from the rear, where a low gray concrete wall surrounded the yard. He was about to step over the wall when Paolo noticed that the French door was already open. He opened his mouth to call out to Lucy. Then he saw something that stilled the air in his lungs. Instinctively, he moved to one side. Carefully, Paolo rested the long-handled weeder against the wall. He sidled up to the French doors, peering inside, cautiously staying out of sight.

There was a man in the living room. He was about five feet nine, stocky with thin graying hair and wearing a faded, black leather bomber jacket over slacks. He had his back to Paolo and seemed to be talking to Lucy. The man's overall stance seemed relaxed, not particularly threatening.

And yet, even though Paolo couldn't see Lucy, he could hear it in her voice.

Terror.

"Who've you told?"

The question sounded casual. Paolo didn't recognize the voice. Lucy was having difficulty replying. She was stammering even before she'd gotten started.

"I . . . I don't know why you—"

"Enough," he said, cutting her off. He reached into his pocket. Lucy recoiled, knocking against the fallen dining chair. He spoke calmly and sounded almost weary. "We can do this the easy way. Or not."

The man was pointing a gun straight at Lucy's stomach.

Paolo flipped the shovel into position as if to return a

serve. One glance at the space between him and the man and he'd computed the precise path, exactly as if a ball were arcing across the net toward that spot.

"Okay, kid, time's a-wastin'."

Paolo took a deep breath and ran, barging through the open French door and into the house.

The man spun to his left, the gun in his right hand. It fired, a muffled sound—*phhooott*. The next shot never came. Paolo's shovel was already swinging, a powerful forehand. It cracked against the man's skull. Paolo watched the man's eyes widen. Just for a second, they bulged. Fingers locked in the trigger, the man's arm fell. His gun hand slammed against the floor.

Paolo stood paralyzed, blood pounding hard in his head: a roar. He could hear nothing else.

After a few seconds, he regained control over his muscles. He lowered the shovel and raised his eyes to Lucy. She stood, rigid with horror, hands by her side, her mouth open, eyes wide, staring, her breath coming in heavy, labored gasps.

Finally, Paolo turned reluctant eyes onto the fallen man. He could see now what a slight, unimpressive figure he was. In his late forties, a cheap haircut, worn shoes, a brown-and-white plaid shirt tucked into charcoal-gray cotton slacks.

Lucy seemed to emerge from her own paralysis. "Is . . . he dead?"

The man lay immobile, eyes staring just the way they

had as Paolo's shovel had connected with the left side of his face. Paolo glanced at the underside of the shovel. There didn't appear to be any blood. But the sight of the dent in the man's head made Paolo's insides clench in cold, churning dread.

MAYA
LIVING ROOM, VENICE BEACH HOUSE,
FRIDAY, JULY 3

Returning from the boardwalk, Maya noticed that the house lights in the front part of the house were all dark. She paused for a second, letting John-Michael catch up with her.

"You think they're all in the backyard?" he asked.

"But why no lights?"

In the doorway, they listened for a moment. Nothing. Maya turned the key, pushed against the wood. That's when she knew for sure that something was terribly wrong. The door wouldn't move. Paolo was inside and was resisting their combined efforts to push it open.

"Paolo, it's me and John-Michael, let us in!" she said, a little desperate.

He let them inside then, held a finger to his lips, and frowned until they fell silent.

Maya's attention went instantly to Lucy, who was crouching on the floor beside the new red couch. A strange man lay crumpled on the checkerboard-patterned rug, his head neatly framed on a russet-colored square. The man wasn't moving.

Lucy looked up, an imploring look in her eyes. "Maya, JM . . . what are we going to do?"

Breathing a Mexican curse through pursed lips, Maya approached. John-Michael, she noticed, hung back with Paolo, who seemed frozen in position by the front door. She stopped short of the body, noting the approximate height of the man, his gray slacks, black leather jacket, and clean but cheap-looking brown leather shoes. There was a pistol in his right hand; a revolver of some kind. He looked like a respectable, middle-aged, off-duty policeman.

Or maybe a private investigator. Maya's heart began to plummet.

This man had to have been sent by Dana Alexander.

"He shot at me," Lucy was saying, pleading, tears in her eyes and her whole body shaking. "It was self-defense."

"I didn't mean for it to kill him," came Paolo's voice. It sounded dull, disconnected, and vague. As though he didn't quite believe what he was saying. "I swung for him with the shovel."

"You thought he was a burglar," Lucy insisted. "It was self-defense."

"I thought some kind of intruder, yeah," agreed Paolo. "He was going to shoot you."

"Obviously an intruder," Maya said briskly. "No one invited him, right?"

"And he shot at us. That's definitely self-defense, right?

It's open and shut," Lucy said, almost pleading.

Not if Dana Alexander has anything to say about this, Maya thought. But she only asked thoughtfully, "Did you find the bullet?"

Paolo and Lucy glanced at each other, apparently mystified.

Maya repeated herself, a little louder. "Paolo? Did you see where the bullet went? Think. It's important."

Paolo straightened up a little, making an effort to pull himself together. "Um, I guess it went over by the stereo."

"Find it," Maya instructed, "but don't touch it." While Paolo hunted, she joined Lucy in kneeling beside the corpse. The man's head had been visibly damaged by Paolo's strike with the shovel. One whole side had been dented. Maya sat back, wondering why she wasn't more repulsed. But the truth was, it felt a lot like seeing a dead body on TV. She rocked back on her heels and turned her head to examine the rug below the man's head.

"We moved him onto the brown square," Lucy explained. "More or less right away, actually. I figured the bloodstain would show up less."

"Cops don't need much blood to connect this rug with his body," Maya said. "Too bad you didn't put a piece of plastic wrap underneath him."

The boys and Lucy were still for two seconds, staring at Maya. Then John-Michael made a dash for the kitchen. "Get some paper, too," Maya called after him. "Something we can burn when we're done."

Looking at Maya incredulously, Lucy said. "What are you talking about?"

Maya ignored her. "Hey, Paolo, d'you find that bullet yet?"

Paolo glanced up from where he was squatting by the baseboard on the wall adjacent to the floor-mounted audio speakers. "Not yet."

"Did you look at the gun?" Maya said.

"Did I look at the gun?" echoed Paolo. "Are you crazy? You think I'm going to tamper with a crime scene?"

Maya said, "You mean aside from moving his head onto the brown square of the rug?"

"That was basic housekeeping," Lucy tried to say, but stopped, gawping as Maya leaned over to remove the revolver from the corpse's fingers. "Omigod, Maya! You touched a dead man!"

The man's fingers were still warm and pliable. It hadn't even occurred to Maya that he'd feel any different than a living person. She noted with surprised detachment that he wouldn't go stiff for a little while. She had no idea how long. But it might be useful to know.

"John-Michael, can you find out how long it takes before rigor mortis sets in?"

John-Michael was already taking out his phone when Maya cried out, "Actually, no, stop!"

Everyone stared at her. "What?" John-Michael asked in a voice that betrayed more than a little fear.

Maya said, "We can't do any suspicious searches on the

internet! We can't behave any differently than we might behave on the night before the Fourth of July."

"His body will feel normal for three or four hours," John-Michael said. His voice was suddenly hard, frosty.

Maya noted the confidence of his response. It was pretty obvious what everyone was thinking.

No one in the house said a word. They couldn't even look at him.

John-Michael had seen his father's body when it was still warm. Which probably put him in the room with his recently dead father. The rest was easy to conclude: John-Michael's arrest for the murder of his father might be a whole lot more serious than he'd led them to believe. But Maya wasn't going to be the one to voice any suspicion. At least not right now.

She examined the gun. It was a Smith & Wesson model 60, she noted, being careful to point it away from anyone and to keep her finger far from the trigger. She opened the revolving cylinder. Inside were five cartridges and one collapsed, metal casing.

"Maya, why are you touching the guy's gun?"

She turned the revolver around so that Lucy could see the inside of the cylinder. "You ever seen a casing all crumpled up like that?"

"Maya, I haven't ever seen a real *bullet*," Lucy said.

"My mom has a handgun," Maya said a little reluctantly. "She's not just a driver—she's also Dana's bodyguard. In Mexico, Mom was a police officer. Maybe you know how things are with the cops and the *narcos* in Mexico? It was safer to leave the country. And believe me—with some of the enemies my mother made as a cop, she'd better not go back. I've been to the range with her a few times. Mom made sure to teach me how to handle a gun. I never fired a shell like this one."

Exasperated Lucy said, "Goddamnit, Maya! D'you have any other secrets you want to share right now? Or you think you're about done for the night?"

Paolo stopped his hunt for the bullet. He straightened up and faced her abruptly. "Maya, just tell us what it is you think you've figured out."

Maya shrugged. "My guess? Mr. Private Investigator here was trying to scare the bejesus outta you both. That was his first tactic. That casing is from a blank cartridge. And I'm betting you won't find a bullet. Maybe a wad of cotton somewhere closer than the wall where Paolo's looking. Yeah, might be a good idea to find that."

Paolo's jaw was slack as he spoke. "A blank? Why would he fire a blank?"

"Like I said," Maya muttered as she removed the collapsed casing from the cylinder. "To threaten Lucy. The rest of the bullets are real enough, though." She slammed it back into position and proceeded to wipe the whole gun carefully with the edge of her shirt. Once she was satisfied that it was clean, Maya handled it through her own shirt and replaced it in the dead man's outstretched hand.

"What the hell did you just do?" Lucy said, her words

heavy with accusation. Maya moved over to the futon, where she felt her knees buckle slightly. Her heart was starting to thud painfully hard as her body responded to the decisions she'd just made.

"Yeah," Paolo said, but quietly. There was an unmistakable note of hope in his voice. "What did you do?"

John-Michael had been standing stock-still through the last few minutes of Maya's actions. Now he knelt beside the dead body and handed Lucy the roll of plastic wrap, still inside its box. "Pull a sheet out and get ready to slide it under the guy's head. Okay?"

Quietly, Lucy did as he asked. Then John-Michael lifted the head and Lucy placed a yard-length sheet of plastic wrap beneath the corpse. With a nod, he was on his way back to the kitchen.

Maya watched for a few seconds and noted with a nod the moment when blood began, now very obviously, to ooze around the dead man's head. She sucked in a few breaths, willing her heartbeat to slow down. Lucy and Paolo were obviously dazed, quite possibly unable to think straight. Lucy's shock was understandable. If Maya's own mind was already beginning to run through the implications of all this to her life and Lucy's, the consequences for Paolo had to be even scarier. Paolo's would be even worse.

A sharp cry from Lucy made Maya gasp. "Omigod. He just moved." She stared at the man on the floor. He didn't budge. She slid off the sofa and once again knelt beside him. This time she listened at his mouth. She gulped down a chunk of air and held it for several seconds, listening. When Lucy made a sound, Maya raised one hand to silence her. Paolo crept closer. Maya released her breath.

"I can't hear . . ."

The man's empty hand twitched. All three of them jerked back at the movement. John-Michael brought a tray and four mugs of steaming cocoa from the kitchen. He alone continued to move. He placed the tray on the wooden folding table near the French doors, then calmly paced over to where the man lay.

As Maya watched, the man began to regain consciousness. First his hand moved, then his whole arm. His chest started to visibly rise and fall.

"Holy crap holy crap holy crap," Lucy intoned.

Maya couldn't drag her eyes off the impossible sight of an apparent corpse returning to life.

"He's not dead," she whispered in a tone of wonder.

JOHN-MICHAEL
LIVING ROOM, VENICE BEACH HOUSE,
FRIDAY, JULY 3

John-Michael spoke quietly. "Now what?"

None of them could reply. A paralytic dread had seized them. They stared helplessly at the would-be assassin. Even Maya, who'd been so cool up until that moment, so *together*. Over the next few minutes, however, John-Michael saw all that resolve evaporating.

The man was alive. He would talk.

Maya groaned, "The gun . . ."

Then they all saw it. The fingers of his right hand were tightening around the handle of the revolver. Collectively, they recoiled as slowly the man began to sit up. He led with his gun arm, which he lifted high enough to be a threat. The rest of him followed in a disjointed, strenuous pattern of movement, like a puppet being slowly dragged upward by invisible strings. When finally he was sitting upright, one shoulder leaning against the red sofa, the man seemed to notice his own blood and cursed roundly, adding, "Which one of you bastards did this to me?"

No one moved.

He raised the gun, this time pointing unsteadily at John-Michael. "I said which one?"

No one spoke.

The hit man swore again, and stared each one of them in the eye. The gun stayed where it was, aiming right at John-Michael's chest. Finally, his eyes settled on Paolo. John-Michael saw Paolo's Adam's apple bob up and down, but otherwise his friend gave no indication of fear.

"You with the tattoo. You're gonna tie up your friends. You make one false move and your boy here takes a bullet to the heart."

The man reached into his leather jacket with his free hand and after a few seconds of fidgeting removed a roll of silver-gray duct tape. He rolled it across to Paolo. "Now."

Paolo picked up the duct tape like it was radioactive waste. With one final, hesitant look at Maya, he began to tape her wrists together.

"Do everyone's hands first," the man said. His voice sounded faint, exhausted. "But the other boy, you do his legs first. Then he does . . . does your hands," he managed to say with effort. "And then . . . then you do his . . ."

The voice trailed off, but still the gun aimed at John-Michael. A sweat broke out all over John-Michael's upper body.

Moving slowly, practically robotic, Paolo moved to Lucy and began to tape her wrists.

The man wiped his free hand across the back of his head. When it came away smeared thickly in his own blood, he gasped. He sounded less angry than resigned. "You stupid children. You have no idea what you've done."

"It was self-defense," Lucy said. And then repeated it over and over, like a mantra.

"Yeah?" the man snarled back. "Maybe you should've killed me when you had the chance."

"Let us call nine-one-one," John-Michael said urgently. "You're bleeding a lot. You . . . your head looks pretty bad. I think you need an ambulance."

The man sniffed. "Not yet. We got unfinished business."

"Look, we know you didn't intend to kill anyone," John-Michael continued. "You fired a blank."

"I can assure you, son, there'll be no more blanks fired today."

But John-Michael didn't stop. "So why *start* with a blank?" There had to be a reason that he'd begun by trying to scare Lucy. If he could get the guy back into that mind-set, maybe they'd get out of this intact. "Let me call nine-one-one?"

"You touch a phone and I'll kill you," the man said, almost casually. He waved the gun, urging Paolo on. "Hurry or my focus might slip. I might let a bullet go, by mistake."

Maya and Lucy were tied up now, wrists and ankles taped together. They were still upright, and looked utterly lost. Finally, everyone was tied up except John-Michael, whose hands were still free. He could barely stand to look any of his friends in the eye.

Why did the guy want them tied up? Obviously it made sense not to let them outnumber him. If he started firing now, he might get a round or two off before they overwhelmed him. But that wasn't likely to happen, John-Michael guessed. Not one of them had the guts to tackle an armed man.

Tying them up would put them entirely at his mercy. Would he kill them, then? Pick them off carefully, clinically, with the five remaining bullets? The more John-Michael thought about it, the harder he felt his heart pounding, until he was certain that the man would hear it, too.

The man's free hand was once again jostling inside his jacket. After three attempts, he managed to extract a small, black, plastic-cased cell phone.

His motor skills are deteriorating, John-Michael noted. "You gonna call nine-one-one?" he asked.

"Everyone, siddown," the man said, ignoring John-Michael's suggestion. This time, his speech was noticeably slurred. He peered at John-Michael, as though staring at him through dark glass. "You. Get over here and kneel down beside me."

John-Michael hesitated. Mercy was their only hope now. "Excuse me, sir, but I think you need a doctor *real* bad."

This time, the hit man exploded. "Shut your mouth and get down on your knees, punk!"

But as John-Michael began, slowly, to fall to his knees,

a sharp cry came from the hit man, followed by a faint groan. Then he clutched both fists to his eyes. Over the next few seconds he began to jerk violently, until his entire body was in spasms.

The housemates looked on, aghast.

"He's having some kind of seizure!" John-Michael gasped.

The air cracked. It took a second before John-Michael realized that the gun had been fired. It was still in the hit man's right hand.

"I'm okay!" Maya called out breathlessly.

"Yeah, me too," said Paolo. "And me," Lucy said.

John-Michael watched in appalled fascination as the man continued to flip and twist like a freshly landed fish.

"What should we do . . . ?" Maya breathed.

An idea was crystallizing in John-Michael's mind, taking form within a cage of icy, implacable logic. The idea became bright and terrible in his mind; irresistible. The answer to so many problems had been within reach—the hit man himself had said it. Who knew where the next bullet would go?

John-Michael moved smoothly. In one swift motion he'd rotated his taped ankles behind him, picked up a large cushion from the back of the red couch, and was on his knees next to the injured man.

He looked at Paolo, who sat helplessly taped up on the floor next to the green futon. Their eyes met with an intensity that made John-Michael shiver. Paolo's lips moved in response to John-Michael's unspoken question. His reply was barely audible.

"Yes."

John-Michael closed a part of himself away as he leaned over the man on the floor, reaching for the flailing hand in which the gun was clenched. He held the cushion firmly over the man's face, jaw clenched tight as he struggled to hold the man down, aware of the man's chin beneath his own shoulder. It wasn't easy; the man's movements were powerful, violent. He shut off his feelings as the man continued fiercely to jerk beneath him. He ignored the objections from Lucy. Maya and Paolo, he noted, made no sound at all. They simply watched as John-Michael held the man beneath him, slowly extinguishing his life force.

It took less time than John-Michael remembered. A sure sign that the hit man had already been on his way out. John-Michael had merely nudged him along.

The silence that followed was lengthy. Heavy and profound. John-Michael released his grip and rocked back on his heels. He glanced first at Paolo, then Maya. They both sat motionless, their eyes full of him. He couldn't look at the dead man; those lifeless eyes would have chilled him to the bones. But he made himself look at Lucy. She was gasping for air, trying to speak words that wouldn't leave her throat. Finally, a strangled cry escaped her and they all realized that Lucy was hyperventilating.

With great difficulty, she choked out, "What . . . what . . . have you *done*?"

PAOLO
LIVING ROOM, VENICE BEACH HOUSE,
FRIDAY, JULY 3

Paolo's skin felt hypersensitive. Looking down, he noticed that all the hairs on his arms were standing up. He felt every whisper of air that moved across them.

We killed him.

Next to him on the floor, Lucy was beginning to squirm, trying to get her fingers to the tape that bound her ankles.

"Let me, it's faster," John-Michael said without emotion as he fiddled with the tape around his own ankles. Paolo watched John-Michael move silently from Lucy to Maya and finally to him, laboriously removing the tape from their wrists so that they could pull off the ankle tape themselves.

Lucy pushed away until she was sprawled on the living room rug, just a few feet from the dead body. The temporary effects of shock that had held her for the last few minutes seemed to be fading. Defiance had returned to her eyes.

"You've ended us *all*," she stated, loud enough for

John-Michael to hear that she included him in the accusation. As if to be certain that he'd understood, she turned to him with a penetrating glare.

John-Michael reacted with a calmness that Paolo couldn't help but admire. "He was dying," John-Michael said. "A seizure like that after a severe blow to the head—you don't go to the emergency room, you die."

"Lucy," Paolo said reasonably, "who knows where his next bullet would have gone? John-Michael saved us."

"Good," Maya said. She sounded relieved. "That's what we'll tell the cops—the truth. They'll call it Stand Your Ground and you'll both go free."

"Actually, in California we have 'castle doctrine,'" Lucy murmured. "Which I guess is the same thing, so long as the attack is in your home."

"I'm *in* my goddamn home!" Maya hissed.

Paolo began to think about that, began to think about the questions that would be asked. How far back would they go? A good prosecutor would dig up everything they could on him. The con. The blackmail. A good investigation might even put him in the car when Meredith died. Maya didn't realize how bad the truth actually was.

"But I hit him," he said, unsure. "When he'd only fired a blank."

"Yes, but you didn't know it was a blank," Maya said. "The other cartridges have real bullets."

"Still . . . I'm not sure we should take this to the cops," began John-Michael.

Paolo, Lucy, and Maya turned to him. Paolo swallowed, his tongue like sandpaper. Yes. Don't tell the cops. That would save him a lot of difficult questions.

"They won't even know he finally died of suffocation," Lucy said. "It'd just be the seizure."

John-Michael barked with hollow laughter. "We have to work off the assumption that they will know. Forensics can tell when someone's been asphyxiated."

"You sure know a lot about this kind of stuff," Lucy observed. "Is this what you did to your father?" Her words practically froze in the air. Paolo watched John-Michael. He visibly reeled for a second, as if absorbing the impact of a shock wave, but said nothing.

"Why is this happening to us?" Paolo asked. It seemed almost redundant, given the heights of terror they'd recently scaled, to be asking such a logical question. But now that he thought about it, he actually didn't know the answer.

"My guess is, he was trying to scare Lucy," Maya said tersely. "But like he said, the other bullets are real. The question is who would try to threaten her. I'd say it's Dana Alexander."

In a small voice, Lucy said, "You really think Dana Alexander might try to have me killed?"

Maya nodded. She bit her lip. "I do."

"This Alexander woman must be a lot worse than I thought," Paolo muttered.

"Lucy went to the cops today to schedule an interview to tell them that she has testimony that could open up an eight-year-old murder case. Dana Alexander might wind up as the prime suspect. If she were trying to avoid death row, I can see it going as far as this," Maya concluded.

"You think the cops told her?" Lucy said anxiously.

"More likely Ariana told Dana the game was up when Lucy kicked her out," Maya said with surprising confidence. "I bet it takes time to organize a hit. More than a few hours, at least."

"Whatever we decide," John-Michael said thoughtfully, "we need to do it now."

Maya shrugged. "Call the cops."

"I'm glad you're so confident that I'd get off with no charges," John-Michael said. "But I'm not."

A tense silence followed. In John-Michael's eyes, Paolo recognized a similar fear to his own.

The police meant questions. Questions would open up the past. John-Michael was already on perilously thin ice with the cops, as far as his father's death went. Maybe he'd get away with dealing with a dangerous hit man, but would it make them reconsider what had happened to his father?

"It's a good point," Paolo acknowledged. "You never know how things will go in a court of law."

"Says the wannabe lawyer," Lucy said.

"A good lawyer can win any argument," Paolo said. "But winning this one might cost some of us."

"A good prosecutor," John-Michael pointed out, "could say that *we* fired the second bullet, to make it look like the guy was a threat."

Paolo and Maya absorbed this quietly, nodding.

"What if we got rid of the body?" John-Michael suggested. "I'm guessing no one is going to report him missing."

"That's just great," Lucy said, her voice thick with sarcasm. "I guess now we're gonna break out the hacksaws and the garbage liners and turn into a bunch of butchers, is that your plan? Or were you thinking of hiring a boat and dumping his ass in the ocean? Without anyone noticing you strolling up to the pier with a big ol' dead body under your arm?"

Paolo licked his dry lips and shook his head. "Neither of those ideas sounds good."

"You got something better?" Lucy flared up, her eyes dark with anger.

John-Michael said, "The best thing for all of us would be if this body and everything that happened here tonight just went away."

"Nothing like this ever *just goes away*," Lucy snarled, her tone suddenly vicious. "If there's one person in this room who should know *that* particular piece of *truth*, it's me."

For a moment, they all paused. Their eyes met above the man's body . . . No one, it seemed, was willing to take the lead.

"I may have an idea," Paolo began. Gooseflesh broke out all over his body as he shivered under the sudden, focused attention of his three friends. He stepped forward. Ignoring the vacant terror of the corpse's wide-open eyes,

Paolo examined the dent on the side of his head. Yes. So familiar.

Just like Meredith's in Malibu Canyon.

Paolo stretched a hand across the man's still-warm chest and into the right-hand pocket of his jacket. His fingers closed around a remote key for an automobile. He stood and addressed all three housemates.

"This head injury. What if it came from a car?"

"A car," Lucy said flatly.

"People get hit by cars, they get this kind of injury. They die by the roadside. It happ . . ." Paolo paused, correcting himself. "It *must* happen."

John-Michael's expression shifted slightly, probably not enough for anyone else to notice, but when Paolo finally allowed himself to glance at his friend, he saw that John-Michael suddenly seemed to let go of some of his tension.

John-Michael understands.

"Sure it does," John-Michael agreed slowly. "Some SUV hits you while you're taking a whiz beside your vehicle on a country road, suddenly you've got a major dent in your head."

Lucy seemed incredulous. "What kind of imbecile stands where a car can hit them?"

"I think JM means, who's to say for sure? A man goes out somewhere like, say, Malibu Canyon." Here Paolo threw another hard glance at John-Michael, who nodded in affirmation. "Gets himself killed by a hit-and-run driver out there with no witnesses. Body rolls down a ravine, maybe? Coyotes and buzzards eat most of the skin off the face before any cop gets a chance to photograph it."

"Malibu Canyon," Lucy repeated. "That's your plan?"

Paolo unfurled the palm of his right hand to show the key he'd taken from the shooter's leather jacket. "His car key. Car's gotta be outside, close by. We drive the shooter up there in his own car. We lay out his body, as though he'd been hit by some truck coming along out of the blue and thrown clean off the side of the road. We leave the car there, key still in the ignition. We drive away."

A long silence followed. Maya eventually spoke. "That's not a bad plan."

"Thank you," Paolo said, relieved. He could feel the creeping reminders of all possible consequences of what had already happened tonight. He wasn't willing to face any of it. Nor should he have to. Just because some murderer wanted Lucy out of the way, just because Paolo had stepped in to help, why did that mean his private life would now be fair game? Why would stupid incidents that had not been Paolo's fault in the first place—Darius blackmailing him into hustling Jimmy out of a Corvette, Meredith threatening him into driving to her country house, the hit-and-run driver killing Meredith on the way to Malibu Creek—why should these things impact him now?

It was like Paolo had stepped into the quicksand again. Struggling wouldn't help. He'd understood pretty quickly that he couldn't just rely on luck and good fortune to twist him out of there. Hesitation and struggling had only pulled him deeper into the mire. No, to get out of that quicksand, he'd had to get down and dirty. He'd gotten onto his belly to spread his weight over the mud and sand. He'd gotten his entire body coated with all that muck and grime, even his face.

That's how you got out of a situation like this. You slithered and crawled like a beast until you finally reached dry land.

LUCY

Lucy continued to be doubtful. "You seriously believe we have any chance to set this up well enough to fool a detective with an actual brain?"

Paolo nodded. "I think we could."

Maya also began to nod. "Lucy, think about it. It's a hard blow to the head. Enough to kill on impact. The cops won't do a detailed postmortem on a body they find that looks exactly like roadkill. They'll never find out that he actually died from being whacked over the head with a shovel."

"How can you be so sure they won't do a detailed postmortem?"

"Because we'll set it up so well that they won't be suspicious," Paolo told her. "They'll see a horrible head wound and blood, they'll assume that's how he died."

John-Michael said, "That's actually pretty good."

"But we all have to agree," Maya said. "Because if we do this, we're all in it together. We put this whole evening in the vault and we throw away the key."

"All of us? What about Grace and Candace?" Lucy said, practically throwing the words at Maya.

Unease settled over the trio once again. "Obviously not Grace and Candace," Paolo said. "They can't ever know."

"They could come home any minute now," Lucy sneered. This was a grandiose, scary plan. There had to be a million ways it could go wrong. She could see why John-Michael might not want his involvement with the man's death to be examined too closely. But really—did the other three housemates have to take the risk, too? "It's not exactly watertight," she said.

"No one walks away from something like this without getting their hands dirty," Paolo said wearily. "You don't want in, you say so right now. And if you don't, then you're gonna keep your mouth shut." He took a breath and raised his right hand. "Who's with me?"

Lucy scowled. "Hell no."

John-Michael and Maya raised their right hands in silence. John-Michael placed both hands over his heart. Imploringly, he said, "Please, Lucy. *Please.*"

"At least come with us," Maya said. "That guy was about to call someone on his cell phone. Maybe it's not safe for you to stay here alone anyway."

Lucy gawped. "You think he was *getting help*?"

Maya knelt down by the dead body and picked up the man's phone. "He wasn't going to be able to handle four of us alone. Not even tied up."

The thought that yet another hit man might be on his way to the house stunned Lucy into temporary silence. Maya pressed some buttons on the phone. "No password. No contacts. He hasn't used this phone in over two hours," she told them. "No calls in or out."

"No one knows he's here," Paolo deduced.

Maya glanced from Paolo to Lucy. "Seems so."

After a moment, Lucy released an exasperated sigh. "I guess we're all screwed anyhow. All right. What do you need me to do?"

Paolo said hopefully, "You're in?"

"What does it look like, dumbass? You did this to save my life. You're gonna need another car to follow you up to Malibu Canyon. Way I figure it, you need at least two drivers, plus someone strong enough to help you hike that body down a ravine. Maya doesn't have her driver's license yet, which means you need me."

"I'm coming, too," Maya said. "Otherwise I'm going to be sitting here answering difficult questions from Candace and Grace about where you guys went."

"Two people per car works best," Paolo agreed. "Lucy, thank you. This means a lot."

"Does it?" she spat back. "You're not leaving me a lot of choice. This is going to come back on all of us, one day."

"Then don't do it," John-Michael urged.

Lucy merely gave a stubborn shake of her head. "Too late. I already gave my word. I'm a fool that way."

Paolo reached for her hand. But Lucy withdrew with a cold, disdainful scowl.

One hour later, she was driving Paolo's Chevy Malibu along the Pacific Coast Highway. Lucy kept her hands steady at ten and two on the steering wheel as they followed the taillights of the hit man's Oldsmobile into Malibu Canyon. It was almost ten thirty at night and the road was quiet; no other traffic was visible on the same side of the road and only the occasional car zipped past heading toward the coast.

Beside her, Maya was uncharacteristically chatty. *Nerves, probably*, thought Lucy. Excessive chatter wasn't her favorite coping mechanism, so the drive was doubly difficult. Not long after leaving the house, Lucy wished that she'd remembered to bring an old MP3 player so that she could at least put some loud music on the stereo to block out Maya's chitchat. Rancid at full blast would be a huge improvement over this.

Paolo had cautioned them against bringing phones, apart from the hit man's, which obviously needed to be disposed of. He'd insisted they all leave their own cell phones in the house. "Someday the cops might want to ask where we were tonight. The answer is gonna have to be that we were all home, all totally distracted, partying or watching a movie or something."

"You need pretty high security clearance to look at cell phone records," Maya had said. "But you're right, we can't allow any risk that we'll be caught. All our phones can be used to link us to a location."

They still needed to be able to communicate between cars, however, as Maya had pointed out, so the housemates stopped at a store on the way to the freeway, and picked up a couple of cheap pay-as-you-go cell phones; one for Lucy and Maya, one for Paolo and John-Michael, who'd waited outside the store in the hit man's car and were now leading the way.

The phone that lay in Maya's lap began to buzz. With a quick glance at Lucy, Maya answered it. After a second, she put the phone on speaker.

It was Paolo. "We're going to head up into the canyon. I checked on the map, if we take Piuma, the road gets pretty twisty. We'll find a blind curve, the kind of place that's a risk spot for accidents. We'll slow down and stop. You guys need to make a note of where we are and then keep driving. Stay out of sight. The last thing we need is for someone else to drive by and see both our cars. In fact, I don't want them to see my Chevy at all. Wherever you stop, get right off the road, somewhere safe, and turn off all your lights. Even inside."

"We're just gonna sit in the dark until you guys do whatever it is you're gonna do?" Lucy asked.

"Exactly. You and Maya sit tight. All we need you to do is give us advance warning if any cars come the other way. Drive until you're at least two minutes from where we are, and call as soon as you see someone coming."

Maya said, "What if someone comes up behind you?"

"Yeah, maybe we shoulda got an extra phone and left one of you behind as a lookout behind us. But I didn't think of that. Sorry. John-Michael and I will just have to hide behind the shooter's car if we see headlights coming up on our side of the road. At least if you give us fair warning of stuff coming the other way, we can do something."

Maya ended the call and then said energetically, "I think five minutes would be safer, don't you? I'm gonna set the timer on my cell phone." She paused. "Oh, damn. I don't have it."

Lucy said dryly, "Just look at the time on the one you bought. You're right, five minutes is safer. Five minutes should give them enough time to arrange the body and get out of sight."

"Paolo's smart for coming up with this idea," Maya said thoughtfully. She was fidgeting with the cell phone now, scrolling through the various options on its tiny, blue-lit screen. "You know, I'm kind of surprised actually."

Lucy found herself agreeing. The *surprise* of it was probably the most interesting aspect—until she reminded herself of what Paolo had actually done. He'd almost killed a guy with a shovel. She'd seen him nod at John-Michael, agreeing that their friend should finish the man off once he started having the seizure.

Maybe it was euthanasia, like it had probably been with JM's dad. Maybe John-Michael had only meant to defend them against the bullets. But then again, maybe he'd intended to kill. Maybe Paolo had intended to kill. She wasn't inside their heads, and no juror ever would be. That was something the boys would have to carry inside for the rest of their lives.

Yet, the reality of it was that Paolo and John-Michael had started to dig a hole into which all four of them had immediately fallen. Climbing out wasn't going to be easy. Like Paolo said, they all had their hands dirty now.

The phone began to buzz once again. Lucy watched as Maya took the call. This time she just listened, said a quiet, "Okay, but we're going for five minutes," and then ended the call.

"They're going to stop at the next major hairpin bend. We should slow to thirty-five miles an hour and then start timing."

Lucy nodded, staring directly ahead. Her eyes felt suddenly dry, like hard stones scraping inside her eye sockets.

We're actually doing this. We killed a guy. Now we're going to cover it up.

PAOLO
MALIBU CANYON, FRIDAY, JULY 3

Paolo pulled slowly onto the edge of a hairpin bend on Piuma Road. With slow deliberation, he turned off all the car lights. Outside, an even layer of clouds glowed with very faint moonlight. Without the cloud cover the Oldsmobile they sat in would have been obvious to any passing vehicle. As it was, there was just enough light not to trip up, but probably not enough to spot a shadowy car and its occupants, pressed to the side of the road.

He turned to John-Michael, who had barely said a word for the whole drive. Paolo wasn't sure what to say to his friend. At some point they'd have to acknowledge that Paolo's action hadn't been intended to kill, whereas John-Michael's was more questionable. Had his friend intended to keep the hit man still during his brain seizure, to protect them from the random firing of bullets? To finish off a man in his dying throes? Or had the intent been to kill? In law as well as ethically, Paolo knew that made all the difference. And yet, John-Michael had very clearly sought Paolo's consent.

They were both responsible. John-Michael had been the one who'd stepped up to the plate, but both of them had agreed about what needed to be done. And now they had to follow it through to the bitter end.

John-Michael spoke with difficulty. "Do you remember exactly how she was, you know, on the road . . . your *friend* . . . when she was dead?"

Paolo winced at the mention. "Yeah. Don't worry about it. Just help me get the guy out of the trunk. It should at least be easier than it was to sneak him out of the house."

The boys opened the car doors and closed them carefully. Paolo popped the trunk and reached in, grabbing hold of the edge of the living room rug they'd wrapped around the shooter's body. Together they lugged the heavy load, which must have been around two hundred and fifty pounds, out of the car and onto the edge of the road, somewhere ahead of the Oldsmobile. He checked several times, making sure that the body lay at the same distance and in the same position as Meredith's had been when he last saw her—that it looked natural, not staged. A constant buzz of adrenaline kept Paolo from feeling anything but the most remote guilt at the memory of her death and how he'd walked away. It was starting to make sense. If it hadn't been for that experience, he wouldn't have known what to do right now.

In Paolo's mind, it felt like a kind of balance. Guilt wasn't a useful emotion in this scenario. Their freedom, their reputations, and maybe even their lives were in danger. Guilt could be banished with impunity.

John-Michael returned to the car and then came back with a wad of plastic wrap in one hand.

"The blood from under his head," he said. "Traffic cops are gonna wonder why there's no blood on the road." Then with precision he peeled back the layers of plastic until the clotting blood in the center of the makeshift package was revealed. Without uttering a word, he slid the ooze under the wound on the man's head. Paolo switched on the disposable cell phone and used the dim light from its screen to help John-Michael. Less than half the blood that coated the plastic seemed to make it onto the road.

John-Michael leaned back to survey his handiwork. "It's not as much blood as was on the rug, or even on the plastic wrap."

Paolo shrugged. "At least there's *some* blood. You really think they'll be checking a thing like that so carefully, when it looks like the dude's been whacked by a hit-and-run driver?"

"I guess not." John-Michael thought for a moment. "What are we going to do with the rug?"

"We gotta ditch it. A long way from here. The plastic wrap, too. Should probably wash it off first, burn it, dump the remains in the garbage. Anything that's touched his blood can be linked to us *and* to the shooter."

"You don't want to take the rug home and clean it, like, industrially?"

Paolo shook his head. "No way. Think about Grace and Candace."

"That's what I am doing. They're going to wonder."

"We'll tell them you fell asleep and peed on it. How hard could it be to get another one? It's probably from IKEA, like everything else."

John-Michael stood up. "We're not saying I peed on it, asshole."

They began to head back to the car, Paolo carrying the rolled-up rug under one arm. He propped it against the rear passenger door, facing away from the road so that it wouldn't be seen by a passing car. Then he rounded on the trunk and was about to close it when he spotted something peeking out from underneath the rug that lined the trunk's base. He raised the flap to reveal a black canvas duffel bag. He felt for the zipper and tried to pull it open, only to find a padlock had been used to secure it. He lifted the duffel bag, experimenting with its weight. John-Michael joined him.

"What's up?"

Paolo handed him the bag. "Feels heavy. But what's inside is, like, all blocky. Books, maybe. Or paper."

They looked at each other as revelation struck. "No way," breathed Paolo. "You think?"

John-Michael nodded. "Money? Uh, yeah, just a little bit. I doubt that hit men get paid by check."

"How much do you think it is?"

John-Michael tested the weight. "A lot," he said, handing it back. "Put it back. When the shooter's people find the car they're gonna want that cash."

"You think they'll know how much is inside?"

John-Michael gave Paolo a curious look. "You're seriously talking about stealing from the kind of people who carry guns and bags of cash? Who'd you think that woman hired to hit Lucy? The local neighborhood watch? This has organized crime written all over it."

"You're saying Dana Alexander is *connected*?"

John-Michael shrugged. "She sure knows who to ask for a job like this. This is way too much money for a single hit."

Incredulously, Paolo said, "Where are you getting all this?"

Sighing, John-Michael said, "It wasn't all sweetness and light, living on the streets for a year, y'know? I met my share of bad men. Never got involved, but I had offers. There's always work if you're willing to do anything. And I'm telling you—compared to this bag of cash, it's pocket change to arrange a hit on a civilian like Lucy. This amount of money—that's from something else. Maybe no one's gonna miss a hit man. But money like this, someone is gonna follow."

The cell phone in John-Michael's pocket was buzzing. He checked the screen and glanced up at Paolo, panic in his voice. "It's from the girls. Car on its way. Come on, Paolo, move it."

Paolo glanced anxiously into the road and closed the trunk. The duffel bag was still in his right hand. "But the mob or whoever, they're not gonna know we took it. How could they?"

The way Paolo saw the situation—they now had to use every possible resource to save themselves. Money could help. It could buy them cars, protection, somewhere to go if they ever needed to run. Money was *insurance*.

"Could we please just get inside?" John-Michael said tensely.

He was right. They'd scarcely closed the doors to the hit man's Oldsmobile behind them when an RV sailed by on the opposite side of the road. Paolo held his breath as it passed. Was the driver going to stop? Had he perhaps caught a glimpse of a body in his headlights? But after a moment the taillights disappeared around a bend, and then another.

"Better wipe down the car for fingerprints while we wait for the girls to come pick us up," Paolo told John-Michael.

"And the guy's cell phone," John-Michael said, adding wearily, "and his gun. We'd better wipe it all down."

"Yeah, I'm not sure we want to leave those things in the car," Paolo said. "It's evidence that could match up with the bullet hole in the wall of our house."

John-Michael thought for a moment. "His people will be expecting his stuff to be with him."

"Why?" challenged Paolo. "Who's to say someone didn't stop by and just take everything outta the car, without reporting the accident?"

Without warning, a ringtone began to sound. Paolo and John-Michael froze. "That's not our phone," John-Michael whispered. "It's coming from the glove compartment."

"What the hell?" Paolo cried out, much louder than he'd intended. His heart was racing, he realized, at the mere spike in John-Michael's fear.

John-Michael's voice was shaking as his hand withdrew from the glove compartment. He opened his fist right in front of Paolo's face. In his palm lay a vibrating, ringing smartphone.

Paolo blinked and then stared at John-Michael, mystified. "Well?"

John-Michael turned the screen toward him. "I'm not answering it!"

"Me either!"

"Well, someone better!"

After another five seconds, the ringing stopped.

"This . . . could be bad," John-Michael said in what sounded like a constricted throat. No more words seemed to want to leave his mouth.

Paolo looked from the phone in John-Michael's hand to the glove compartment. "Hey, look," he said, smiling. "A key ring. You suppose this fits the padlock on the duffel bag?"

"Forget about the bag of money for one second, could you?" John-Michael said, exasperated. "Paolo, look at this phone, will you? At the house, the shooter was using his second cell phone. A *burner*. Come on, man, what the hell is wrong with you? Have you lost your mind? He had *another phone*. Don't you understand what's going on here?"

A dull realization began to wash over Paolo, stripping away all the bravura and hubris, until he felt nauseous from it.

"Oh no," he said, his voice empty. "Oh God, no. Maya said he didn't make any recent calls from the burner . . . but if he used this *smartphone* to call someone else, then . . ."

John-Michael's eyes seemed to bulge in his head. He stared at Paolo in horror and disbelief and said, "Then that *someone* is gonna come looking for the money."

LUCY

MALIBU CANYON, FRIDAY, JULY 3

"He said what now?"

Lucy glanced over at Maya, who apparently couldn't believe what she was hearing on the cell phone. "Maya! I need to hear this, too. Put him on speaker."

". . . plus there's the fact that this *fancy* smartphone has been switched on this whole time, so we probably need to get rid of that, too," John-Michael was saying as the phone's speaker kicked in. His voice sounded flat, resigned, dull. It felt totally at odds with the magnitude of what he seemed to be saying, which made Lucy wonder if maybe she'd misunderstood.

"Excuse me, you're saying he had a second cell phone?" Lucy asked, incredulous. "'Cause if he had a second *goddamn* phone then we are screwed six ways to Sunday!"

"Yeah," John-Michael admitted. "Yeah, we may as well just accept it; the shooter's people are going to know by now that he didn't finish the hit, for whatever reason. Look, we're headed your way on foot now. If you leave in about a minute we should meet up somewhere far enough away from the shooter's car that if some other car happens along, they won't see the two cars together."

Maya interrupted, "You've got the rug? And the plastic wrap, and all the dead guy's stuff, his gun and everything?"

"We got it all," John-Michael confirmed. There was a wry chuckle. "We're going to be hitting a whole bunch of Dumpsters tonight, I'm pretty sure."

Lucy released a trembling breath. She turned the key in the ignition. Then she was driving Paolo's Chevy Malibu at a steady thirty miles per hour around the tight bends, back toward the spot where they'd last seen the boys parking the hit man's Oldsmobile.

Beside her, Maya seemed quiet and thoughtful. Lucy couldn't understand how she did it. If it wasn't for the distraction of having to drive, and rather cautiously at that, in the dark on such a high, twisting road, then Lucy knew she'd be going nuts. She felt a raw, itching sensation, as though a nail file was being rubbed gently against the insides of her hands and wrists. A constant irritation that made her want to scream and twist in frustration. And it was slowly building up. With things the way they were, however, there was no way to release her feelings, at least not as violently as she needed to. It would totally freak Maya out, for one thing.

"What if the shooter told whoever he talked to on that second phone that he was about to go into our house?"

Lucy tensed. "I . . . uh, no, actually . . . What d'you mean?"

Maya spoke slowly, considering each word. "It means that there's a potential witness out there. That's a best-case scenario."

Lucy scarcely dared to ask. "And the worst?"

"And the worst," Maya said softly, "is that the guy who's been trying to call the *smartphone*, is the same guy who Mr. Shooter was about to call right in front of us. Remember? To get help with the four teenagers he'd gotten all trussed up like chickens."

"Oh jeez," Lucy breathed. "In which case we're finished."

"Unless we hit back first."

It took several seconds before Lucy was able to grasp what Maya was saying. Lucy was sure there was something wrong with Maya's icy calm. What kind of person could be so cool under such horrific pressure?

"I don't . . . what are you saying, Maya?"

Maya rubbed the back of her neck with one hand. "Just a thought. We should probably discuss it with the guys."

When two minutes later they rolled to a stop by the side of the road, the boys dropped the rolled-up rug into the trunk of the Chevy and Paolo swapped into the driver's seat, giving Lucy's hand a quick squeeze before she moved into the back with John-Michael. As before, Lucy didn't respond.

Abruptly, Maya said, "What are we gonna do about the second guy?"

Lucy watched Paolo and John-Michael exchange a

wary look. "Yeah," Paolo admitted. "We've been talking about that."

"Good," Maya said firmly. "Because it's a major hole."

"Hole?" Lucy asked uneasily.

"In our story," Maya said. "Think about it: we're hoping that the cops find this guy's body and assume it's a hit-and-run. They've got a body in the road, a massive blow to the head, blood on the asphalt. The dead guy's car is *empty*, fingerprints all wiped. So what do they conclude? One hit-and-run car and another one with some kind of fly-by-night thief? Or the hit-and-run car who also happens to be the thief?"

"Either one works," Paolo agreed.

Maya nodded. "Sure. Until someone comes forward and says that he or she talked to the dead guy when he was still alive in Venice Beach."

Paolo appeared to think for a second or two before he replied. "Not an issue. The shooter could have done his thing, then driven here afterward."

Maya shook her head and said vehemently. "No, it *is* an issue."

"A hit man's buddy isn't going to talk to the cops," he objected. "He's probably a hit man, too."

She took a deep breath and then exploded. "We don't know for a fact that he is a hit man, and even if he is a hit man, that fact is not necessarily known to the cops, and even if it *is*, the cops might be dirty, and even if they aren't, the existence of a potential witness against us, Paolo, that is something I know is gonna keep me awake nights, even if the guy doesn't involve the cops but instead decides to come looking for us himself!"

Behind them, a car approached. They all ducked down low and waited until they'd heard the car pass. It didn't appear to slow down. Once the car's taillights had disappeared around the bend they'd just taken, Paolo started the car hurriedly. He began to drive. "We've got to find a way off this road. We're just too prominent here."

"You're right," John-Michael said. "The cops will want to interview anyone who was on this road tonight. All someone needs to say is that they saw a Chevy Malibu parked nearby."

"What do you suggest we do then, Maya? Since it's obvious you've thought it through so much better than the rest of us?" Paolo insisted, his attention on the road ahead.

Calmer now, Maya said, "Whoever called Mr. Shooter on that second cell phone is going to be wondering why they didn't get the confirmation call."

"What confirmation call?" Lucy asked.

From the front passenger seat, Maya gave Lucy a sympathetic look. "You know. The one where he tells *whoever* that the job is done."

"Oh," Lucy managed to say, barely suppressing her disgust.

"Assuming that whoever it was on the call had anything

to do with the hit on Lucy," replied Paolo.

"Will you just accept it, man?" John-Michael said. "That's our nightmare scenario, so obviously we have to take it into account." He looked across at Paolo. "Okay, Paolo? Can we please agree?"

Paolo, however, seemed to be miles away. It took a couple of prompts from John-Michael before he responded, and even that was reluctant and noncommittal. "I guess."

Lucy noticed that John-Michael was staring at Paolo with a measure of frustration. So, he'd also picked up how strangely detached Paolo was choosing to be, all of a sudden.

"We should tell them about the bag," John-Michael said. The tone of his voice made the hairs on the back of Lucy's neck stand up. There was an unmistakable hint of threat.

Paolo winced, but he didn't turn around. He didn't say a word. When Lucy looked at John-Michael, he shifted back to the other side of the passenger seat, avoiding her eye.

"What bag?" said Maya curiously.

"Yeah," Lucy said, more insistent. "Tell us about the bag."

"We found a canvas duffel bag in the shooter's car. Cash," John-Michael said. He spoke slowly. "A lot of it. We're thinking half a million at least."

"You counted it?" Maya asked, baffled. "When?"

"We took a quick look before we transferred the bag to the trunk of the Chevy. Each roll looks to be about twenty grand."

Into the taut silence that followed, Maya whispered, *"En la madre."*

It was suddenly crystal clear why Paolo was so distracted.

"A half million dollars? You're thinking of keeping the cash!" Lucy cried, lashing out with a foot into the back of Paolo's seat. The car swerved for a second and Paolo swore loudly.

"Lucy, Lucy." John-Michael gripped her forearm. "We already made it look like the shooter's car was robbed anyhow. We had to—or else they'll wonder where his phones are, his gun. The shooter's people will assume that the thieves took the bag with the money."

"And then what?" Lucy grunted, pulling free of him.

John-Michael shrugged. He didn't look nearly as relaxed about the idea as his words suggested. "Then I guess whoever has a claim on the money comes looking for anyone who might have committed the robbery or the hit-and-run."

"But what are the odds they ever find us?" Maya said pensively. "We've seen, like, two cars drive by. The Chevy has been in the dark the whole time."

Lucy could see with a sudden and dreadful clarity where Maya was going with this. She tried to swallow. "No," she said very quietly. "We've got to go back. We have to put the bag back in the shooter's car exactly how you found it, leave the cell phones, leave everything."

"We can't leave those things," Paolo snapped. "They could lead right back to us. The money, *maybe*, we could leave. It was underneath a rug in the trunk so someone who was just stealing whatever they could lay their hands on inside the car might not notice it . . . but the cell phones, Lucy, and the goddamn weapon? They have to go!"

"Stealing cell phones is a knucklehead move even by your standards, King," Maya said, exasperated. "Cell phones can be traced."

"Which is exactly," Paolo said between clenched teeth, "why we're going to destroy them."

"This is awful," breathed Lucy.

John-Michael immediately moved to her side and put one arm around her shoulders. "I know, Luce, but we're gonna think it through, all of us. Together. We're gonna come up with a solution. We're not gonna let anything bad happen to you."

Lucy wanted to shake his arm away again. She was on the verge of tears. Something terrible was definitely going to happen to her, whatever her friends did. Fear was building inside, all mixed up with a horrible sense of vulnerability. She recognized both. Her recently dredged-up memories of Tyson Drew's death were stirring into the mix. If she went to the authorities with what she knew, she risked being killed. The witness protection program would be her only hope. But she couldn't talk about any of it, not while the atmosphere inside the car was dense with such pigheaded determination.

They talked about solutions but didn't seem any closer to one. Lucy felt her insides squirm like roiling snakes. She was afraid that they were about to take an even darker path than any of them might have imagined was possible. People lost their way, in times like this. They got lost so bad they never found their way home.

MAYA

"Give me the guy's other phone," Maya said. "I want to see it: the smartphone." John-Michael took the object from his pocket and handed it over the front seat to Maya. Her fingers moved nimbly over the keypad. "Hmm. Classic hackable password. Huh." She paused, shocked at what she found. Within the next two seconds she was shaking with rage and disbelief.

She turned to face them in utter dismay. "Are you guys actually this stupid?"

The other three stared at her. John-Michael sputtered, "Maya, what is your problem?"

"*FoneTrackr*?" she said, eyes bulging. "Why didn't you mention right from the beginning that his phone was running that app?"

John-Michael gave a helpless shrug. "I have no clue what you just said—I have an iPhone."

"This brand of phone has an app you can use to locate and manage any of its devices from a remote location. This smartphone," she pronounced heavily, "has been GPS-tracked *the whole time*. What did I tell you about cell phones? So, the other guy? He already knows that Mr. Shooter went to Venice. He knows he parked near the house. He knows he stalled awhile in Malibu Canyon. And now," she finished, "now he knows where we are, too. Paolo, stop the car. We gotta go back."

Anxiously, Lucy said, "Go back? I thought you didn't want to go back."

"To replace the money, no. But now we have to," Maya said shortly. "Right away."

"Maya." John-Michael struggled to stay polite. "You gotta explain why you want to go back."

"Seems pretty obvious to me," came Paolo's voice from the front. "The second guy is coming for us."

"For us, or for the cash," agreed Maya.

"Good," Lucy said. "You're finally seeing sense. Put the money back and let's get out of there."

Maya continued to check the phone. "There's a voice mail," she said, putting the device to her ear.

"It must be from when that call came in," John-Michael said, "when we found the phone."

She listened to the message. "Omigod."

Lucy said, "What?"

Maya played the message again, after switching on the speakerphone function.

"I'm at the house. Our friends seem to be out for the evening. You want me to wait? What is going on with your location? Why aren't

you here, man? Getting a little concerned about our special delivery. Check in as soon as you get this."

"You hear that?" Maya demanded. "He's *at the house.* Our friends are out for the evening? That means Grace and Candace didn't get home yet. The *special delivery*?"

"The money!" murmured John-Michael.

"We have to get back to Venice!" Paolo cried. "Grace! Candace! They're in danger!"

"They are if he stays there," Maya said.

John-Michael spoke quickly. "So we get him to leave."

"And do what?" Lucy said.

No one answered at first.

"I can think of one solution," Maya said mildly.

"Which is?" John-Michael said.

"Like I said to Lucy a while back. We strike back first," she replied, still perfectly calm.

Lucy snorted. "Seriously? You want to *kill* him?"

Maya looked over her shoulder at where Lucy sat with her back pressed to the rear passenger seat. "No–I don't want to kill anyone, Luce. But I don't want a dude with a gun to hang out at our house, waiting for Grace and Candace and eventually us. I'd do pretty much anything to stop that from happening."

"You're not shooting him," Paolo warned.

Maya observed bluntly, "I'm the only one who knows how to handle a gun."

Sardonically, Lucy said, "So, this is what's happening right now, is it? We're driving back to Venice and shooting a guy. Well, I gotta say, this sure has turned into an interesting evening."

"We're not going back to the house," Maya said. "There, he has the advantage over us. He can lie in wait. We're going back to where we left Mr. Shooter, Mr. Hit-and-Run Victim."

Lucy shook her head. In the wildness of her eyes, Maya caught a glimpse of desperation. "Okay," Lucy muttered. "This isn't making any kind of sense."

"The second guy is at our house—probably," John-Michael said. "Or at least he was when he made that call. We have to get him away from there."

"Exactly," Maya said. "I say we lure him to the Oldsmobile. When he sees the car, and his dead friend, he might believe he finished the hit on Lucy, then started to drive home or wherever and got taken out by the hit-and-run."

"Really," Lucy said skeptically. "He's gonna believe that? He's not gonna wonder what his friend is doing driving around in the *middle of goddamn nowhere*?"

"Maybe he's disposing of a body," John-Michael said. "I mean—*we* were."

"The thing is," Maya said, "the guy doesn't have a clue what happened to his friend, apart from that he was at our house. He knows he left the house—I'm gonna assume he thinks his friend was alive and well when he did."

"Why's he gonna come running?" Lucy said. "Didn't he ask, on the message, if he should wait at the house?"

"That's why we have to lure him away," Maya agreed.

"Send a text," Paolo blurted. "Something vague. Like 'need help with the cash.'"

"No," Maya said decisively. "Let's go with John-Michael's idea. Let's imply that Mr. Shooter is out dealing with a body. Maybe more than one."

"Good point. He was about to kill all four of us," John-Michael said. "If his buddy gets the chance, I'm sure he'll finish the job."

"Okay," Maya said, typing on the phone's keyboard. "How's this? *All done. I got some heavy lifting to do. Could use some help. The package is safe with me.*"

"It's good," decided John-Michael.

"Yes," Paolo said. "Send it right away. And then we need to call the girls. Stop them from going home."

"Oh, how's that gonna go?" Lucy said. *"Hey, Grace, Candace, don't go home, m'kay? There's a killer on the loose."* She took a huge breath. "Or, hey, you know what, guys? We could call the frikkin' police!"

"And say what, exactly?" demanded Paolo, furious. *"Yeah, so, we, like, totally killed this guy who was in our house with a gun and everything, but we decided to make it look like he'd been hit by a car up in the hills, and, like, now he's sent this real salty dude to kill our friends so, like, could you kind of take care of all that for us, m'kay?"*

Out of the corner of her eye, Maya could see Lucy seething, arms crossed tight across her chest. "You believe you could actually shoot someone? Until he's dead?"

Paolo exhaled through his nose. "It's him or us. And we are not the ones who started this."

"I'm not okay with going to prison for killing a guy who tied up me and my friends and threatened us with a gun *in our own house*," John-Michael said. "That's for damn sure."

"You can't be sure that would've happened," Lucy shot back. "You both *could* have gone for Stand Your Ground."

"Lucy, nothing's been *sure* since that dude walked into our house," Paolo said in a harsh whisper. "That was then. This is now. Things. Change."

Silence. Maya took a few breaths. Paolo was right—their options looked bleak.

"Lucy," John-Michael said soothingly. "We're *all* scared. But we have to deal."

"Let's get this clear now," Maya said to Paolo. "How far to where you left the car?"

"Six or seven minutes," he replied.

"We have to act fast," she said, watching the screen of the smartphone. "The other guy will get the message. Hopefully he'll start out for Malibu Canyon right away."

Lucy leaned against the window and looked over at Maya. She seemed vague and lost. "This all happened because of me," she muttered.

Maya closed her eyes, turning to face the front of the car. If she'd followed up on her suspicions about Ariana, this might have been avoided. She might have been able to persuade Lucy that her rehab buddy was a spy and gotten her to kick Ariana out of the house a week earlier. Then she wouldn't have known that Lucy had finally gotten to the point of questioning her own memories of the night of Tyson Drew's murder.

If only the offer of investment from Alexa Nyborg hadn't happened when it did. But Maya had to admit that the investor's offer had entirely consumed her attention, from the minute the prospect had entered her life. She should never have spied on her friends. She should have acted sooner on her suspicions of Ariana. She shouldn't have let her work take absolute control of her life.

Why was everything going so horribly wrong? It was so unfair, Maya wanted to cry. All she'd ever wanted was to work hard, to create something extraordinary, and to make enough money that she and her mother would never again be under the thumb of a person like Dana Alexander. And she had worked—like a slave. Almost every waking minute she was either in school, studying, or coding.

But for what?

To end up going to prison for conspiracy, at best? Or even worse—to be killed by Dana Alexander's hit man?

Maya drew a ragged breath. There'd been a ton of bravado in what she'd said about killing the second hit man. Words spoken before she'd really thought them through. And yet—there was an implacable logic to it. What other solution was there that wouldn't land all six friends dead or four of them in jail? Now they were hurtling forward to a destination from which she knew there would be no return.

The smartphone in her hand began to vibrate. Maya read the text and looked up.

"He's on his way."

JOHN-MICHAEL
MALIBU CANYON, FRIDAY, JULY 3

The hit man's Oldsmobile was just barely visible, farther along from where they'd parked at the side of Piuma. "Give me the gun, John-Michael," Maya said. She reached over the front seat, holding her hand out. John-Michael didn't move. He could feel the gun beside him, digging into his thigh. For a few seconds, no one said anything.

Then Paolo guffawed. "You're being ridiculous."

They'd switched off the interior lights, but John-Michael could hear the tension in Maya's voice when she replied with a harsh whisper, "You think because you've seen a gun fired on TV, that it's *nothing*? C'mon, Paolo, I'm the one who's fired a gun before. I'm a good shot."

"I don't doubt your ability to shoot," Paolo said. "I doubt your ability to kill. Take the compliment, Maya." He held his hand out, too. "The gun, JM. Hand it over."

John-Michael hesitated. "Why not Maya? Is this some kind of macho shtick, Paolo?"

Paolo groaned. "We're *so* not getting into gender politics

right now. Just gimme the gun, John-Michael. I need to get into position."

John-Michael kept his hand on the revolver. "No, Paolo. You have to explain. Why not Maya?"

"Are you out of your mind?" Paolo's face twisted in disgust. "What kind of a person lets a fifteen-year-old girl do a thing like this, when it was his fault in the first place?"

"We all agreed that it needs to get done," Maya said briskly. "We're protecting ourselves. And I'm the best woman *or man* for the job."

Beside him, John-Michael felt Lucy stiffen.

Paolo swore. This time he lunged at John-Michael. "Give it to me!"

John-Michael picked up the gun and held it in his left hand, gingerly, as though it were a piece of fetid trash. The gun was well out of anyone else's reach as he threaded a finger through the trigger. "If you'd killed that guy outright," he mused, "then none of this would have happened, Paolo. You could have stuck with Stand Your Ground or castle doctrine or whatever and everything would have been fine."

Maya said, "Until Dana Alexander sent someone else."

"But Lucy would have told the cops everything *tonight* . . ." John-Michael said.

". . . and they'd have put me in witness protection," Lucy finished, finally speaking up.

John-Michael's fingers tightened around the handle of the gun. "Now we're both killers, Paolo," he reflected contritely. "You and me." In the gloom of the unlit car, he peered at Maya. "And that's why it can't be you, Maya. Paolo and me, we did this. We're the ones who wanted to cover up what we did."

Paolo breathed a huge sigh. "Yes!" he said. "Exactly. Give me the gun, John-Michael. I started this. I'm going to finish it." He leaned across the front seat and grasped John-Michael's left hand in both of his. John-Michael resisted for only a moment before allowing his friend to take the weapon.

Paolo opened the driver's-side door and stepped out onto the rough ground at the edge of the road. "Drive far enough to get out of sight, but make sure you can see when our guy shows up."

"Take one of our cell phones," Maya said, offering the one in her hand. "We can use it to text you when he's close."

"*If* he happens to be approaching from our direction," John-Michael remarked. Maya *tsked* at this, which irritated him a little. It made sense to try to anticipate all the angles, not to dismiss anything.

With an air of vague disinterest, Paolo took the phone. It was as though he could no longer see his companions in the car, as though they were no longer connected to him.

John-Michael recognized that feeling.

Is this how everyone feels when they're about to kill someone?

He watched Paolo walk the short distance to the shooter's Oldsmobile. No one in the car moved. John-Michael looked at Lucy, beside him in on the backseat. It was obvious from her body language that she had zero intention of driving the getaway car. Maya didn't have a license, which left only him. John-Michael heaved a sigh and climbed over into the front seat. He started the car and drove past the Oldsmobile and along Piuma, until he reached a spot about sixty yards away where the side of the road was broad enough for the car to completely leave the asphalt. He pulled off the road as well as he was able and then switched off all the lights.

All around them was darkness and the sounds of the hills: crickets, rustles from the undergrowth, the rumble of distant traffic. Inside the car, no one made a sound. Eventually, though, Lucy spoke again. John-Michael could actually hear the dryness of her mouth.

"And you're just going to let him do this?"

Neither Maya nor John-Michael answered. Lucy responded only with a resigned sigh.

John-Michael said, "You got a better idea?"

"All this is to protect you, Lucy," Maya pointed out.

Lucy gave a short, breathy laugh. "No. When Paolo hit the guy with the shovel it *was* to protect me. Now it's to protect *you*," she said, stabbing a finger at John-Michael.

"It's to protect all of us, Lucy," John-Michael said wearily. "How do you not see that?"

"We're the same as Dana Alexander, don't *you* see *that*? She sent some goon to shut me up, now we're going to shut up a goon . . . we're doing exactly the same thing."

"Dana Alexander is ready to see an innocent man get executed for a murder she committed. She was ready to see you hurt or dead, and God knows how many more of us," John-Michael said. For the briefest instant, it was on the tip of his tongue to remind Lucy that if only she'd tried to recover her buried memories earlier, Dana Alexander could have been taken out of the running before she was ever a threat to any of them. But that would be cruel. Lucy already had to be suffering enough guilt about the whole situation. In a flash of insight, John-Michael wondered if this was why she seemed so blocked when it came to taking action.

Lucy had been treading water for almost a decade, hoping and praying that the shadow of murder in her past would remain forever hidden. With John-Michael, it was different. He knew that hope wasn't always enough. There were times when you had to be prepared to take that extra step. To *push*.

He stared into the black road, nerves jolting as a car approached. All three fell silent, waiting to see if it slowed down. Once again, they dipped below the windows as the car passed. It didn't slow down. They sat upright and breathed again.

"I can't take much more of this," Maya admitted.

John-Michael ignored her. He ignored Lucy's frustrated squirming. Instead, his thoughts settled on Paolo, alone, waiting in the dark. Another car would drive up soon, park behind the Oldsmobile. A man would get out. Unsuspecting, he'd step up to the dead body of his associate. Perhaps he'd even bend down to touch him. Had the two been friends? Family, even? Then Paolo would step out from his hiding place. Arm outstretched, he'd pump three bullets into a defenseless man. And that would be it.

A matter of seconds that would transform them both. The hit man's associate would be moved from the land of the living into the land of the dead. And Paolo?

The thought slunk through John-Michael's chest until he could feel it move like ice water through his guts. He was already a killer. Twice. Now Paolo was about to join him.

JOHN-MICHAEL
MALIBU CANYON, FRIDAY, JULY 3

Time passed—too much time. Something snapped inside John-Michael. A decision. Before he could begin to doubt himself, before the echoes of alarm, the warnings from the two girls in the car could take effect, John-Michael opened the rear passenger door and leapt out of the car. Just as he reached the Oldsmobile, he saw the tracks of white headlights on the road. Behind the car, John-Michael dropped down to one knee, tucked against the front wheel. He breathed slowly, waiting for the car to drive by.

When it slowed to a crawl John-Michael held himself rigid. He could hear the crunching of rubber on the pieces of gravel that had been thrown up onto the road. He felt the pounding of his heart inside his rib cage. After the slowest fifteen seconds that John-Michael could remember, the car's tires screeched into action. Then it was gone.

From somewhere in the shadows at the side of the road, John-Michael heard a hissed warning. "Dude, get out of here! I almost shot at you."

John-Michael looked around, locating the source of the voice. He began to walk toward where he could just see Paolo stepping into the road.

Somewhere up the road, the car that had just passed by was turning around. John-Michael bolted toward Paolo, and tackled him. They both dove and slumped against the thick trunk of a tree. Then suddenly, John-Michael was stepping out onto empty air, falling. Too late, he realized that the ledge behind the tree was narrow. His second foot scuffed the edge, sliding down a sickening angle. His entire body began to follow. Then, like a solid rock, Paolo's hand shot out, grasped his upper arm and held on, the fingers gripping him painfully tight.

Paolo cursed as he hauled John-Michael back from the cliff edge, one arm wrapped around a low branch, the other dragging John-Michael up. With one huge tug he hauled John-Michael to the ledge. The force of the motion slammed John-Michael against the tree, trapping him between the tree and Paolo's own tensed-up torso and thighs. The ground sloped downward just behind them, so that both had to lean hard into the tree to stay upright and hidden.

"What are you doing here?" he heard Paolo whisper roughly against the back of his neck. "This isn't part of the plan."

"I won't let you do this," replied John-Michael as evenly as he could. He twisted around gradually until he was facing Paolo. And then he reached for the handgun. Paolo seemed paralyzed for an instant, and then tried to pull his hand away. But John-Michael resisted, grabbed Paolo's wrist, and looked directly into his eyes. "You're not a killer."

Paolo shook his head, once. His eyes brimmed with confusion. The sound of a second car scraping up loudly behind the parked Oldsmobile made them both jolt. For just a second, Paolo's attention flipped to the road.

John-Michael moved swiftly, pinning Paolo in place for a moment with one elbow under his throat while his hand gripped Paolo's wrist joint and twisted. As Paolo let out a sharp gasp of pain, he slid firm fingers around the hard metal of the revolver, wrenching the gun from Paolo, who reacted too late. John-Michael jerked sideways, swerving to keep his balance, so close to the edge. The gun was now in his grasp. He gave Paolo a quick shove to counterbalance himself, then shifted out of reach. Then they stopped moving, their attention focused on the newly arrived car.

Paolo's sharp exhalation was the only outward sign of his anger. The need for silence seized them both. Less than ten yards away, the door of the second car was opening.

John-Michael transferred the revolver to his right hand. He held the handle firmly, feeling the weight of the weapon.

Point and shoot.

He moved farther into the shadows, away from the precarious edge behind the tree.

Paolo remained pressed against the tree. His eyes followed John-Michael, yet he made no attempt to stop him. All he said was "Don't."

John-Michael shook his head. Everything was so much clearer now.

Paolo had some big problems, sure. But he'd never actually taken a human life. Whereas John-Michael had done it twice. And one of those hadn't begged for it.

"It has to be me," John-Michael mumbled. It had to be done—for his housemates. A light-headed sensation began to flood him. As though reality was separating out, trapping him on the wrong side.

The man inside the second car was stepping out onto the gravel at the side of the road. There was a sound of slow footsteps crunching toward the dead body. The headlights of his car, some kind of sedan, had been left on. They lit up the driver from behind, casting a shadow across the dead body. John-Michael watched the man stoop briefly, to give the dead body an almost cursory check. The man seemed to pause over the hit man's burner phone, which they'd positioned close to the shooter's right hand.

To John-Michael's surprise, the man straightened up and took a quick look up and down the road. Surely he hadn't been down there long enough to check whether his associate was actually dead? Why wasn't he calling 911? In fact, his demeanor was entirely casual. He stood for a full minute in silence, apparently to satisfy himself that the road was indeed empty. Then he made a prowling move around to the trunk of the Oldsmobile.

John-Michael lurched forward. The ten yards that had separated him from the man were rapidly lengthening. He had no idea if he could make an accurate kill shot at that distance. It would be even harder if the target was retreating. Moving softly, he closed as much distance as he dared behind the man, following him halfway to the trunk before his target froze. Slowly, the man began to turn around.

"Get your hands up," John-Michael heard himself speak. "Up where I can see 'em."

He could see the man's face now. He looked to be around thirty years old, maybe six feet tall, with dark, short hair and a square jaw that was clenched in determination. He wore a dark suit over a white shirt. Not exactly the dress code of a hit man, John-Michael thought fleetingly.

The man hesitated. "Did you have something to do with my buddy here dying?"

"Don't move," grunted John-Michael.

The second man's arms were raised, obligingly, palms open and facing John-Michael. He began, very slowly, to walk toward the teenager.

"Looks like a hit-and-run, kid. Did you do this?"

"Stay where you are!" John-Michael cocked the gun threateningly.

"Calm down. Does it look like I'm armed? I came by to see what's up with my friend here. Well, it looks like he's a goner." The man's tone was friendly, relaxed. Still he kept moving closer toward John-Michael and the gun.

Do it now. Shoot him. Do it.

John-Michael's finger was on the trigger, his gun arm outstretched, his right hand sticking out at his side, for balance. He willed himself to squeeze the trigger, kept the words running through his brain. Yet somehow, it was as though there was a blockage in his neurons. His mind was issuing the commands, but the cells of his body refused to obey.

"Practically point-blank range," the man said quietly. He was close enough now that John-Michael could shoot him straight in the forehead. Their eyes met, John-Michael's angry and frustrated, the man's wide and puzzled, almost hurt. "How old are you, kid? Sixteen? Seventeen? Look, I know that's my friend's gun you're holding there. I recognize it. Which suggests to me that you don't own a gun. Probably never shot one, am I right?"

"One more step and I will end you," John-Michael managed to grind out. "Now who the hell are you and what are you doing here?"

The man raised a single eyebrow. His forehead was less than six inches from the barrel of the revolver now, both hands open and held at the side of his face.

John-Michael bristled with aggression. His left hand joined his right on the revolver. This was it. No mercy. He had to get rid of the witness. Suit or no suit, this guy was clearly in league with the hit man.

"Oh," the man said softly. *Dangerously*, John-Michael realized, but far too late. The man's mouth opened and he gave a half smile. "Questions . . ."

What happened next was a blur of activity that John-Michael could scarcely comprehend. Somehow, the second man went from a helpless victim inches from the business end of a gun, to moving at lightning speed. The man snatched at the gun, clamping John-Michael's wrist in his hand. Suddenly, John-Michael was pulling at the trigger only to have it fire upward. The sound of the gunshot felt deafening, roaring into the empty canyon, seeming to echo for seconds. It turned his legs to jelly. Then, inexplicably, the gun was in the other man's hand.

As if through a long tunnel, he heard the order to get down on his knees. A jagged breath escaped him as he stumbled to the ground, feeling pieces of gravel digging into his kneecaps.

"All right, calm down," the man was saying, "everything is okay. So—we've learned that some of us know how to do this kind of thing and some of us don't. That's all right. Between you and me, kiddo, I've been in this business a long time. It's quite a grave matter, to shoot a bullet into a perfect stranger. That's a solid piece of mental preparation, right there. Unless you're some kind of psychopath."

Then John-Michael heard the catch in the man's breath. "*Are* you a psychopath?"

PAOLO
MALIBU CANYON, FRIDAY, JULY 3

Paolo gripped the tree trunk so viciously that splinters of bark pricked beneath his fingernails. From the instant the man had wrested the revolver from John-Michael, Paolo had held back, his limbs locked against the tree. Fear and fascination mingled as he witnessed the older man's almost balletic movements in snatching the weapon. It was obvious— the guy was an expert in some kind of martial art. Even with a gun stuck in his face, he'd disarmed John-Michael in less than two seconds.

He watched John-Michael, the misery plain in his features, lit up by the second man's car headlights. The man now towered above him, the gun aimed squarely at John-Michael's head.

"I asked you a question."

John-Michael cringed. "No. I'm not a psychopath."

The man stuck his right hand inside his suit jacket pocket, withdrew something that he tossed over to John-Michael. It took a moment for Paolo to realize that they were plastic zip ties. A charge of pure fear jolted him.

In the steady, neutral voice that he'd been using since he'd taken the weapon, the man said, "Put them on."

Paolo saw John-Michael's hands shake as he did what the man said. He tried to guess from the man's tone and stance whether their lives were now in danger. It was impossible to tell.

What kind of man could disarm someone like that? What kind of person carried plastic handcuffs?

The answers that were forming in Paolo's mind were pretty terrifying.

"Now you're going to stay there, on your knees, while I take a little look around my buddy's car. If I hear you move, I'll shoot, you understand?"

John-Michael nodded. The man sighed in irritation. It was the first aggressive sound that Paolo had heard him make and instinctively, he snuck a little farther behind the tree.

"Answer me, so I know you've understood."

In a small voice he heard John-Michael say, "Yes sir."

The man seemed pleased with John-Michael's sudden submissiveness. He brought the revolver in for a closer examination and quickly opened the cylinder to look inside. "Interesting," he murmured thoughtfully. He tucked the revolver into the waistband of his pants, and reached under his left arm. When his right hand withdrew it was holding an automatic pistol.

"Now we're getting somewhere. If everything is in

order we can just finish up here and both get on with our evening. But if I'm not happy, we're going to have a serious problem."

He retreated then, quickly, made his way to the car, tried to open the trunk. When he couldn't, he blasted the lock open with two shots. For a moment, Paolo couldn't see what he was doing. But he could figure it out, and the thought electrified him.

The man hadn't come up to Malibu Canyon to help his friend. He'd come looking for the bag filled with cash.

Before Paolo's legs could obey the urgent message from his brain to go over to his housemate and free him, the man reappeared from behind the Oldsmobile, storming toward John-Michael with teeth bared. Paolo saw the man swing a kick straight at John-Michael's back. Groaning, the boy collapsed.

"Okay, kid, the fun is over. You're about to get the beating of your life. Or you can tell me what the hell you did with my money."

Paolo winced in sympathy as he saw the second kick approach, now farther around John-Michael's back. This time his friend curled up into a fetal position, gasping, trying to get his wind. Paolo fought down the urge to go to his instant rescue. One mistake and they'd both be killed.

"Listen to me. I can count, therefore I know that my buddy fired his weapon twice. One blank cartridge has been fired, and one bullet. Now I also know that he sent me a message, but not with this phone. Also, he didn't answer any calls. You with me so far?"

The man swung in with another heavy kick on John-Michael, who released a low moan, curling up even tighter. For the first time, real anger began to surge through Paolo alongside the fear.

Stupid, stupid, allowing John-Michael to take the gun.

"Now—and let me be clear—I do this for a living. So when my partner starts to act a little odd I think something's up. You know what else I think? I think *you* maybe had something to do with my friend being dead. I don't know whether you tried to rob him, or whether you hit his car, or whether—and this seems unlikely—whether you somehow actually took his *own* gun from him and shot him with it. That's to say, I assumed from that head wound that a car hit him. But maybe I should have looked harder?"

He punctuated this last sentence with two more kicks. John-Michael barely reacted above another lengthy groan. Paolo could hardly bear to watch. But it was obvious that the man suspected something. He wasn't just going to let John-Michael go, nor was he going to kill him quick.

"You're wondering why you didn't kill me when you had the chance," the man said, spitting on the ground near John-Michael. "Well, it's like this. You've heard of Darwin, yes? Natural selection, all that? This lifestyle, it's very, what I would call *Darwinian*. People like you and me, who've been in the situation that you're in now, if we survive it's because we learn. We adapt. I won't lie to you, not everyone makes it. *You* may not make it. But if you do, you'll know for the next time. *Do not* pull a gun on someone unless you mean to use it."

Another kick, this time to the backs of John-Michael's thighs. Paolo welled up—tears of empathy and frustration.

The man suddenly slid down on one knee beside John-Michael, the pistol pressed firmly to the crook in his leg.

"Now. Five seconds to tell me where the cash is. Or you take the first bullet, right through the knee."

PAOLO
MALIBU CANYON, FRIDAY, JULY 3

There was no way that Paolo could physically tackle the man. John-Michael was going to give up the location of the cash any second now. He'd be beaten into revealing Paolo's position. They'd probably be forced at gunpoint to call the girls.

Then all four of them would be potential hostages. Plenty of spare blood, in case the guy felt like throwing his weight around, killing or maiming one of them, just to show that he meant business.

All their lives would be at risk. And Paolo would be directly responsible.

He had to act before John-Michael gave him up. He crouched low, fumbling for any kind of fallen stick. The ground fell away so sharply underfoot that he had to use one hand to hold on to a low branch of the tree he'd been hiding behind. As the branch bent, Paolo's teeth sunk into his lower lip, his jaw clenched in the desperate hope that the limb wouldn't snap, or make enough noise to betray his position. But there was nothing within reach. John-Michael's groans had gotten louder with every kick. And the seconds were ticking by.

Paolo swung to his feet and emerged from behind the tree. He moved swiftly, using John-Michael's groans to hide any sounds he made. But he wasn't quite fast enough. The man had already begun to turn his head as Paolo threw a punch.

It was a fierce strike, hurled with all the energy of Paolo's fastest serve. The blow would have hit the back of the man's head. But Paolo caught his right cheek instead.

Paolo's fist connected, hard. His knuckles crunched into the man's eye socket. The impact shot straight up Paolo's right arm and into his shoulder. The shock of pain took his breath for a few seconds. Shaken, he watched the man reeling, his left hand clutching at his face. But it was a momentary victory. Then the man's gun arm was swinging up. An automatic weapon was bearing down on Paolo, fast. He managed to swerve backward, narrowly avoiding the swipe.

"On your knees," hissed the man. Paolo held still. His attention flicked back to where John-Michael had been only a second ago. He caught a glimpse of two legs disappearing into the darkness at the edge of the road. The man's eyes followed Paolo's glance, but he didn't take his focus off him for a second. "Your boyfriend left you."

He shoved the gun into Paolo's face, pressed the muzzle up against his ear. The air of arrogant confidence had vanished. His eyes were narrow slits of steel, his upper teeth bared. Paolo dropped slowly to his knees, raised both hands in the air. The knuckles of his right hand dripped blood. He felt the cold metal of the gun roving across his skin, from his ear to his right eye.

"That. Hurt." The man inhaled noisily. "I'm going to get a goddamn black eye." He leaned forward. Paolo could smell tobacco on his breath.

"I know your little boyfriend can still see us," the man whispered conspiratorially. "Better tell me where you got the money. Better tell me *soon*. I swear to God, I'll hunt him down and skin him alive."

"Behind the tree," Paolo said suddenly. He said it again, louder. And began to mutter a silent prayer, a telepathic message to John-Michael, willing his friend to hear, to listen, to understand.

"The cash. It's in a duffel bag behind the tree. We only just opened it. We didn't touch your friend. Seriously. We were just cycling past. Our bikes are back there, behind where you parked your car, right at the side of the road." Paolo risked a gesture then, his left hand raised, pointing behind him. He opened his eyes wide, shook his head slightly. "I'm sorry I hit you. But you were hurting my buddy, I didn't know what to do."

"Where'd you find the cash?"

"In the trunk," Paolo said. The ring of truth could only help them now. Somehow, he had to get the guy to move over to the tree. "There was a padlock."

"Where'd you find the key?"

"In the glove compartment. The whole car's open."

"Why didn't you call nine-one-one?"

Paolo felt tears spring to his eyes. He decided to encourage them. "He was dead, man," he whined, managing a sob. It was a relief to release some of his fear. "We couldn't help him."

A sneering note entered the man's voice. "But you could help yourself to his gun and his goddamn *money*, is that what you could do?"

Paolo shook his head. The terror that had seized him a moment ago, that had filled him with self-pity, faded rapidly. Instead, his mind sped ahead, trying to figure out any way to escape his fate. "We didn't know what was inside, we were just curious. Look, I'm really sorry, please just let us go. We won't say anything. The bag's just there, where I was hiding. You can take it and . . . and . . ."

The man snickered. "And what? Let you go? We'll see about that. First off, I'm gonna need to see these bicycles. Where's your spandex, kid? You sure don't look like cyclists. And I don't remember seeing any wheels up here except the ones on my pal's Oldsmobile." He stood back. "On your feet." He raised his voice so that John-Michael could hear. "Hey, 'cyclist' number two, I know you're still around. If you leave this one alone with me, it's not going to go well for him. I'm an artist when it comes to breaking bones. I'll snap at least six before I get started with the bullets. You're gonna be amazed how badly a person can be messed up before death finally settles on a body."

In the silence that followed, Paolo listened for any response. There was nothing. John-Michael had vanished in the direction of the two girls. The smart move would have been to get out of there ASAP. Maybe the older man was right, maybe not. But somehow, Paolo couldn't quite believe that his friend had stuck around to take another battering.

"Start walking. Let's see these bicycles."

Paolo's hesitation earned him another shove with the barrel of the gun. "Don't you want to pick up the cash?"

The man stared, suddenly curious. "Why?"

Paolo forced himself to shrug. "It's right there."

"*You* get it."

"Me?"

The man nodded once. "Yeah."

Paolo managed a dumb nod. He began to shuffle toward the tree. This wasn't what he'd been aiming for. This was going terribly. No sign of John-Michael. Now he was in the middle of nowhere, facing a sadist with a gun. He reached the tree and stared helplessly at the empty ground behind the tree trunk.

"Hurry up."

Paolo stepped into the shadows, slipped behind the tree. There was only one thing left to do now. He pressed himself up against the back of its trunk and remained motionless, waiting.

A beat went by. Then the man called out, incredulous,

"You're actually hiding? We're doing this?" There was a guffaw. "Do you have any idea what I'm gonna do to you?"

Paolo's eyes closed. He could taste iron in his mouth from where he'd bitten his lip. He could hear the roar of his own pulse as blood rushed past his eardrums. His chest was rattling so hard with the hammering of his heart that he couldn't believe the man couldn't hear it.

But he didn't move.

Footsteps. Paolo looked at the ground. There wasn't more than a foot of ledge behind the tree. Then the ground fell away to blackness. There might be a ridge just below. Then again, maybe not. Maybe it went straight down to the ravine.

"Last chance," said the man. He was right beside the tree now. He'd only have to lean forward, to peer around the tree trunk and see Paolo, shivering, desperately trying to melt against the bark.

Paolo shifted around the tree, further out of reach. He heard a hitch in the other man's breathing as he waited for Paolo to reveal himself, probably wondering whether to risk taking a look.

Comeoncomeoncomeon . . .

The gun came first, stretched ahead of the man's arm, almost skating against Paolo's head before he could duck out of the way, but he managed to maneuver his way out of reach, behind the tree. "Now you're being silly," the man reasoned as he stepped onto the narrow ridge behind the tree.

Just as John-Michael had that first time, the man skidded a little, losing his footing. His arms reached out for the tree and grabbed a branch, one hand still clutching the revolver. Paolo was already speeding around the tree, his head down in a sprint as he aimed for the Oldsmobile. He had to get some cover.

He barely noticed the slender silhouette of John-Michael as he emerged from the shadows, hands clasped together and brandishing a large, heavy stick. Paolo heard but didn't see the wood swing through the air and connect with something low. He heard the anguished scream of pain as the man stumbled—and, heard the strain in John-Michael's voice as he raised the stick for a second blow. Two shots rang out. Then there was silence.

Paolo made his way back behind the tree. John-Michael stood breathing hard, a three-finger-thick piece of tree leaning against his shoulder. There was no sign of the hit man.

"Paolo. I think he's gone."

MAYA
MALIBU CANYON, FRIDAY, JULY 3

In the east, the moon cast a teal-colored glow behind the hills. Directly above, the sky turned midnight blue. Through the car windows, Maya glimpsed a few stars. They wouldn't last. In an hour or so the moonlight would be powerful enough to obliterate anything but the light of Venus. She reached absently for her phone, planning to check her night-sky app for the positions of the planets. Then she remembered that it was still in the Venice Beach house.

Candace and Grace would be home by now. They'd probably have tried calling everyone, only to find the calls going to phones that had been left in the house. They'd look at the gaping expanse of maple wood flooring in the living room and realize that the rug had gone, too. From there to the truth of what had actually happened a few hours ago, however, would require a radical leap of imagination. Maya tried to guess what conclusion she'd have drawn, if she'd been the one in their position. They arrive home to find the house newly empty, all the housemates' cell phones apparently abandoned.

"They're going to think we went to the beach," Maya concluded aloud. She turned to see Lucy's skeptical glance.

"*That's* what you're worrying about?" Lucy gave a dubious shrug. "Me, I'm more concerned about what our boys down the road are doing with that gun. It's been a long time since we heard from them, don't you think?"

"I guess if they'd used the gun we'd have heard the shots," she continued.

"Don't be so sure," Maya replied doubtfully. "We've got at least two hills between us."

Maya felt herself redden, but she didn't respond. As the ensuing silence enveloped them both, Maya began to reflect on Lucy's words. It had been well over fifteen minutes. They should have agreed to check in with each other at regular intervals.

"Okay," Maya conceded. "Maybe we should go back."

"What if they're in the middle of it? Better call first."

"If they're in the middle of it then surely they won't answer?"

Lucy made a sound of irritation. "How should I know? Make the call!"

Maya picked up the phone in her lap and called the boys' burner phone. When it just kept ringing, she held the phone up to Lucy, askance. "See? Not answering. I say we head over there."

Lucy started the Chevy Malibu. She said nothing, her

movements languid, almost bored. She seemed closed off from what was happening. Physically and emotionally rejecting her role in the middle of it all. Maya felt pretty certain that if Lucy hadn't been the only licensed driver right now, she'd have walked away.

Who'd have thought that Lucy would be the one to pick the law over surviving a battle with a murderer? That punk persona, it didn't seem to count for much, Maya noted. Not when you came right down to it. Lucy was more like her parents than she cared to admit.

Minutes later, they arrived at the bend higher up the road. Maya saw instantly that a second car had driven up close behind the Oldsmobile. Its headlights had been left on, beaming yellow light off the edge of the road, no more than three yards away.

Hearing Lucy inhale shakily, Maya concentrated on what little she could see beyond the two parked cars. There was no sign of movement. Ahead, obscured by the cars, a scattering of trees framed the edge of the road. She couldn't quite tell where the road ended, however; the light beam blasted a hole into the darkness but either side was merely shadows.

"Leave the engine running," Maya murmured. Then she unfastened her seat belt and climbed out of the front passenger seat. Lucy made a squeal of displeasure, but did little else to discourage Maya.

She jogged across to the second car, noting that it was another Chevy, a Cruze. Passing the Oldsmobile, Maya turned her attention to the shadows. It took her eyes a moment to adjust. After a few seconds she made out two figures close to the largest of the trees at the side of the road. One of them was kneeling, apparently staring at the ground.

Paolo and John-Michael. It had to be. Maya felt a jump in her pulse rate as she put everything together. The second car was here. That meant that the plan had worked. The hit man's associate had taken the bait. And now, he was nowhere to be seen.

Paolo must have killed him.

With the portion of her brain that was detached, calmly reviewing the day's history, Maya noted: *John-Michael and Paolo are both killers now.*

"Maya." John-Michael rose to his feet as she approached. He didn't sound surprised to see her, or relieved. Just neutral. His hands hung together in front of him, as though clasped in prayer.

Paolo was more effusive. "Is Lucy here? My car! I need a flashlight–there should be one in the glove compartment." Then he was gone, rushing past Maya. He returned a couple of minutes later, this time with Lucy. In his right hand was an aluminum tube the length of Maya's forearm. Paolo hurried by, switching on the flashlight as he reached the tree. When its beam aimed down, it became obvious that whatever they were looking for was over the edge of the cliff.

All four housemates stood precariously close to the

precipice, peering over. Maya wasn't sure what they were looking for but she could guess.

The driver of the second car. Did the boys shoot him? Maybe cause him to fall over the edge? Her eyes went immediately to Paolo's hands, wondering how many bullets it had taken. When she didn't see the revolver, Maya began, confused, to look for the weapon in John-Michael's hands. The weapon wasn't there, either. Catching a glimpse of narrow white plastic zip ties between his wrists, she felt her mouth go dry at the thought of what must have happened.

It could only mean one thing.

Lucy had come to the same conclusion. "You didn't shoot him." The air wasn't particularly cold, but just the same, Lucy clasped her hands across her chest, gripping both shoulders as she shivered. "What happened? Where is he?"

"I knocked him down," John-Michael said. He sounded utterly drained. "He fired his gun as he was falling, like, a couple of times."

Paolo confirmed this. "I heard two shots."

Maya faced John-Michael. "He had a gun and you hit him?"

"With a stick," John-Michael said, using his cuffed hands to raise up a thick stafflike tree limb that he'd been holding at his side. "So he'd fall down the edge, over there."

"That was a long drop," Paolo said to Lucy. "The guy is not moving. I'm guessing that, basically, y'know, it's over."

Maya peered down again, this time aiming the flashlight to follow Lucy's horrified gaze. Yes, Paolo was right. A body in a two-piece suit lay about fifteen feet below. The head wasn't visible from this angle, but as Paolo had stated, the rest of him wasn't moving. There was no sign of the gun.

"You couldn't have killed him with that," Lucy said with a nod at the stick. "It's nowhere near heavy enough."

"No," John-Michael agreed. "But maybe the fall? Someone should really go down there, check that he's dead. I can't do it, so don't ask. I feel like I just went ten rounds with Rocky Balboa."

Lucy gasped. Even Maya was astonished by John-Michael's mild, matter-of-fact delivery. He seemed to notice their shock, because he followed up with, "I wasn't trying to kill him," he said in his gentlest voice. "He was about to torture Paolo. I just lashed out. I'm pretty sure he broke one of my ribs," he added, wincing as he inhaled. "My whole body hurts like you wouldn't believe."

"We need to get you some painkillers, dude," Paolo said. "There was really no other option. He found his friend dead. He wasn't messing around."

"I went into basic survival mode," John-Michael agreed. "I didn't know how far he'd fall."

"But he . . . you were . . . he attacked you?" Lucy asked, stumbling over the words. Maya guessed that Lucy had yet to notice that John-Michael's wrists were bound. She was still only grasping at the edges of the horror of what the boys must have been through. The more Maya thought about it, the more apprehensive she grew.

"I wasn't going to just stand by and watch him take Paolo apart," John-Michael growled.

"We need to get out of here right away," Maya announced, nervous as she backed away from the edge. "For real. It's a miracle no one has stopped in the past fifteen minutes."

"A couple of cars passed by," John-Michael commented. "But they didn't stop."

"Well, now we have Paolo's car back there. That's three cars at the side of a deserted canyon road. It's starting to look like a sideshow."

"Maya has a point," Paolo said. He reached for Lucy's hand, a little tentatively, Maya noticed. "Let me drive."

Lucy reached into her jeans back pocket, handed him the key to the Chevy Malibu. Paolo took it, released his temporary, light grip on her fingers with evident reluctance. "We should all go now," he said.

Inside the car, Paolo drove while Lucy joined him in the passenger seat. A silence descended on them all, weighty and dense. Maya wanted to speak, to ask about John-Michael's cuffed hands, to say something about the bag full of cash that now sat in the trunk of Paolo's car, about the two dead shooters. About the fact that Dana Alexander, if she'd sent these people to scare off Lucy, wouldn't be deterred by the fact that a couple of her hit men had disappeared.

Maya wondered what Dana Alexander would do when

she found out. The conclusion she arrived at wasn't pleasant.

"Lucy," she began, and leaned against the front passenger seat until her face was close to Lucy's. "Giving testimony on Monday may not be enough. You have to find that bottle of nail polish, the one with Dana's fingerprints or whatever and you have to take it to them. If that's the only thing that can convict Dana Alexander then . . ."

Maya felt her breath come quickly then, her tongue thick and heavy as the words dried up. All hell would break loose once Alexander was arrested. Alexander would get Maya deported, definitely. They couldn't even be sure that she wouldn't lash out from inside prison. Killers like Mr. Shooter and his friend were never more than a phone call away.

Lucy was almost certainly destined for some kind of protective custody, maybe even witness protection. Maya's thoughts turned to Jack Cato. Had he tried to call her this evening? Would she return to unread messages and missed calls on her cell phone? The sudden memory of him was such a sweet and tender contrast to the violence and terror of the past few hours that it brought instant tears to Maya's eyes.

"Are you crying, Maya?" John-Michael asked, amazed. She felt the touch of his fingers on her cheek. "Hey now. The worst is over."

Maya leaned into his fingers, screwed her eyes tightly shut, and imagined that she was touching Jack. She felt exhausted. There were still so many details to iron out, details that would mean the difference between prison and freedom, between safety and danger. Yet, Paolo and John-Michael seemed dazed after the events of the night. They weren't thinking straight.

If only she could believe that John-Michael was right; that the worst was over. More than anything, she longed to relax. But she didn't dare. Deep inside, Maya was beginning to understand that this was very far from over.

GRACE
PACIFIC AVENUE, VENICE BEACH,
FRIDAY, JULY 3

"Still nothing?"

Grace answered with a glum shake of her head. Candace spread her fingers on the steering wheel, brow furrowed in confusion.

"Every last one of their cells is going to voice mail," Grace said.

"Guess this explains why no one bothered to text us what they wanted from the store," Candace said, yawning.

It did, Grace thought.

She had sent a group text to the housemates: Getting supplies for the 4th. Any requests?

But, nothing.

Now this: total radio silence. It couldn't be good.

A sense of misgiving had been building slowly inside her, ever since she and Candace had left the house. The argument earlier that evening had been of epic proportions. When Candace had suggested they escape the pressure cooker atmosphere, Grace had been only too happy to follow. She'd assumed that everyone else would, too, but the others had hung back. Glancing over her shoulder as she and Candace hurried toward the boardwalk, Grace had eventually spied John-Michael and Maya leaving the house.

The household had fragmented. The way it had happened tugged at Grace's heart. They shouldn't be splitting off into little cliques, but they had. She with her stepsister. Paolo with Lucy—the girl he'd once had a thing for. John-Michael with Maya—as though they were the natural "outsiders."

Grace had kept her eyes on Paolo throughout much of the explosive drama of Maya's revelation. Normally, she tried to hide her feelings, but in that situation, the focus wasn't on her. While they'd all been distracted, Grace had allowed her eyes to be drawn to Paolo's anxiety and disquiet, to the way he'd scratched the raw skin of his tattoo, to the way he'd grimaced at his own touch. He'd been uncharacteristically introspective.

Ever since Candace's reaction to the news about Grace's father, Grace had felt a burden of guilt. Candace was right. She should have told her about her father sooner. Maybe things would have been different if she had? When Candace had suggested that they go for ice cream together, she'd decided it was time to come clean. Grace had told her all the details of her relationship with her father, from the time when she first realized she'd have to keep his fate a secret.

Secrets had almost torn their Venice Beach household

apart. But now that everything was out in the open, maybe all six friends could start over.

So they'd gone straight from the ice-cream parlor at Santa Monica Pier to Candace's Prius, which had been parked a few streets along, and from there to Trader Joe's.

The house was empty when they got home, but not dark. Dimmed lights had been left on in the living room and in the second-floor bathroom. It was as though everyone had stepped out a few moments ago. Grace tried calling John-Michael again. When she heard his familiar *Death Note* ringtone coming from the red sofa, she felt even more confused.

"Their phones are here," she called out to Candace, who was in the kitchen, putting away the groceries. After a moment she'd confirmed it: all four cell phones had been left in the living room.

"Where the hell is the rug?" Candace said, walking over from the kitchen, hands on hips as she surveyed the room.

Blankly, Grace stared at the empty wooden floor in front of the red sofa. "Oh yes," she intoned, feeling stupid. "There's also that."

Candace stooped, peering down. "Dear God, is that blood?"

Where one corner of the rug would have been close to the base of the red sofa, a few drops of a dark fluid had collected. One of them had smeared, leaving a trail like a bleeding comet, where something had been dragged through one of the larger drops.

"There must have been an accident," Candace concluded.

"Or a fight."

"Maybe they took the rug out to clean it?" Candace suggested.

"Without their phones?"

"Why would they need their phones? Maybe they went to the beach."

Grace looked at her, baffled. "You think they took the rug to the beach?"

"How the heck do I know?" Candace was getting annoyed now. "It's not here, so *clearly* they didn't leave it."

Grace sat back on the futon and folded her arms across her lap, staring up at her stepsister. "You think they've gone to the beach for–what–a midnight picnic?" She shook her head, bewildered. "You really like to look on the bright side, don't you?"

"What's your solution?" Candace said, resentful. "You think they called Olivia Pope from *Scandal* over to help them dispose of a body, or something crazy like that? And by the way, d'you think maybe we could discuss it while we put the groceries away? I'm not doing it by myself."

Grace followed Candace to the kitchen, where five large brown paper bags awaited them on the dining table. "What about the blood on the floor?" she said, stacking cobs of sweet corn in the refrigerator.

Candace said, "Maybe they went to the emergency room. And not the beach."

Grace shrugged. "And they all forgot to take their cell phones? I mean, if they left in such a hurry, at least one person would still have a cell phone in their pocket."

"You'd think," Candace admitted.

"Let's see if Paolo's car is still here."

"It won't be."

Candace was right. And the absence of Paolo's car wasn't going to do anything but intensify their fears.

"Kind of odd, though, all their cell phones being on the sofa like that." Candace spoke slowly, and Grace thought she caught a tremor in her voice at the end. "Almost like they took them out of their pockets and left them behind on purpose." Candace looked up. "Why would they do that?"

Grace packed four pints of Ben & Jerry's ice cream into the freezer and turned back to look at Candace. "I can only think of bad reasons."

"Try to think of a good reason, will ya?" said Candace, her voice rising to a high-pitched whine. "Look, I know you're freaked out and all about your dad, but you have to trust that it's going to be okay. Lucy's gonna talk to the cops on Monday and then you'll see."

"I'll see what?"

Candace shrugged and tried to sound bright as she said, "That the wheels of justice will turn in your favor."

But even Candace's forced optimism couldn't distract Grace from the sensation of dread that had crept inside. "I think . . ." Grace clenched her right hand into a fist. "I think maybe we ought to call the cops."

"What about John-Michael? He won't like that."

She nodded slightly, by now barely aware of Candace. Grace's thoughts had gone to him, too. The cops and John-Michael were never a good mix. More than anyone else in the house, Grace understood that.

Anxiety pulled at her now, a heavy sensation dragging her where she'd rather not go. The air inside the house seemed itself to have shifted. There was a *strangeness* to the house, as if all life had been sucked from it. She sensed a pulsating, insistent knock at her consciousness: a warning.

"Something bad has happened," Candace said, suddenly giving voice to Grace's own fear. Grace could only tremble faintly and nod. "But I don't think we can call the cops," Candace continued. Her words were slow, considered, each one falling onto prepared ground. "At least, not yet."

Grace clasped her hands together so that they wouldn't shake. Where could they hide, where would they wait, in fear of what might be coming?

JOHN-MICHAEL
JACK IN THE BOX, FRIDAY, JULY 3

"We need an alibi."

Paolo passed around the burgers he'd just bought from Jack in the Box in Pacific Palisades. Maya had insisted that they didn't stop in any public place closer to the house or to Malibu Canyon—"just in case." All four housemates unwrapped their sandwiches.

Lucy looked at hers and put it back in the paper bag.

"Yes," Maya said vigorously, "an alibi. Probably easiest if we say we were hanging out at the beach."

"Or the pier at Santa Monica," suggested Paolo.

John-Michael held his burger an inch from his mouth, waiting to hear the plan. Paolo seemed pretty calm after their ordeal. Almost happy. Whereas John-Michael had collapsed onto his knees and vomited as soon as he was out of sight of the others and dumped the various items that could link them to the two deaths. Even now, he felt queasy.

"Not Santa Monica Pier," Maya said. She seemed a little antsy. "We need to think of a place where there wouldn't be security cameras. But before we get into that, let's just do one last checklist of everything else. Okay, John-Michael, rug?"

"Burned and then dropped in the second Dumpster we saw after got off the 1."

"The burner phones?"

"Ours—crushed and dumped in the trash can right over there," John-Michael said, pointing. "The other guy's burner phone is on the ground beside his hand. Where he left it after he texted his partner."

"The zip ties they used on you?"

"Trash can of the men's room at Jack in the Box."

"Mr. Shooter's smartphone?" Maya said, a little insistent. "There's a lot of evidence there. Not least of which, the GPS tracking."

"That's more difficult," admitted John-Michael. "We're going to have to hit it pretty hard with something heavy."

"All right, but the sooner the better. I've already disabled the app that allows it to be traced," she said. "Guns?"

"The revolver? Fingerprints wiped and back with Mr. Shooter. And the other gun is with Mr. Fifty Ways to Mess You Up."

Maya frowned. "Huh?"

"You wanna take a look at my bruises?" John-Michael said resignedly. "I'm gonna turn seven different shades of purple in a day or so." His stomach was finally settling down, so he took a bite from the cheeseburger. But when he tried to swallow, all John-Michael could think about was the yelp of pain that the hit man's associate had made when he'd finally lost his footing on the edge.

He'd have killed us both if he'd had the chance.

Three deaths on his hands now. Unexpected, for someone who found it hard to kill a spider.

For a few moments, the quiet sounds of chewing were the only noises in the car. All four housemates seemed content to settle with their own thoughts. Or maybe they were as choked up as John-Michael. Maybe their emotions were teetering, on the verge of letting go with a scream like the one that refused to be shaken out of his memory.

Maya finished her food and wiped her fingers carefully with the napkin before speaking. "We may need to discuss the situation with the cash."

"You want to split it up?" Paolo said.

"You better not spend a dime of that money," Lucy piped up, adamant. "You don't know who's gonna come after it."

"Who's going to come after it?" Maya asked, frowning. "The only two people who know about it are dead."

"Unless the money is from Dana Alexander," said Lucy.

"All that money?" Maya said, unconvinced. "No *way* can it cost that much to scare one defenseless teenage girl."

"Until we changed things," pointed out Lucy.

John-Michael agreed with Maya. "If any part of the money was from Dana, it's a small part. There are a ton of reasons they might be carrying that much cash. Most of them illegal. Unless Dana Alexander has a secret life as one scary-ass crime boss, all she knows is that they got what-ever payday she agreed on—probably via a third party."

There was no way the cash could be traced to them. Even if the second guy had called someone on his way out to Malibu Canyon, he couldn't have known who he'd be dealing with when he found the hit man's body.

Lucy shook her head. "Still, I say we get that under lock and key and leave it until this whole situation goes extremely cold."

"You're right that Dana Alexander's still an issue, though," Maya said thoughtfully.

It was a good point. Alexander would find out soon enough that her attempt to silence Lucy hadn't worked. Better that she found out from inside a jail cell. "Grace's dad will get taken off death row," John-Michael added. "It's win-win."

"Not necessarily," mumbled Maya. For a second or two it seemed to John-Michael like she was maybe thinking of saying more, but she didn't elaborate.

John-Michael just nodded and took another bite. How much would Lucy tell the cops? If they knew what had happened tonight, they'd probably take her into protective custody. Much as John-Michael worried about not seeing her again for who knew how long, Lucy needed to be safe. And simply telling the cops that Dana had planted a spy in their household wasn't likely to cause all that much concern.

"Maybe we should tell the cops that Mr. Shooter

threatened Lucy," he said cautiously. "And that he went away."

"I don't know," Maya said, shaking her head. "Seems to me that if we say anything about him at all, it could come back on us. What if they investigate?"

"Why would they?"

"When they find the body," Lucy said, sounding jaded.

"Oh," he said. "Oh yeah. Well, maybe you make up a description? How would that be?"

"Uh-uh," Lucy said. "For once, I'm gonna agree with Maya. We keep quiet about the whole thing. The guy was never there and we don't know *anything*. Same goes for telling Grace and Candace what happened tonight," Lucy said, sounding more confident. "We say *bubkes*."

"Bubkes?" echoed Maya.

"*Nada*. Zip," said Lucy. "If you expect me to go to the cops, you'd better be damn sure that everything that happened tonight is inside of a full-scale Armageddon containment field. The 'vault' won't cut it here—I'm talking Pentagon inner-circle-level secrecy."

"Also, it's kind of unfair to expect the others to keep this secret," Paolo said. "It's not that I don't trust them, that's not it at all, it's just that—"

"Yeah," Maya agreed, grimacing. "It's a burden. And they don't deserve to have this dumped on them."

"Also, they weren't here," Lucy added pensively. "They might not understand."

The housemates seemed pretty unanimous, at least on

this point. "So that's decided then, is it?" said John-Michael. "We're protecting them?"

"And ourselves," said Lucy.

"Yes," Paolo said. "But where do we tell them we've been all night?"

John-Michael thought for a moment. "Why don't we just tell them that we can't say? That way we admit that bad stuff went down, but we don't get them in any deeper."

"Yeah," murmured Paolo. "That might work." Maya nodded her agreement. John-Michael looked across at Lucy, hoping for a reply. She'd lapsed into a pensive silence, staring at her hands, folding and wringing them in her lap. After a minute she went for the door handle. "I need a milk shake. Anyone want anything else?"

"I could go for a chocolate milk shake," Maya said with more than a hint of relief.

John-Michael said, "Can you get me a strawberry?"

"I'll help, Lucy," agreed Maya. She unbuckled her seat belt.

The minute the girls were out the door, John-Michael was astonished by the sound of Paolo whimpering, as though he were gulping back a sob. Watching him, John-Michael inhaled sharply. The moment passed mercifully fast. Whatever emotion had risen so hard and fast to swamp Paolo was soon under control.

"I'm sorry, man," Paolo managed to say, struggling to breathe across his gasps. "I don't know what got into me."

John-Michael watched his friend for a moment. He

resisted the temptation to reach out with a hand and touch Paolo's shoulder. "It's okay," he said after a while. "This is how . . ." John-Michael paused, swallowed. "You're going to feel up, and then you're going to feel down. This is how it feels after something like . . . like what we did."

Paolo said nothing. His eyes were large and round, open with sudden understanding as he studied John-Michael's face. For a second or two, John-Michael could practically read his thoughts.

Maybe John-Michael actually did kill his father.

You couldn't blame the guy for thinking that way. Not after what had happened tonight. After tonight, Lucy, Paolo, and Maya had to be thinking the same exact thing.

LUCY
GROUND FLOOR, VENICE BEACH HOUSE,
FRIDAY, JULY 3

Lucy was the first into the house. The lights were off in every room except the living room, where only one of the two floor lamps was switched on; dimly, at that. Grace and Candace were stretched out, one on each sofa, half asleep. As Lucy and the others walked in quietly, the two girls pushed themselves into an upright position. And stared, bleary with confusion.

With every minute that passed, the bag of money worried Lucy more. They should have left it behind. She'd felt this at the time, but had been too shocked, too generally overwhelmed to make any kind of argument. The other three had been so confident that it was safe to keep the money.

Theft was theft. Maybe it *wasn't* as bad as killing, but it might end up being more dangerous.

The night's events were already coiling into a knot of hideous complexity. She could barely stand to think back on any part of the evening. Earlier that day, Lucy had still been struggling with the immensity of her own revelation, after the hypnosis. A huge deal at the time; something to be absorbed slowly and considered.

Right now, Lucy would give anything to be back there. To be able to rewrite history. Why had she even waited until the afternoon before going to the cops? Maybe if she'd gone first thing in the morning, they wouldn't have been so busy?

Grace cleared her throat, struggling on sleepy legs as she stood. "Where have you all been?"

"Has anyone come by the house?" Maya asked, ignoring Grace's question. Maya was all about that, tonight: ignoring what didn't suit her, acting like some weird kind of cold-blooded badass. A teenager playing out a life she'd only ever seen in the movies—totally relatable. Real life had no context for what they'd been through in the past few hours. At times, Lucy had felt like she was back on a studio lot, sleepwalking through a scene straight out of a cop show.

"No one," Grace answered, shaking her head. She was examining each one of them curiously. "Which one of you got hurt?"

Paolo was the last into the house. In silence, he went up to Grace and hugged her. Lucy noticed the girl's eyes closing for the briefest moment as he held her, the way her limbs instantly relaxed, and it was like a light going on. Briefly, a tiny smile found its way through her anxiety.

Grace and Paolo have started something.

After a second or two, Grace pushed Paolo off her gently. "Was it you?"

Paolo shrugged, trying to hide a guilty expression with a puzzled grin. "Was *what* me?"

This time, Grace shoved him, hard. "Stop lying. We saw the blood."

Candace stepped forward. She also looked angry. For Grace, however, Lucy could sense it was personal. Something was brewing there, for sure.

"You've made us sick with worry," Candace said, agitated. "We were about to call the cops. The only reason we didn't, the *only* reason . . ." She paused as her voice cracked. "Don't even think about lying to us."

Lucy was still as she watched Candace struggle to control her emotions. You were never quite certain, with an actor, what was true, what was fake. But Candace did seem kind of overwhelmed.

"Thank you," John-Michael said. His voice was sincere with gratitude. "Please do *not* think about calling the police."

Grace stared from Lucy to John-Michael. She couldn't seem to look at Paolo, Lucy noticed. At her sides, Grace's hands tensed and relaxed, over and over. "So we were right, something bad happened?"

Lucy checked with her coconspirators. One by one they responded with the slightest of nods. She turned to

Grace and Candace. It was time to lay out the story they'd prepared. "We knew you'd worry. And we love you all too much to lie to you," she began, her voice shaky.

"Good," Candace said. Her lower lip was trembling. "Don't."

"But that means that we can't tell you a whole lot. Because anything you know could be used against you. And us."

The sisters' facial expressions crumpled. Candace said, "What the hell?"

"Yeah," Grace said, gasping. "You don't get to leave us hanging."

"We thought about it a lot," John-Michael admitted.

"Yes," Paolo added firmly. "We thought about telling you the truth, we thought about lying. We can't do either one of those, because, like Lucy says, we love you guys too much for that."

"You love us, so you won't tell us where the four of you have been, why you left your cell phones here, presumably so we couldn't contact you, why there's blood on the floor, why you took the stupid rug?" Grace stopped abruptly, incredulous.

"Which is where, by the way?" Candace asked.

No one answered that.

"We care about what happens to you. Which is why we can't tell you. It might . . ." John-Michael paused. "It might put your lives in danger."

"Oh," Candace said blithely. "That's okay, then. I mean—it's not like you did something bad and didn't want us to get you into trouble."

"It's also that," Lucy confessed. "If we want them to trust us, we have to be honest about whatever we can."

"Lucy," Paolo said softly, "of the four of us, you're the one who did nothing wrong. Not a thing. You're not going to take any heat for this from anyone. I'll see to it."

Grace stared at both with undisguised hostility. "Which is it, then? You *all* did a bad thing? Or just some of you?"

"All of us," Lucy said, now decisive. "The details don't matter." She may not have delivered any of the damaging blows, but she also hadn't stopped any of it from happening. She'd driven the car, she'd aided and abetted, at least. This night had made criminals of all of them. There was no pretending otherwise.

Candace ran one hand through the straggles of her hair. "So, let me get this straight. You've put *all* our lives in danger?"

Lucy forced herself to nod. The two hit men were dealt with, but the person who'd ordered the hit was still out there. The idea that Dana Alexander, movie star, Shakespearean actor, could have any involvement with the kind of people who arranged murders . . . It sure *sounded* delusional.

And yet. Lucy knew what she'd seen, that night at the Hollywood party. Dana Alexander, holding a man down underwater. Until all the struggling stopped. Until he bobbed, motionless, to the surface. And she knew what she'd experienced afterward, Dana Alexander's seductive persuasion, bending reality to her own ends.

Who knew what kind of people Dana Alexander was mixed up with? Who she could buy? If the housemates were right about Ariana, the movie star had managed to plant a spy in Lucy's life years ago. And when Lucy had moved to Los Angeles, another spy had been found–Maya.

Someone like that must move smoothly in pretty scary circles.

"I know I'm in danger," Lucy admitted. "And I can't tell the cops how bad it really is. Please don't ask me why, Gracie. But I *will* give that testimony." She paused. "I'm going to find that nail polish, the bottle that Dana gave me that night. I know it's in my room in Claremont, somewhere. Then the cops will know that I really did talk to Dana that night. We'll make her sorry that she ever made me feel like a dopey little kid who couldn't tell the difference between a dream and reality. When she tries to change her story about what happened, you'll see, the cops are going to become real interested in her background. Who knows what else they'll find?"

Grace stepped back. Her eyes grew large. She wrapped both arms around her chest, trembling. "Thank you."

Gently, Lucy smiled. "I will do whatever it takes to make this right. Your dad's been in prison for long enough."

At this, Grace burst into tears. This time it was her

stepsister who was at her side in an instant, taking her into her arms for a close, comforting hug.

Lucy felt tears of her own, stinging and hot at the corners of her eyes. Not just from relief, but fear. It was long past time that she faced up to the truth of that night, almost nine years ago. But that didn't make the possible consequences any less terrifying.

MAYA
GROUND FLOOR, VENICE BEACH HOUSE,
SATURDAY, JULY 4

Grace quivered as she wept against Candace's shoulder. It was past midnight now. The room filled with a palpable sense of relief that a day they'd remember chiefly for its hideousness was finally over. At this point, Maya reflected, they'd latch on to any good outcome for the evening. Grace's father might go free. It was important to focus on something positive, make it easier to forget the horrors of the night.

But Maya couldn't bear to watch. How could she forget her own part in keeping Dana Alexander's secret? It made her sick to think that she'd ever sent that woman information about her housemates. Discreetly, she crossed the room, toward the French doors. On the side table beside the red chair, were the cell phones they'd left behind. Maya picked up her own, saw a text from a number she didn't recognize.

Her fingers fumbled, searching for the button to click on the text. *Strange number*, Maya thought. *Never seen it before.* Then she read the text.

O JUDGMENT, THOU ART FLED TO BRUTISH BEASTS.
AND MEN HAVE LOST THEIR REASON.

"Huh, weird," she said.

Candace asked, "What's weird?"

Maya held out her phone. "Take a look."

Candace released her grip on Grace, who seemed calmer now, took the phone, and read aloud: "'O judgment, thou art fled to brutish beasts. And men have lost their reason.'" She looked straight at Maya. "I know that line—it's from *Julius Caesar*."

"Yeah," nodded Lucy. "It's that 'Friends, Romans, countrymen' speech. We had to learn it by heart last semester."

"But what does it mean?" Maya said, mystified.

"Antony says it," Lucy told her. "He's telling everyone that they have lost their minds, basically. That their judgment is shot to pieces; that they've lost the power to make good decisions. That they're reacting like *animals*."

For a few seconds Maya's mind was wiped clean. All she could do was fixate on the screen, hunting for a coherent response.

"Maya, what's wrong?" she heard John-Michael say. He sounded nervous.

Maya lifted her head to look up at him. Whatever showed in her face must have really scared him, because John-Michael moved fast, caught her as she crumpled, falling to her knees. For a moment, Maya braced herself against John-Michael's shoulders and rose to her feet. With a slight cough to clear her throat, Maya said as evenly as possible, "It's . . . I think it's from Dana Alexander. She's going to rat me out to immigration."

The others stared at Maya dumbly. There was a protracted silence. Eventually, Paolo said, "Is this a joke?"

Maya sighed. "Yeah, Paolo, I felt this was a good time for jokes."

"Well, I don't understand," was all he said.

"Seems pretty clear to me—Maya lied to us," Candace said.

"No." Maya shook her head, forcing herself to remain calm. Of course they would think that, *of course*. "All I know for sure is that my mom may have used forged papers to get my US citizenship. Dana Alexander knows, she's always known. That's why . . ." She stopped, took a huge breath, and released it slowly before continuing. "That's why I was doing stuff for her. All those reports. If you'd been a little less enraged earlier on, I would have told you but, honestly, I just wanted to stop talking about it."

Candace sniffed, apparently disdainful. "Hmm. You got 'ratting you out to immigration' from that Shakespeare quotation?"

"Presumably this is Alexander's fancy-ass way of letting me know she does *not* appreciate my decision to stop spying on all of you."

Lucy took Maya's phone from Candace's fingers and read the text for herself. "So, so, so screwed," she pronounced slowly.

Maya looked at Lucy. "You think I'm right?"

Lucy tried to laugh. "Oh yeah. That's from Dana Alexander, I'd bet this house on it."

Paolo said, "Seriously?"

Lucy shook her head. A sad, amazed little smile touched the corners of her mouth. "Dana Alexander *knows*. She's telling us that she knows about everything. About me, about how we sent Ariana away, about Maya, about Candace making out with her precious little sister's boyfriend. I'm guessing she's not too happy about *that* particular piece of news. She's saying that *we've* lost our minds, our reason."

On this final statement, Lucy fixed John-Michael with a deeply significant stare. Watching, Maya could feel her knees giving way once again.

Dana Alexander knew *everything.*

What if she even knew what had happened tonight? From the anxious, pale glances that she was getting from Paolo and John-Michael, Maya could tell that they were thinking the same way. They didn't dare articulate their fears, naturally. Not while they'd sworn to keep Grace and Candace out of the horrors of the past few hours. Maya forced the rising tide of panic out of her mind and stumbled backward until she felt the sofa against the backs of her knees. She slumped onto the couch, furiously trying to think.

Alexander couldn't know absolutely everything. Could she? Surely not about what happened up in Malibu Canyon? But she might know that her plan to keep Lucy quiet had gone awry.

One of the two hit men could have gotten word to Dana Alexander. Sometime before the second guy had fallen off the cliff, Maya guessed. He must have called Alexander to tell her that the hit hadn't been carried out. Now the woman would be wondering. Should she act quickly? Send someone else to silence Lucy? Or wait?

They couldn't afford to take the risk.

"We can't be here for the next few days," Maya said with sudden and absolute conviction. "And if we're gonna make any calls, they can't be traced. So we need to buy some new burner phones."

Candace frowned at this. "New?"

"We have to get out of LA." She stood up. "Tonight. All of us. Now."

GRACE
INTERSTATE 5, SATURDAY, JULY 4

Wind trailed through Grace's fingers as they rested lightly on the open window of her sister's car. The night was warm and Candace liked to keep the air-con of the Prius turned off to be eco-friendly. For someone who'd initially sneered at her mother's choice of car, Candace was turning into quite the proud owner.

From the backseat, Maya spoke up. "I just got a text from John-Michael. They're going to get gas at the next service station. We should fill up at the one after. Our cars shouldn't be photographed together anywhere."

Neither Candace nor Grace said anything. It was just another mysterious element of what was now a thoroughly troubling night. And they couldn't even ask why.

The car stereo was playing some electronic dance music, dreamy and pulsating, the kind of thing that Candace liked to play at the end of a party—total contrast to the chaos that was tearing Grace up on the inside.

This music only made her sad; nostalgic for a time

that Grace now realized had gone—perhaps forever. A time when they'd all been happy together, closer than she'd ever believed it would be possible for a group of friends to be. Closer than she'd ever felt with her family.

The saddest part, Grace reflected, was that only now did she see that time for what it was. The time they'd first met. Their first party. *Seinfeld* marathons all day long, eating John-Michael's amazing sandwiches. Lazy afternoons on the beach, watching Maya surfing, chatting around a campfire. The warmth of knowing she was surrounded by people who cared for her, who understood what it was to be right there, in that time, in that place, who understood and accepted in a way that no one else did.

All that—it was gone.

Whatever had happened tonight at the house, whatever had caused Lucy, Maya, Paolo, and John-Michael to disappear for around four hours with absolutely zero explanation—it had to be *really* bad. There was trust between the group now. It had been sorely earned, months of struggling with individual problems; John-Michael and the death of his father; Lucy and the nightmare visions of her past; Candace and her indiscretion with her costar; Maya being blackmailed into spying for Dana Alexander. Tonight, finally, all of that had exploded, scattering the housemates as they reeled, shell-shocked.

And yet, they'd instantly gravitated back to one another, to the Venice Beach house.

Paolo alone had no secret. He'd been frank about

wanting Lucy, even though it had led to rejection. His transformation by that disappointment was almost disturbing. Grace doubted that Paolo was happier since being emancipated. Yet, he shared the depth of his frustration with no one, as far as she knew. Instead, he wore it on his skin.

Perhaps Paolo was the only one who truly understood how to keep something *in the vault.* Grace caught herself smiling at the irony of that. She was still holding out on her own feelings for him, after all.

"How long do you think we can stay at Alexa Nyborg's house in Napa?" Candace asked Maya, breaking across Grace's troubled thoughts.

"Nyborg just emailed to confirm that she's going to Washington for the weekend and the invitation is still open."

"How long will we need to stay?" Grace asked. But Maya didn't seem to want to commit to any specific time frame.

Candace sighed with longing. "Hey—the show is on summer hiatus until the middle of August, so I'm in no hurry to rush back. How seriously cool is it that you know a billionaire?"

Unbelievable. Candace wasn't paying the slightest attention to their dilemma. Grace wanted to scream at her: *Do you get what's happening here? Have you listened at all to what they've been saying? You still believe this is some kind of vacation?*

"A paper billionaire," Maya protested quietly. "I bet most of her shares are still in escrow."

"Alexa Nyborg is a real-life billionaire, and she's chosen you to be her little protégé. She even replies to emails you send her at midnight on the Fourth of July. Girl, you've won the lottery," mused Candace. "Aren't you gonna tell Hottie McBrit?"

Maya didn't answer. She sidled up to the car window and stared into the darkness beyond. Grace could almost hear the ache in Maya's shallow breathing. Whatever Maya felt about her newfound business angel and her English crush, it was somehow tainted by whatever had happened tonight.

The new secret was a fault line in the group. The collective understanding that had once existed between them was finished. Grace touched a finger to a button and closed her car window. The interstate road was climbing higher into the hills and the air had turned cold.

The fault line between the friends might become a chasm, but Grace resolved that she would find a way, somehow, to heal it.

She closed her eyes for a moment. Behind her eyelids she saw the pale green sky of a late evening on Venice Beach, the silhouetted palm trees, the sound of hard plastic wheels on the concrete path that wound through the low, grassy dunes, the smell of grilled maize tortillas near Andy's fish taco place, of board wax at the surf rental shop, of freshly baked funnel cakes at Santa Monica Pier. It would be waiting for them, everything they'd left behind. One day, they would return.

Uneasy in her position, Grace turned to observe Maya. The girl was scrunched up, folded like an ironing board, knees drawn up to her chin, arms wrapped around her legs and her head resting lightly against her kneecaps. Sitting behind the driver's seat, Maya was staring through the side window. The next moment, she flinched so hard that her limbs unwound as if released from a spring.

The sudden movement was enough to jolt Candace, who lost control of the car for a moment, causing it to swerve into the next lane. When the momentary scare was over, Grace saw Candace looking fiercely at Maya in the rearview mirror.

"Freak!"

"I'm sorry," Maya muttered miserably.

"What the hell is wrong with you?" Candace demanded before adding, with thick sarcasm, "Oh yeah, that's right, I'm too precious to be told."

To Grace's surprise, Maya neither replied nor reacted. Instead, she simply continued to gaze through the window with a kind of drawn-out expression, breathing in little gasps, through parted lips. After a moment she said, "Did either of you see that white Buick earlier on, the one that passed us just now, did you see it before we left the PCH?"

Exasperated, Candace said, "I have no idea what you're talking about."

Maya's voice dropped to a whisper. "I think I saw it before."

Grace faced Maya, tried to catch her eye. "Why do you

care? Why would someone be following us *now*, Maya? Maya? *Maya?*"

Maya didn't reply at first, instead she rolled her head against the backseat like a cat trying to get comfortable and lie down. A minute passed, then she mumbled, "Forget it."

Grace stopped trying to get any further response after a while, she just sat back in her seat and considered, focusing on the darkness beyond.

Maya should have been happy, on the way to enjoy the first rewards of her hard work. But she wasn't. Maya was *afraid*. And try as she might to think soothing, rational thoughts, Grace couldn't ignore it for another minute.

She was scared, too.

ACKNOWLEDGMENTS

From the beginning I speculated about how I would take things to a dark place in this second installment of the Emancipated series. What was conceived as a somewhat escapist story line—six emancipated teenagers living the SoCal dream—felt like the perfect opportunity to explore morality. If things went badly wrong, what would each one of them be prepared to do to protect their "perfect" life?

The entire Malibu Canyon section of this story was inspired by a twisty drive with my good friend Hoku Janbazian through the Hollywood Hills and down to Malibu beach, where we ate some terrific fish tacos. A lovely day dreaming up some hideous drama—I thoroughly recommend the location.

Huge thanks are due to Katherine Tegen for supporting this incarnation of the "escapist" teen story. Two fantastic editors have been massively helpful in finding the Goldilocks zone between "dark enough" and "too dark." Thank you, Elizabeth Law and Maria Barbo!

Thanks to Emily Wheaton, a former US soldier and

fellow member of the *Once Upon a Time* fandom, for all her great advice about firearms. Thanks also to California resident and fellow Oncer Cyndi Burke for additional advice about her home state and also about guns!

Team Emancipated at Katherine Tegen Books and HarperCollins ran a terrific internet-based marketing campaign for book one, including videos and a cool quiz. Thanks especially to Kelsey Horton for all her creativity, energy, and enthusiasm. Other members of our wonderful team include Bethany Reis, Veronica Ambrose, and Rebecca Schwarz. A virtual cookie to you all now and a real one later!

Fellow children's author and friend Michael Grant continues to be a source of steady encouragement and support with the promotion of the Emancipated series—thank you, Michael. Thanks also to my agent, Robert Kirby, at United Agents in London; to my husband, David; and daughters, Josie and Lilia. The kids were especially eager to further their favorite "ships." One gets her way—but #nospoilers.

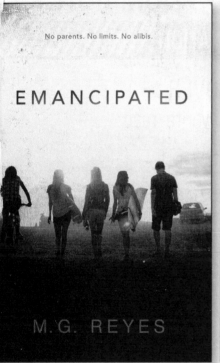
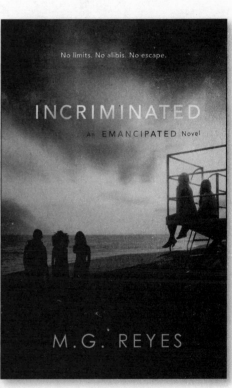

JOIN THE

Epic Reads
COMMUNITY

THE ULTIMATE YA DESTINATION

◀ **DISCOVER** ▶
your next favorite read

◀ **MEET** ▶
new authors to love

◀ **WIN** ▶
free books

◀ **SHARE** ▶
infographics, playlists, quizzes, and more

◀ **WATCH** ▶
the latest videos

◀ **TUNE IN** ▶
to Tea Time with Team Epic Reads